MURDER IN HARROGATE

Stories inspired by the
Theakston Old Peculier Crime Writing Festival

EDITED BY VASEEM KHAN

ORION

First published in Great Britain in 2024
by Orion Fiction
an imprint of The Orion Publishing Group Ltd,
Carmelite House, 50 Victoria Embankment
London EC4Y 0DZ

An Hachette UK company

3 5 7 9 10 8 6 4 2

Typeset by Born Group
Printed and bound in Great Britain by Clays Ltd, Elcograf S.p.A.

www.orionbooks.co.uk

To the Harrogate International Festivals team whose blood, sweat and tears allow the crime fiction community to come together to rejoice in murder and mayhem each year

Contents

Foreword

Are you sitting uncomfortably?

What you now hold in your hands is a collection of dark and deadly stories penned by some of the most well-known and experienced writers of the genre *in the world*. Collectively, this outfit have created beloved characters, penned innumerable bestsellers, sold millions of copies in dozens of languages, engendered popular screen adaptations, won every award imaginable and occasioned endless reading pleasure in the masses.

Assembling such a crew is no easy feat.

In Hollywood, this sort of thing is par for the course. A gang of desperadoes brought together for that one impossible mission (think *Avengers Assemble* but without the Lycra), a mission that usually ends up with everyone but the hero blown to bits, cut down by a hail of bullets, crushed under a tank, skewered by a rusty sword and so on and so forth. I had to promise our authors that none of these fates would befall them. I'm not sure they all believed me – this being the publishing industry – but, given that they are all my friends and I have a reputation as being (generally) honest and trustworthy, they agreed to pen a story for the collection.

Having assembled my gang of writing ninjas, why constrain them to writing about Harrogate? What's the big deal about Harrogate anyway?

The answer to this question lies with the Theakston Old Peculier Crime Writing Festival.

The festival, which celebrated its twentieth year in 2023, holds a unique place in the crime and thriller firmament. It is the largest such festival in the world, each year bringing thousands of crime-fiction-loving pilgrims to the quaint British town of Harrogate in Yorkshire, England. In 2023, I was asked to chair the festival, acquainting me further with the town and its environs. (And with the notorious Bettys Café Tea Rooms, which has been responsible for adding unwanted inches to the waistlines of many an author – and reader – over the years.)

The town is, of course, synonymous with the genre, thanks to a certain Agatha Christie. On 3 December 1926 Christie vanished from her Berkshire home in the south of England, sparking the sort of nationwide hysteria that would not be seen again until the great Covid toilet-paper shortage.

Eleven days later, the creator of Hercule Poirot and Miss Marple turned up at what is today known as the Old Swan Hotel in Harrogate. From that day to her death she remained close-lipped as to the exact circumstances behind her disappearance.

Theories abound, of course. Marital difficulties. A nervous breakdown. Alien abduction. A massive bender. (Strangely enough, it's the last of these that is the most unlikely – Christie was a teetotaller.) Ultimately, Dame Agatha was found safe and sound and would go on to pen many more bestsellers. Her canon has now sold over two billion copies – only Shakespeare and God (by way of the Bible) have sold more. Her enduring fame means that Harrogate will forever be linked to her legacy.

And this was one reason that a local brewery, based in the nearby village of Masham and led by urbane brewer and Yorkshire businessman Simon Theakston, decided to sponsor a crime festival in Harrogate back in 2003. That first edition took place under balmy skies with nary an inkling for the organisers as to just how popular the annual event would go on to become.

Chairing the festival in 2023, I was struck by the roll-call of excellence that has graced the festival for two decades – a veritable Who's Who of crime, mystery and thriller writing. The festival engenders a collegiate environment that allows authors to mix with readers, reviewers, critics, agents, editors, publicists, bloggers, booksellers and the occasional random nutjob.

During my year as chair, I almost didn't make it to the ball. I was hospitalised just days before the festival, with an excruciatingly painful kidney stone. A dour-faced surgeon came to visit me just two nights before the opening day to tell me that I would have to 'go under the knife'. Perhaps it was my crime fiction brain – or the morphine in my system – but I thought I detected a Hannibal Lecterish undertone in his voice, as if he could think of nothing better than having me at his mercy with scalpel in hand.

That night I prayed to the gods of crime fiction . . . and, lo and behold, a miracle! The stone popped out just hours before the op, upon which, like any crime author worth his salt, I immediately took a picture of it and sent it to some writer friends.

Around the same time, I was approached with the idea for this anthology.

I was, of course, flattered to be asked to edit the collection. (Flattery will get you *everywhere* with authors. Authors are like cats. Stroke our bellies in the right places and you can convince us to do anything.) A full writing schedule of my own meant that finding time was always going to be a factor. But, with publisher Orion and the Theakston Old Peculier Crime

Writing Festival joining forces, I couldn't help but be dragged into the mad scheme – and the end result is everything we all hoped it would be.

This collection represents a high-water mark for crime anthologies. The authors are not only individually hugely successful, but also long steeped in the dark arts, working in domains ranging across the genre. Historical crime, contemporary killings, mini-thrillers, there's something here to sear everyone's tastebuds. Our authors' warped minds have been given free rein and they have outdone themselves.

But what exactly makes a good short story? How does a crime short story differ from a novel? Here's my take. A novel puts its arms around you, leads you in, gives you time to smell the roses before the putrid stench of the corpse works its way into your nostrils. A short story, by contrast, has no patience for that sort of mollycoddling. It's a shovel to the back of the head, followed by a shallow grave in the woods.

I write a lot of short stories. For me, a short story is a chance to experiment. My story for this edition is a departure from the two series that I write. It's a story about the murder of Macbeth – or, to be more accurate, an actor playing Macbeth. I began writing it last year, 2023, which marked the 400th anniversary of The Bard's First Folio. And if there's someone out there who *still* isn't convinced that Shakespeare was a crime writer . . . Well, there's plenty more space in that shallow grave.

For those used to penning full-length novels, it can be quite a shock to the system, changing gears like this, especially if an editor such as myself is walking up and down the anthology galley, cat o' nine tails in hand, just looking for a back aching for the lash.

I am pleased to say that the authors in this edition were a dream to work with. I expected nothing less. I am certain that had we all found ourselves in the trenches at the Battle of the Somme, they would have willingly charged over the top and into a hail of bullets at my command. (They might not have been happy about it, but they would have done it.)

For me, personally, this anthology allowed a moment's reflection on my career, the long and torturous path to being asked to helm such a prestigious venture. I wrote my first novel aged seventeen – a comic fantasy in the vein of the late, great Terry Pratchett's Discworld series. Even then I loved the notion of being a tweedy writer, a man of letters, admired, envied, a doyen of the literary establishment. I also thought it would be a good way to avoid having to get a real job. There was one small problem with my cunning plan . . . that first book was rubbish.

I wrote six more novels across twenty-three years before finally being published at age forty with *The Unexpected Inheritance of Inspector Chopra*, a novel about an Indian policeman who is forced into retirement in his forties and, while solving a murder, also has to deal with the unusual predicament of inheriting a one-year-old elephant. The book became a bestseller and effectively gave me a career.

After five books in that series, I moved back in time to 1950s India and historical crime. Beginning with *Midnight at Malabar House*, I explore a nation still reeling in the wake of Gandhi's assassination, the horrors of Partition and Indian Independence. My protagonist, India's first female police detective, is banished to Bombay's smallest police station, Malabar House, and forced to work with an English forensic scientist deputed to Bombay from the Met Police. Collectively, these books allow me to explore that turbulent period just after Britain's colonial adventures in India.

Which brings me to another theme of this anthology, namely, the use of crime fiction as a lens with which to examine the world around us. The writers of this collection are very different individuals, but the one thing that unites us is passion. Passion for subjects that move us, anger us, fill us with joy. Crime writing allows us to explore the societies in which our stories are embedded. And why not?

After all, isn't it so much better to learn while you're being entertained? (Presumably, you *are* the sort of person who finds murder entertaining otherwise you wouldn't have shelled out your life savings on buying this anthology.) And so, in this collection you will find crime and passion fused together in myriad delicious ways. You will find: a missing actress; a deadly park run; a gruesome Victorian mystery; an art theft; a vanished sister; a dicey dentist; a frustrated writer; a deadly treasure; a body in the bath house . . . and a murdered Macbeth.

It isn't easy being an author. Contrary to public perception, we don't swan around in velvet smoking jackets, sipping port in our studies. Limos don't pick us up from our castles to sweep us to gala events, to be feted by the masses, rose petals strewn before us, chilled champagne buckets waiting in the green room.

Sometimes it's a packet of stale crisps, a warm glass of something yellowy, a shared Uber with seven other writers and an event in some grubby corner of the country with the only attendees a gang of sinister-looking Morris dancers who were given the wrong invite.

Writing can be a lonely, brutal business. And the *act* of writing never gets any easier. Sometimes it is simply about sitting down at our kitchen tables, mug of tea in hand, a wild idea running around our head like a sex-crazed squirrel, a vision hovering before us of some future reader – i.e. you – grimly enjoying the dark and murderous words we are about to pen.

At least I'm fairly sure that's how the authors of this anthology approached their task, though, in truth, they might have written their story while sitting in a Turkish mudbath; or in a yurt on the Mongolian steppe as part of a research trip for a new cosy crime series featuring Genghis Khan; or on the Eurostar wearing a false moustache while on the run from the police, a dead body cooling in their garden shed.

The end result is a collection second to none.

I leave you with a final thank you, for giving us your time and trust, and with a few appropriate lines from Shakespeare's *Henry VI*, Part III:

> *And from that torment I will free myself,*
> *Or hew my way out with a bloody axe.*
> *Why, I can smile, and murder whiles I smile.*

NOTHING LIKE A DAME

Mark Billingham

'Dame Agatha? Well, what can I say? She's a giant of our genre, obviously . . . certainly one upon whose shoulders the likes of myself are standing. If you're a serious crime writer, and I would classify myself as one such, you must honour your debt to the greatest of them all. She was, and remains . . . untouchable.'

This was the kind of meaningless twaddle Marian Fairley would spout if she found herself being interviewed on stage at some low-rent festival, or on one of the increasingly rare occasions she was doing her bit on local radio, because . . . well, it was expected, wasn't it? The truth was that she'd never read a Christie novel in her life and had no intention of starting now. She'd seen one or two of the films of course, and had once spent several hours she'd never get back sitting through *The Mousetrap*. So, Christie was the Mistress of Plotting, was she? Well, as far as Marian was concerned, there were holes in *that* particular plot you could drive an articulated lorry through. So, while Marian would happily trot out the usual tributes when pressed, she knew more about Formula 1 or bee-keeping than she did about the works of the peerless dame.

She knew *all* about the disappearance, though.

Those eleven days in 1926, when the search for the famous novelist became a national obsession. A vanishing act that played out on the front page of every newspaper and had the country gripped. Over a thousand police officers had been involved in the hunt for the missing crime writer. Aeroplanes were used for the first time in such a case and even Sir Arthur Conan Doyle had got involved in his own quirky fashion; trying to get to the bottom of the mystery with the help of a spiritualist and one of Mrs Christie's gloves.

Marian had read all about it in several books and watched three different documentaries, so she was more than au fait with the theories. She was unconvinced that Dame Agatha had suffered a nervous breakdown following the death of her mother *or* that she was attempting to frame her unfaithful husband for murder in the wake of his request for a divorce. Having considered all the available facts carefully, Marian was of a mind with those who believed that Christie had spent those eleven days in some sort of fugue state; that she had quite simply lost all sense of herself. It was not, as the *Daily Mail* had said at the time, a 'heartless practical joke' and it most assuredly had not been a cheap publicity stunt.

I mean, she hardly needed the publicity, did she?

She certainly got it, though.

More publicity than any writer these days could possibly dream of and, best of all, it hadn't cost her a penny . . .

Marian Fairley was under no illusions. The unpleasant fact of the matter was that her career, in recent years at least, had been somewhat less than spectacular. Her idiot of an editor always found very polite ways to tell her that her sales were down – 'the market's in a very bad place, darling . . . not been the same since Covid' – but politeness didn't pay her mortgage. She fought against any suggestion that her books were old-fashioned. No, there was precious little blood and gore and her detectives did not listen to jazz or take drugs or beat up suspects, but she knew there was still a market for what she liked to think of as traditional mysteries.

She tried to avoid using use the C-word – no, not *that* one, she would never dream of using that one – but she repeatedly pointed out that . . . ugh . . . *cosy* crime fiction was making a comeback. She reminded anyone who would listen how many gazillion copies that bloke off the quiz show had sold, not to mention the one who used to be a vicar, but her bloody publisher stubbornly refused to spend any more than the bare minimum on publicizing her work.

She wasn't even sure that she had a publicist anymore.

The last one – some twenty-two-year-old bimbette called Felicity or Georgina or something – had been about as much use as an ashtray on a motorbike, but she'd *been* there, at least. It was disgraceful, the way Marian had been treated, with no respect shown in editorial discussions, a noticeable disdain for her marketing suggestions and cover ideas and scant regard paid to a long and moderately successful career.

Thirty-seven novels and countless short stories, one of which had been adapted very successfully for the stage by an amateur company in Ipswich. She had been longlisted for a Dagger and highly recommended by several notable critics. She was briefly published in America and had even toured there once – paid for out of her own pocket, but all the same. She had appeared at festivals in Scarborough, Wolverhampton and Dundee, opened her local fête on more than one occasion and had, in better days, been the most popular author in Dorset libraries two years running.

She'd once shared a stage with Val McDermid, for heaven's sake!

Well, if all went according to plan, it would not be too long before Ms McDermid would be bragging about sharing a stage with *her*.

Marian dropped her bags at the desk and turned to take in the lobby of the Old Swan Hotel in Harrogate. She felt a tingle of excitement. This was where it had all happened; where Dame Agatha had finally been discovered. The hotel had been called the Swan Hydropathic back then, when people came to the town to take the waters. Marian didn't know if that was even a thing anymore, but there *were* some lovely shops.

She waited ten full minutes for someone to collect her luggage and, having finally run out of patience, she took the matter up with the young woman behind the desk. The receptionist – 'Tiffany', according to the badge on her bosom – muttered a half-hearted apology. Something about being short-staffed because there was a wedding on. Marian would have wagered a fair amount that Agatha had not been treated so shabbily, but this was the way of the world now, wasn't it? Whoever should have been carrying her bags to her room was probably messing about on Instabook or skiving off somewhere with their feet up, Twittering.

Tiffany thrust a registration form across the desk and Marian dutifully filled it in, providing the false information she'd chosen carefully in advance. She told Tiffany that she wouldn't need to leave a credit card on file because she would be paying for everything in cash. In 1926, Agatha had registered under the name of her husband's mistress, so Marian did likewise; signing in under the name of the woman with whom her own husband – now somewhat too dead to appreciate the joke – had once had a silly fling.

A drunken fumble at a work Christmas party, a tryst or two in the West End, no more than that.

She handed the form back and picked up her cases.

'Will you be all right with them, Mrs Dawson?'

Marian smiled. 'Don't worry,' she said. 'I can manage.'

*

The next morning, Marian caught someone staring at break-fast. Not staring at the *breakfast*, but rather, at Marian herself, while she was eating breakfast. Marian *thought* the woman was staring at any rate, though she might easily have been looking at someone behind her, one of the wedding guests perhaps. Either way, she realised, this was something of a quandary.

It was lovely to be recognised, there was little point in denying it, even if that was most definitely *not* why she wrote. It would not be an enormous surprise were she to be spotted, least of all here. There was a famous crime festival held each year at this very hotel, shamelessly milking the Christie connection, so this was somewhere a member of the public might almost *expect* to see one of their favourite crime writers.

Marian herself had been invited to the festival – though just the once, disgracefully – and it would be fair to say that her appearance had not been an unmitigated triumph. It had not been her fault. She had, as always, acquitted herself admirably, but the event had been derailed by an oikish and over-refreshed crime writer from Birmingham who, having described his own somewhat turgid prose as 'edgy' and 'relevant', went on to accuse Marian rather forcefully of being a 'third-rate Dorothy Sayers'.

All these years on, the phrase still made her shudder.

Marian looked across at the woman on the other side of the dining room – who was *definitely* staring – and smiled.

Yes, a quandary . . . because she really did not *want* to be recognised, certainly not straight away. She needed time, a few days at least, for her disappearance to be noted, then reported and for the search to begin in earnest. Which it would, she was certain. Her agent did not call her as often as she once had, but they were due to have an important conversation about the paltry offer Marian had just received for translation rights in Lithuania. Some members of her family would obviously miss her and alert the authorities, even if – when she came to think about it – there weren't too many she was still in touch with. A daughter from whom . . . well, *estranged* was probably the polite word for it, and a sister in South Africa she had not spoken to since the unpleasantness over their mother's will. No, there weren't sackloads of Christmas cards arriving these days, but that was fine because Marian had her characters for company; men, women and domestic animals whose lives, loves and murder investigations she had skilfully charted for over three decades and who were beloved by legions of readers from Doncaster to Dungeness.

Inspector Withers of Scotland Yard.

Marjorie Duff, sleuthing suffragette.

Mrs Tibbles, feline detective.

There would be enough people who cared about her whereabouts to get the ball rolling, Marian was sure; to worry themselves silly and report her missing. Then it was just a question of staying below the radar while the mystery of the missing crime writer built to fever pitch. The newspaper reports, the TV specials, perhaps even a dramatic reconstruction on *Crimewatch*. Did they even make *Crimewatch* anymore . . .?

She was knowledgeable enough about police procedure, of course, to have taken all the necessary precautions. Agatha might have known a fair bit about poisons, but Marian knew just as much about CCTV cameras and cell-site signals. There would be no credit card transactions to trace and her mobile phone would not be getting switched on until all this was over; when she would doubtless have to answer the hundreds of concerned emails and wade through the inevitable slew of posts on social media.

#WhereIsMarian?

So, for a while at least, she would be living incognito. A mysterious guest at a grand old hotel, brilliantly disguised—

'You're Marian Fairley, aren't you?'

She looked up to see that the woman who had been staring at her a few moments before was now hovering at her table. Clearly the dye job and spectacles had not been quite enough to mask Marian's identity.

'Well, actually—'

'There's no point trying to deny it,' the woman said. 'I've seen the author photo on the back of all your books. I know it's rather an out-of-date one, but I still recognised you.'

Marian stared down at the remains of her toast and kippers. This was awkward. 'The thing is, I'd be awfully grateful if you could—'

'I am *such* a fan of Inspector Withers.'

Marian looked up and beamed, despite herself. 'Oh. Thank you, that's so kind.'

The woman, who Marian guessed was fortyish – slight and mousy – sat down without being invited and shuffled her chair a little closer to Marian's. 'Celia Bignall.'

Marian shook the proffered, bony hand. 'Lovely to meet you, but would you mind terribly keeping your voice down?'

Celia leant close and whispered. 'Oh yes . . . *Withers on the Hunt, Withers Strikes Back, Withers to the Rescue* . . . that's my personal favourite. All the early ones, really.'

'I see . . .'

'I mean, if I was going to be *super*-critical, I'd have to say that some of your later books haven't cut the mustard in quite the same way, but then those early ones were *so* good that you have a lot to live up to. Do you mind . . .?' She leant across and helped herself to a piece of Marian's toast from the rack.

'It's only my opinion, obviously, but my instincts tell me you're a writer who respects the opinions of your readers.'

'Right . . . yes, of course.'

Celia clapped her hands together and sighed happily. 'Oh, I *thought* you would be, and I hope you don't mind me blathering on like this, but I've always been a bit . . . full on, you know, especially when I'm nervous and yes, I know I can put my foot in it sometimes but I've never been shy about letting folk know what I think, because I've always believed that honesty is the best policy.'

'That's absolutely fine, but—'

'"The truth is always your best friend." I think Inspector Withers said that in *Withers at Large*, didn't he?'

'He did, yes.'

'As I say, those early books were spot on, but sometimes a series can go on a bit too long, don't you think?' Celia nodded, chewing her toast enthusiastically.

'Well, that's always a concern for those of us who—'

'I mean it's almost impossible to *keep* writing good books and the last few . . . well, the last dozen or so, if I'm being honest . . . definitely felt a bit . . . phoned-in.'

'Oh, I'm not sure that's fair.'

'I know some critics called them *lazy*, but even I think that's a bit strong.'

'Which critics—'

'It's more like tiredness, if you ask me.'

'I can assure you—'

'Nobody could *blame* you. You've been doing this a long time, and a degree of boredom is bound to set in eventually, especially when you're knocking out three or four books every year.'

'No, I don't accept—'

15

'I mean the most recent Marjorie Duff novel was a long way below par, you'd have to agree with that, and as for Inspector Withers' last outing . . .'

Marian pushed her chair back. 'I'm very sorry, but I need to—'

'Maybe it's because your intrepid detective hasn't aged at all. He's still racing around like a randy whippet when he must be seventy-odd by now—'

Marian stood up so suddenly that the teacups rattled and the ketchup dispenser fell over. 'Oh, put a bloody sock in it!'

Marian spent the rest of the day in her room and had lunch and dinner delivered. She watched hours of dreadful rubbish on the television, flicked through all the complimentary magazines and read a few pages of some tiresome thriller – written (or most probably *not* written) by a television presenter she'd never heard of – which had annoyingly been on the bestseller list for weeks. In truth, she was more than a little shaken by her encounter with Celia Bignall and could only hope the wretched woman would be checking out very soon.

The following morning, keen to avoid the possibility of running into her again, Marian decided to skip breakfast and instead walked to the nearest newsagents. She bought a copy of every daily paper and carried them all back to the hotel, then, after ordering coffee and biscuits from a passing member of staff, she settled down in the hotel lounge to read.

She began to leaf through the pages, looking for her name, her picture below a headline. It was vain and silly, she knew that, but she very much hoped they'd used one of her earlier author photos; one with a few less lines, but hopefully not that one where she was staring wistfully off into the distance as though waiting for her muse to descend. She thought photographs like that always made one look rather pretentious.

Made one look a perfect arse, in fact.

Half an hour later, having rifled with increasing frustration through every paper – even the sports pages, because Marjorie Duff was a keen badminton player – Marian had found no mention of her disappearance. It was still a little too soon, she decided. There was, as yet, no reason for concern. She would check them all again tomorrow and there was always the evening news, of course . . .

On her way back to the lobby she was stopped by a young man who identified himself as the assistant manager. 'How's your stay been so far, Mrs Dawson?'

'Couldn't be better,' Marian said. 'Thank you.'

Waiting at the lift, keen to get back to her room, she became aware that someone was standing behind her and turned to see Celia Bignall, smirking.

'What?' Marian asked, somewhat snappily.

The smirk quickly disappeared, to be replaced by a nervous smile and a sorrowful shake of the head. 'I wanted to apologise,' Celia said. 'For being a little disrespectful yesterday. A little too . . . forthright.'

Marian turned back and stared at the doors, willing the lift to arrive quickly. 'Apology accepted.'

'I get a bit . . . carried away when I'm nervous.'

'I understand.'

'I've always been the same. Ask any of my friends. I don't know when to shut up sometimes.'

'It's fine,' Marian said, doubting that the woman *had* any friends and wishing that she would shut up immediately.

'Thank you,' Celia said.

The lift finally arrived with a welcome *ping*, but as Marian moved forward to step inside, she felt herself being held back. She stared, horrified, at the hand Celia had laid on her arm and turned to see that the smirk had reappeared on her face.

'Why are you using an alias?'

'Excuse me?'

'I heard the manager call you Mrs Dawson.'

'Well . . .' Marian could do nothing but wonder how best to respond and watch as the lift doors closed and it began to ascend without her. She could hardly tell this woman the truth, could she? 'It's just . . . something I do occasionally. You know, when you're a public figure . . .'

'A *what*, now?'

'When you have a degree of celebrity, the fact is that you need to guard your privacy. I'm not saying I'm one of those – what's their name? – Kardashians or anything.'

Celia laughed. 'Right, but it's not like you're Stephen King, either. Or J.K. Rowling.'

'Well, no, but—'

'With all due respect, Marian, you're not awfully well-known.'

Marian raised her chin and looked the woman in the eye. 'I once got an email from P.D. James!' That appeared to impress Celia every bit as much as it should have done. At the very least it left her, mercifully, at a temporary loss for words. Marian studied her. The woman's hair was clumsily cut and a little greasy. She had bad skin and a lazy eye. Perhaps her rudeness was a defence mechanism of some sort, or a way of compensating for her own obvious shortcomings.

Much as she longed to tell Celia Bignall to get lost, perhaps even using rather more industrial language, Marian was far too polite to stoop to her level.

'So, Celia . . . what are you doing in Harrogate?'

That smirk was back in a flash, along with the woman's alarming capacity for offence. 'Me? What are *you* doing in Harrogate?'

'Well—'

'The crime festival's months away and anyway, I've already seen the line-up and I didn't see your name on the programme.'

Marian's restraint evaporated and, once she'd barked out an instruction which was both physically impossible and unlikely to *ever* escape the lips of Marjorie Duff or Inspector Crispin Withers, she pushed past Celia Bignall and marched away, having decided to take the stairs.

Later that same evening, Marian snuck into the wedding disco and danced alone at the back of the room. Yes, she'd probably had one glass too many of Merlot, but there was nobody around to judge her, so she didn't care a great deal. She'd read somewhere that Agatha had danced during those eleven days, had mingled happily with fellow guests and cut a rug one evening to a popular song of the day. Marian did not know the name of the tuneless racket to which *she* found herself dancing, but it was a long way from *Yes! We Have No Bananas*.

Celia was sitting with a book in the lobby and glanced up as Marian made her way from the ballroom. 'You're quite the mover,' she said. 'Who would have thought?'

Marian ignored her, moving a little unsteadily to the lift, then stabbing at the buttons.

Celia returned to her book, half-smiling as she turned the page. 'I suppose that you can do whatever the hell you feel like when you're being someone else,' she said. 'That must be so . . . *liberating*.'

The following day, Marian rose good and early and, having donned a wig and dark glasses, set out to explore the town. She stopped at the newsagents again, but the raft of papers she purchased were deposited unceremoniously in a litter bin once she'd established their repeated failure to report her disappearance.

Celebrity gossip and royal tittle-tattle keeping stories of *genuine* public interest out of the news.

It was shoddy journalism, simple as that.

She wandered into shops and, having wandered quickly out again as soon as she'd seen the prices, headed for somewhere she felt rather more at home. Unusually, there were *two* book-shops in town; a branch of Waterstones and a rather charming indie. Predictably the big chain had none of her backlist in stock – there was fierce competition for space, she knew that, what with all the literary masterpieces from TV chefs and soap stars – but Marian was delighted to find one of her Mrs Tibbles titles in the small independent. For obvious reasons she was unable to let the man behind the till know who she was, but she discreetly signed the copy of *Foul Play and Furballs* anyway, smiling as she did so; thinking that, when her plan came to fruition, the shop would be ordering an awful lot more.

She imagined a whole shelf lined with her titles.

A front-of-store display with a large cardboard cut-out.

An entire *section* . . .

A few moments later, once she'd put the book back – face outwards – on the shelf, she thought she'd been rumbled when the member of staff stepped out from behind the till and sidled up to her with a knowing smile. She guessed that he'd seen her sign the book and, feeling as though she had little choice in the matter, she was about to say, 'Yes, I *am* the author,' but the man didn't give her the chance.

'Is there anything I can help you with?' he asked, cheerfully. 'The new Richard Osman is *very* good.'

'Just browsing,' Marian said. 'Thank you . . .'

After another hour spent aimlessly walking, hunger got the better of her and she found herself, along with dozens of other people, standing outside Bettys. This was hugely irksome.

Tempting as one of their famous 'fat rascals' was, she simply could not risk hanging around in a queue for half an hour and being spotted.

It didn't happen often of course, and that, in many ways, was the joy of being a writer. One of the many joys. You could be celebrated – treasured, even – and yet remain largely anonymous.

Well, *that* was all about to change . . .

'Is there anything I can help you with? The new Marian Fairley is very good.'

'Ooh, she's the one who disappeared, isn't she? I've read all about it . . . I'll take ten of them.'

Marian turned disconsolately away from Bettys, deciding that she'd have to make do with a sausage roll from Gregg's, and all but bumped into Celia Bignall.

She tried not to look too horrified.

'Oh, hello.' Celia smiled, as though she'd completely forgotten their somewhat sweary exchange the previous afternoon. 'I was wondering if you'd checked out. Fancy a coffee?'

Marian mumbled something non-committal and turned to stare forlornly at the window of Bettys. The food those inside were eating looked wonderful, but the queue wasn't getting any shorter.

'Oh, that's such a faff,' Celia said. 'Pretty flipping pricey, as well. Come on, let's find somewhere it doesn't cost twenty quid for cheese on toast . . .'

If someone had put a gun to Marian's head, she could not have said why she agreed. If she were being brutally honest with herself, she might have put it down to the fact that she hadn't factored the lack of meaningful human contact into her plan. Disappearing, as it turned out, was an awfully anti-social business. It had been necessary, of course, but those hours spent mooching around or hiding away in her hotel room had been long and lonely, and in truth, despite the time she spent alone when she was working, she was not altogether comfortable in her own company. Certainly not as comfortable as she had been, once upon a time. Celia Bagnall could be nobody's idea of a dream companion, but, for whatever reason, the woman had latched on to her and such a thing had not happened to Marian before.

It wasn't altogether pleasant, yet strangely it was rather thrilling.

Ten minutes later, they were sitting close together at a small table in the corner of a Costa. Celia had bought them both lattes and a large slice of carrot cake to share.

'It's the least I can do,' she'd said. 'I think I upset you again yesterday.'

'I may have overreacted,' Marian said.

They drank their coffee and quickly demolished the cake.

'I wanted to ask you about writing,' Celia said.

'Right.' Marian braced herself for the snarky remark, the poisonous dig, but it didn't come.

'I'm guessing it's a hard life.'

'Well, yes, on occasion,' Marian said.

'It must be a struggle sometimes.'

'It certainly can be, but that's usually only because you're doing it correctly. Writing *should* be difficult. Good writing, at any rate.'

Celia looked rapt.

'Yes, there's most certainly been struggle in my career and there's been a good deal of sacrifice.' Marian nodded, sadly. 'No, a *great* deal of sacrifice.'

'Oh, I'm sure.'

Marian shrugged. 'That's only one small part of the burden a creative artist must carry, but trust me, one letter from a grateful reader makes it all worth it. The knowledge that I've brought pleasure into someone's life. The fulfilment I feel, knowing *my* words have enriched it.'

'That's all very helpful,' Celia said.

'You're more than welcome,' Marian said.

'Actually, I do a bit of writing myself.'

Marian's heart sank a little. 'Of course you do.'

'Nothing in your league, of course, but I did win a couple of short story competitions.'

'Well done, *you*.' Marian conjured a half-smile. 'Who knows, perhaps one day you and I might be battling it out on the bestseller list.'

Celia sniffed. 'Do you actually *make* the bestseller list?'

'Do I . . .?'

'I'm only asking because I don't normally look at them.'

Marian said nothing, her fists clenching slowly beneath the table while she smiled sweetly, as though modesty forbade her from blowing her own trumpet.

Over breakfast in bed on what would be her final day in Harrogate, Marian came to a difficult decision. Difficult because she had never been one to give up easily. She had persevered in the face of countless rejection letters and later, once she was published, she'd stuck fiercely to her guns in writing the sort of mysteries her brain-dead editor had insisted were hackneyed and past their sell-by date.

Now though, she had little choice but to cut her losses.

She remained convinced that her plan had been a good one and that, given time, she would have been greatly missed; worried about. That the authorities would have come looking for her. That a great deal of welcome publicity would surely have followed. Major profiles and full-page interviews in the serious newspapers, perhaps even one of those daft reality TV shows she'd been watching up in her room. Now, as she set aside her breakfast tray and slunk into the ensuite, she could only imagine where it might all have led.

The sales.

The signing queues that wound twice around the bookshop.

The *demand*.

But the money she'd saved up was running out. The hotel wasn't cheap and Marian simply could not afford to wait any longer.

She got dressed and went out to take a final turn around the town. She bought a shawl and treated herself to some jam from Bettys. Then she trudged back to the hotel to pack.

With an hour before her train departed, she walked one last time around the hotel gardens. She thought about getting home to the cat – she'd left him plenty of dry food – and wondered briefly what she'd tell people about where she'd been. Then she realised that she was being silly because clearly, up to this point at least, nobody had asked the question.

It had been a little break, that was all.

That's what she'd tell people, if they *did* ask; that she'd gone away to recharge her creative batteries. Plotting out the next Inspector Withers mystery, trying to decide how many of her nine lives Mrs Tibbles had left, or pondering a radical new direction in which to take Marjorie Duff.

Marian heard her name being called and looked up to see Celia waving from a quiet corner of the garden. Hoping the woman couldn't see the grimace, Marian waved back and ambled across. Yes, the woman was rude, tactless and altogether unpleasant, but good manners cost nothing, so it couldn't hurt to say her farewells, could it?

'Will you join me?' Celia was sitting in front of a sumptuous-looking afternoon tea. 'I always over-order, so there's plenty for two, and these scones are seriously delicious.' Without waiting for an answer, Celia poured Marian a cup of tea from a heavy silver pot.

Marian sat down. She had some time to kill and those scones *did* look awfully good.

'You off, then?'

Marian stared.

'I saw you checking out.'

'Oh, yes . . . well, I need to be getting back. I'm on a deadline for the next book, so . . .'

'Successful trip?'

'Most definitely.'

Celia sipped her tea. 'Well . . . it wasn't *really* though, was it?'

'I don't know what you mean,' Marian said, taking a sip of her own.

'Don't get me wrong, it was a nice idea. I mean, I worked it all out fairly quickly. The hotel, the false name, you looking through the papers every day—'

'I like to do the crosswords—'

'And I understand exactly what you were thinking. The *angle*.' She raised her hand to 'write' out the headline. '*Mystery writer vanishes, only to be discovered in the same place that the most famous mystery author of them all was found.* Yes, it was a very clever idea.'

'You have quite the imagination, Celia.' Hoping that she was not looking quite as alarmed as she felt, Marian began buttering a scone. 'I can see why you have authorial ambitions of your own.'

'It was always a flawed plan, though. Two major problems with the plot.'

'I'm all ears,' Marian said.

'For a kick-off, the fact is that in this day and age, with mobile phones and social media and what have you, it's pretty much impossible to disappear. All very different in Agatha's day of course, but now it could simply never happen.'

'I see. What's the other problem?'

'Well, without putting too fine a point on it, nobody missed you. I'm sorry if that sounds harsh, but it's the truth, isn't it?'

Marian began spooning on the jam. 'Like I said, quite the imagination.'

'I'm not imagining it though, am I?' Celia leant across the table, eyes wide and bright, even the lazy one. 'Was there a single paragraph printed in any of those papers? Even one radio report? Agatha had legions of fans desperate to know what happened, publishers and agents, family and friends all frantic with worry. And you . . . didn't. I'm sorry for being so blunt.'

'No need to apologise.' Marian popped half a scone into her mouth. It was every bit as delicious as Celia had promised.

'I've never been one to beat around the bush, but I think you know that already . . .'

Perhaps it was that use of the word *beat* but, for whatever reason, the idea plopped right into Marian's head and she knew immediately that it was an extremely good one. That as plots went, this one would have no holes.

There was one thing that *always* generated publicity, after all. Yes, there would be a heavy price to pay, but knowing how many sales would be generated, how much money and fame would surely follow, Marian decided it was a price worth paying.

Infamy was probably more accurate, but it was close enough.

'Why don't I get us some more tea?' she asked.

'Lovely,' Celia said.

Marian reached for the teapot and stood up. She moved to stand behind Celia, as though on her way to the hotel's rear entrance.

'We could probably do with a smidge more jam, as well.'

'Not a problem.' Marian carefully emptied the teapot, pouring the dregs of the lukewarm tea onto the grass. She knew that the Queen of Crime had dispatched people in all sorts of ways over God-knows-how-many books, but felt confident that this was a murder weapon of which even Dame Agatha would have been proud.

Terror at Teatime, would be a nice title. Or *Potted Murder. Scones and Bones* might work, Marian thought, but only if people pronounced scone incorrectly, to rhyme with *alone.* She decided that it didn't much matter.

'They're good and solid, aren't they?' Marian raised the blunt silver object up high. 'These teapots, I mean.'

'Oh yes.' Celia slurped her tea, oblivious. 'Perhaps, with things being as they are, you don't get to stay in expensive hotels quite as often as you once did, but that's the sort of quality you pay for here . . .'

'To whom shall I sign this?' Marian asked.

The large woman in front of her shrugged. 'Make it out to "Maureen", would you, babe?'

Marian began to write.

'No, on second thoughts, just put "Big Mo". That's what everyone calls me in here.'

Marian did as she was asked and handed back the somewhat battered copy of *The Murderer Who Wasn't Missed,* which was currently spending its eighteenth week on the bestseller list. 'Where did you get it from?'

'My old man brought it in,' the woman said, admiring Marian's inscription. 'The screws had a good old nosey in case there was a phone or whatever hidden inside. Stupid really, because if he wants to smuggle something in he just puts it up his bum.'

'Thank you for that,' Marian said.

As Big Mo left the cell, another equally scary woman squeezed past brandishing a copy of her own. 'I nicked mine from the library,' she said, handing it to Marian. 'Last one they had, as it goes, because you're really popular in here.' She grinned, displaying a large gold tooth; pretty much the only one in her mouth. 'You and Jeffrey Archer . . . for obvious reasons.'

'That's lovely to hear.' Marian raised her pen. 'What shall I . . .?'

'Just put anything you like,' the woman said. 'Doesn't matter because I can't read anyway.'

Marian scribbled, thinking it best not to ask the woman why she'd bothered stealing the book in the first place. She was probably going to swap it for cigarettes or some such. Marian had learnt so much these last six months.

'So you got another book coming then?'

'Oh yes,' Marian said. 'And the one after that is almost finished.'

The woman nodded, impressed. 'You're like a machine, you are.'

'Well, what else am I going to do?' Marian looked at her new friend and smiled. 'And it's not like I haven't got plenty of time.'

'. . . *and it's not like I haven't got plenty of time.*'

Marian Fairley had a mischievous twinkle in her eye as she read the final line and, no sooner had she closed her copy of *Nothing like a Dame,* than the packed crowd at the Theakston Old Peculier Crime Writing Festival burst instantly into rapturous applause.

A few of them even stood up.

The Q&A that followed was predictably hit-and-miss.

Do you write on a Mac or a PC?
When's Mrs Tibbles coming back?
Are you a millionaire yet?
But then there were these:
'It's so incredibly realistic. Like you were actually there.'
'That final scene, when you're both having tea . . . I could *feel* how much you hated her. Well, the character, I mean. Bravo, Marian.'

And best of all: 'I have to say it's just so fiendishly clever, the way you inserted yourself into the narrative. Yes, I know that the whole "author as character" thing's been done before, but never as skilfully as this, and to me that's the sign of a writer at the height of their powers.'

'Here, here,' someone shouted from the back.

'You're awfully kind.' Marian waved the praise away, then blew a kiss to the questioner; a rather handsome middle-aged gentleman in a linen jacket and salmon-pink corduroy trousers.

'It's almost a . . . *meta* mystery and the way you employ the myths surrounding the Christie disappearance is a stroke of . . . well, I don't think "genius" is too strong a word. So, thank you. Thank you for being a genius.'

The audience began to clap again, even louder than before, and it seemed as if they were in no hurry to stop. There was cheering, and even some *whooping* from the Americans in the crowd. Marian let it all wash over her like a warm bath and wondered what ever happened to that oikish writer from Birmingham.

An hour later and the queue in the signing tent seemed to be getting longer. Marian was well-used to the routine by now.

Smile, chat, sign, wait. Smile, chat, sign, wait . . .

It was actually becoming a trifle tiresome.

She was certainly not going to complain, although she might ask the organisers of the next festival to put a time limit on things, and another glass of wine wouldn't go amiss, and she was *definitely* not doing any more selfies.

'Would you mind . . .?'

As if on cue, a mobile phone was produced and Marian dutifully posed, because nothing could spoil her mood, not while she was still basking in the praise from the man in the pink trousers. 'Genius' was a *little* over the top, she thought. However beautifully written her book was, however many shortlists it would probably end up on, it was no more than a straightforward roman à clef at the end of the day.

Well, perhaps not *altogether* straightforward.

Fact and fiction had very definitely parted company where the denouement was concerned.

Whatever her intention had been when she'd put a major dent in that teapot, things had worked out even better than Marian could ever have dreamt. Because she did not go to prison, was never so much as questioned. Because Celia Bignall *had not died*.

Though the poor darling would not be winning another short story competition any time soon.

All the way back to London on the train, Marian had been expecting the police to be waiting for her at Kings Cross. When they weren't, she'd sat nervously at home, wondering just how well she'd cope at His Majesty's pleasure and waiting for a knock on the door which had never come.

By the next morning, she was starting to wonder just how inept the detectives in North Yorkshire really were. She could barely believe it, knowing full well that had Inspector Crispin Withers been on the case, it would have all have been done and dusted by now and she'd be rolling around in the back of a prison van.

It was thanks to the internet that Marian had eventually discovered why she had not been arrested and just how hard-headed the dreadful Celia had actually been.

How wonderfully, *perfectly* hard-headed.

'Can you sign it to "Colin" please . . . and if you could put today's date that would be marvellous.'

Marian looked up at the next fan in line, though her smile was not for him. Rather, she was smiling at the memory of the story she'd seen the day after she'd left the Old Swan, curiosity having finally driven her to the online edition of the *Harrogate Advertiser*.

MYSTERIOUS ATTACK AT SWAN

Police were called to the Old Swan Hotel yesterday following the discovery of a seriously injured woman in the grounds. The victim – Ms Celia Bignall, 42 – appears to have been attacked by person or persons unknown and suffered a near-fatal head injury. Police remain baffled and can get no help from Ms Bignall, who not only has no memory whatsoever of the attack or those responsible, but cannot even remember why she was at the hotel in the first place. A police spokesman said, 'It's a mystery worthy of Agatha Christie herself, who coincidentally suffered her own bout of amnesia at this very hotel almost one hundred years ago . . .'

OLD PECULIAR

Steve Cavanagh

'"Milly Porter has . . . *issues*",' said Dr Braycott, reading aloud the referral letter.

Milly had heard this sentence spoken many times in her life. At school, in the headmaster's office, as her father sat nodding his head beside her, wearing his special, *concerned* eyebrows; at the Girl Guides, as she sat on the cold gym floor of the local community centre while the leader explained to her father's eyebrows that Milly's behaviour fell short of the Girl Guide Promise when she tried to strangle a fellow guide with their neckerchief and woggle; and more recently in dull offices with a plaque on the door reading 'Human Resources', as she sat on uncomfortable chairs and tried to mimic her father's eyebrow trick with varying degrees of success.

That word.

Issues.

There was always a pause before they said that word, as if the speaker were searching for the right one. Something sympathetic, something more polite than *problems*, something typically middle class and unmistakably English, yet honest. And when that word was eventually spoken, it was always stretched on the lips, pronounced carefully and slowly, as if the word itself was not nearly big enough to define Milly's multifarious capacity for making a full and comprehensive bollocks of almost any situation.

'*Issues* . . .' Dr Braycott repeated. 'That's what your boss says. What might those be?' he asked, as he folded his fingers together over his stomach.

Milly, sitting across the desk from him, shrugged, and then concentrated on pushing her eyebrows closer together.

At least this was a pleasant office. With a comfy chair. There were even some plants scattered about the shelves behind him, and one of them was still alive.

When Dr Braycott realised that he wasn't going to get anything more than a troubled expression from Milly, he leant forward and put his elbows on the desk. Always a bad sign, thought Milly. Nothing good happens when men put their elbows onto their desks.

'As you know, I have to write a report for Clive. The recommendations from Occupational Health always carry a lot of weight. I want to help you, but you need to help yourself. Now, I know it might be painful, but it would be good to start with the reason why you're here. Could you tell me more about the incident, please?'

'Didn't you listen to it?' asked Milly.

'I heard the interview live on air while I was driving home. But I want to know what you were thinking at the time.'

'I was thinking that the prime minister is a lying scumbag.'

'Yes, you said as much on the radio . . .'

'I didn't know the mic was live. I've said this publicly, on Twitter, Facebook, and to Clive in person. Look, I don't know how many times I can apologise.'

'I know what happened, Milly. But I want to know what led to this . . .'

'Thirteen years of catastrophic government?'

Dr Braycott sighed. 'That's not what I asked, Milly. Come on, this isn't an isolated incident. There have been a number of HR issues . . .' and to emphasize the point, he stared at a thick file of papers. This wasn't Milly's first clash with HR, and not the first time she'd been to OH.

'I've read your files. I don't need to go into the other incidents you'll be glad to know, but this . . . anger . . . is a problem.'

'I'm not *angry*.'

Now it was Dr Braycott's turn for an eyebrow manoeuvre, raising both of his almost to the top of his head.

'Sorry, look, I know you want to help. I try to do my job, but there are always people who wind me up . . .'

'Let me stop you there. I have your initial occupational questionnaire that you completed when you joined in 2015. Under "family history", it says both your parents and your sibling are deceased. Is there anything in your past you want to discuss?'

'No, not really.'

The desk groaned as Dr Braycott's elbows dug further into it.

The silence in the room began to make Milly's stomach feel weird. She needed this job. There was rent to pay for her flat. Wine to drink. Cheese to be eaten. Books to be bought and occasionally read. She had no partner in her life, and was content with that for now. And the job was her life. It was the one thing she was good at, apart from eating cheese and drinking wine, of course, but those endeavours do not pay rent. Milly knew journalism was the only job she could do. As well as the fire of resentment that crackled inside her, it burned alongside another flame – curiosity. The two were natural partners. Milly loved being a journalist. Asking questions. Getting to the truth. And when she hit on a big story, for a time those twin fires were quelled. Like standing barefoot on cold tiles after a hot bath.

'Milly, I want you to think carefully about this. I have to write a report and I don't want to say that you were anything less than cooperative, if you understand me?'

She had to talk to this man. She needed him. Elbows and all.

'I've always told people my sister is dead, but to be honest, I don't know that for sure. Things were really good until my sister, Susan . . . until she went missing. My mother couldn't handle it. She left Dad, ran off with a New Age guru and died a year later. She took LSD and jumped from the top of a cheap hotel somewhere in Yemen. My dad, he was so loving, but it destroyed him. He could barely cope after Susan disappeared and Mum . . . he was never the same. We moved to London after Mum's funeral, but he never got over it. It wasn't fair, what happened to us. What happened to Susan . . .'

'Have you tried counselling?'

'Oh yes, many times.'

'How did that go?'

'There were . . . *issues* . . .' said Milly.

'I see . . . well, I'm going to recommend some more counselling . . .'

'It doesn't work,' said Milly, then instantly regretted it. Dr Braycott was trying to help and she wasn't making this easy.

'You have to deal with this and I'm going to recommend you are given some time off to do so. Your past is going to keep ruining your future unless you find a way to resolve it somehow . . .'

Milly had heard this before, but right at this moment, in this office, she felt like she was really hearing it for the first time. Pain and loss was to be hidden, deep down. But with Milly it always seemed to come to the surface at the worst possible times. Dr Braycott was right. Unless she dealt with this there would be more uncomfortable chats in uncomfortable chairs in uncomfortable offices, and very soon one of them would be her last.

'There is something I can do,' said Milly, softly. 'I was ten when Susan went missing. I don't know what happened to her, or what the police did about it. I want to know what happened. I want to investigate.'

'What, as a journalist?'

'As a sister who is also a damn good journalist. I have a better understanding of these types of cases now. It might help if I understood more about what happened to Susan.'

Dr Braycott finally took his elbows off the desk and leant back in his chair.

'I'll sign you off work on health grounds for a month. By all means speak to people, find out what you can, but I also want you to see a counsellor afterwards. Deal?'

'Deal.'

'So where will you start?'

'I have to go back to where it all happened. Where Susan went missing – Harrogate.'

Milly found a taxi outside Harrogate train station. She put her case in the boot, got into the back and wound down the window. It was the beginning of summer and while it wasn't a long walk from the station to Bettys Café Tea Rooms, carrying a case in this heat would make her sweat and she was already nervous.

She arrived at midday to a queue of people waiting outside under the ornate awning for a table at the famous tea salon. Standing behind an elderly couple, Milly checked her phone. A text message from John Asquith – he'd arrived early and secured a table. Milly made her excuses as she stepped out of the line and made her way to the entrance, past a few mumbles and complaints. She explained to the waiter at the door that she was meeting John Asquith and he showed her inside.

Bettys hadn't changed much since she'd last visited. When she'd lived in Harrogate, coming here was a special occasion, usually reserved for birthdays or exam results; as long as they were decent results of course. It was a typically English tea – delicate sandwiches, small cakes, sausage rolls, scones with thick hills of cream and tart jams, all served with the greatest amount of unnecessary pomp and ceremony. Even the milk for coffee came in a silver jug that was so hot she remembered having to pick it up with a napkin wrapped around the handle. Milly always thought it funny that Bettys, who served the most English of teas, in the most English of tearooms, was founded and made famous by a Swiss baker.

John Asquith rose when he saw Milly and extended a hand and a warm smile. He was dressed in a black jacket, white shirt, no tie and grey trousers with a sharp crease running down each leg.

'It's been a long time, Milly,' said John. 'You were only a bairn when I last saw you.'

Milly remembered John, he was older now and something else about his appearance had changed but she couldn't put her finger on it immediately.

As she said hello and sat down, she studied John further.

When the police came to the house she wasn't allowed to linger downstairs, she was sent to her room straight away so the adults could talk. At ten years old this had felt like a punishment, but now Milly understood her parents were trying to save her from hearing the worst, or being crushed by the desperate fear that strangles a house when a child goes missing.

'Did you used to have a moustache?' asked Milly.

'I did. Retired the 'tache when I left the force, didn't I. I'm sorry to hear about your father,' he said, with an earnest tone.

Milly's dad had passed in his sleep two years ago. He had been ill for some time and not told anyone. He didn't want to worry Milly. At least he had a peaceful death. For that small mercy, Milly was thankful.

'Thank you, and thanks for meeting me. I'm sure going over old cases is the last thing you want to do . . .'

'Not at all,' replied John. 'You can only play so much golf and the wife doesn't like me hanging around the house, getting under her feet. Plus, I want to help. I like helping.' And he reached down and retrieved five notebooks from a bag at his feet. They were old and well-used and bound together with elastic bands. He slipped his hand under the elastic and flicked it onto his wrist, freeing the notebooks. The top one he placed on the table in front of Milly. Just then, the waiter arrived and they ordered coffee and sandwiches.

'I don't have access to police files now, and even if I did, I couldn't hand them over, but these are my personal notebooks. Not police property. I write things down; it helps me think. Every detail of Susan's case is in that notebook.'

She opened the book and looked at John's neat handwriting. Pages and pages of notes, with headings and sub-headings. A map of Harrogate and surrounding areas had been glued into the centre pages, colour-coded to show locations of searches and their dates.

'Susan went out to meet friends that day,' said Milly. 'What do you think happened?'

John cleared his throat. 'She never met them. We interviewed all of her mates, they didn't see her that day. They usually hung out in the town, Birk Crag or the Pinewoods. There was CCTV showing Susan heading towards Birk Crag from your house up in Bilton about eight in the evening. That was probably the last we saw of her. Although, one property had CCTV footage of a young girl passing by, around half past eight, but neither I nor your parents could confirm one hundred per cent it was definitely Susan. We couldn't rule it out though.'

'Which property?'

'Oh, it were a big posh house in the Duchy Estate. Kent Road. Lots of those houses have security cameras, but most of them don't record unless someone wanders up the driveway – motion-activated, you see.'

'Could it have been Milly?' she asked.

'I thought it were. I think your dad agreed with me, but your mother wasn't sure and I don't think he wanted to argue with her. Poor woman's nerves were hanging by a thread. The CCTV never formed an official piece of evidence. There's an old copy of a still taken from the footage in the back of the book.'

Milly flicked to the end of the notebook. Folded in half, stuck to the back pages, was a photocopy of a black and white, grainy image. A young female figure. Walking past the entrance to a driveway, she was looking over her shoulder, her hair flicked away from her face by the movement. Jeans, trainers and a black T-shirt with a distinctive logo. A smiley face, but with a wiggly-lined smile and Xs for eyes. The name of the band sitting above the image.

'Susan had that Nirvana T-shirt,' said Milly.

'I know. Trouble is, a lot of young people did. You think that's her?'

Milly looked again at the picture. The face was overexposed, caught in the light from a security camera. But the clothes, the hair, the shape of this person. It all seemed so familiar and yet, it was so long ago since she'd last seen Susan.

'I know it's her. I can feel it,' said Milly, touching the centre of her chest, feeling the throb of her heart. 'What do you think happened to my sister?' she asked, as much to herself as John.

John sighed. 'We conducted forty-one searches, mostly woods and scrubland, fields. Whoever took Susan didn't want her to be found.'

'Did you ever have any suspects?' she asked.

John leant back in his chair and took a sip of coffee, considering his answer.

'We hauled in a few likely scumbags. Men with previous. Took a good bit of manpower but we were able to eliminate them from the inquiry,' he said, then paused and added, 'well, nearly all of them.'

'Who couldn't be eliminated?'

John thought carefully before he answered.

'One local paper had a picture of him, coming out of the station after questioning, so I'm not telling tales out of school. Local man. Lives in Kent Road . . .'

'Where the CCTV saw Susan?'

He nodded, continued, 'He's not well-liked in the area. Bit of a loner. Just to be clear, there's no evidence linking him to any crime. Remember that, but there's something not right about him. There's been reports from neighbours of strange behaviour. I can't tell you his name, but I'm sure a journalist like you can find it out right quick. Folks in the Duchy have a nickname for him – Old Peculiar.'

Milly had never heard of this man before. She always knew something terrible had happened to Susan, and the reason she never came home was because she was dead. But somewhere in the back of her mind was always the possibility that it may have been an accident. Now there was a man. Someone who was the reason her sister was dead.

'I'm sorry, I have to go now. The missus is waiting for me to take her shopping,' John said and then stood.

Milly shook hands, thanked John for his help and for everything he had done for Susan. As Milly was about to turn and go, John called her name.

'Don't you want the rest of these notebooks?' he asked, holding up the other four.

'Are they all notes on Susan?'

'No, these are the notebooks on the other girls who disappeared.'

Harrogate was a spa town. The old Victorian hotels that had been built to accommodate those who came for the healing qualities of its natural springs were largely still in use. Milly sat at a desk in one of those quaint old hotel rooms, pouring over the notebooks.

She loved these old buildings – the thick stair carpets, the grand entrances and even the faint smell of cabbage which permeated throughout the oak-panelled halls and corridors. It was likely, of course, that cabbage wasn't on the menu in the hotel restaurant that day and hadn't been for some time. It was the pots and stoves that carried the odour, haunting the place with aromas as old as the buildings themselves.

As she read John's notes, his final words rang in her ears.

We never officially connected the disappearances of the other girls, but I know they're all linked. Copper's instinct. Be careful, don't go knocking on Old Peculiar's door, neither. There's summat not right about that fella.

After several hours, Milly got up from her desk and stepped outside into the grounds of the hotel to light a cigarette. Even though she had a light breeze in her room from the open window, the heat had still managed to stick her blouse to her back and she was glad to be outside. The hotel was busy hosting a wedding reception and men in shirts and ties, their jackets abandoned, stood talking loudly and swilling Pimm's and pints of beer in plastic cups.

Milly, craving a little quiet, found herself wandering out of the hotel grounds while she smoked her Regal and then lit another. She had skimmed the notebooks, lingering on the notes on her sister. Five young women between the ages of fifteen and twenty-one had gone missing from Harrogate in the last ten years. Susan had been the youngest. With three of the other young women being over eighteen, they hadn't gotten the same press coverage. Milly knew that in nearly all missing persons cases, after an initial flurry of media coverage, the broadcasters, newspapers and websites lose interest. Someone going missing is a story – a person who remains missing is not.

Her feet took her north, through the old town streets, past the long stretches of public gardens and flower-beds that made Harrogate so pretty this time of year. Harrogate in Bloom. The place was always full of flowers. As she walked, she remembered long summer afternoons with Susan, Mum and Dad, lying on blankets with the smell of the grass in her nose and the sun in her eyes. Mum read magazines and sipped lemonade, Dad read his war novels and Susan listened to music on her iPod. The Cure, Suede, Manic Street Preachers, Siouxsie and the Banshees and, of course, her favourite – Nirvana. Sometimes she would share one of her earbuds with Milly.

The five-year age gap wasn't small enough, nor quite big enough, for either of them to fully appreciate the other's taste in music or films. But they loved each other, and her big sister was always there if she needed her. It was easier to talk to Susan than Mum. When Milly was younger though, Susan played with her a lot. They would have tea parties in the garden for Milly's teddies, and sometimes Susan's old dolls would be invited. Milly smiled at the memory. The warmth and the innocence of their laughter.

As they'd grown older, the gap between them seemed to widen as Susan grew out of toys and found bands, concerts, people with nose piercings and friends who could get served in a local off-licence. Susan was entering a new world, one which Milly was not yet ready for. Milly was sure that if Susan had not gone missing, they would be close today. The age gap doesn't matter when you're older. Sometimes, usually after Milly's *issues* had risen to the surface and she'd done or said something foolish, while she nursed a glass of wine in her London flat, she thought of Susan. How good it would be to have her in her life. To have someone she loved and could trust.

Milly felt the loss of her sister anew in different stages of her life and it felt like losing her all over again.

And that made Milly angry, because Susan had not been lost. Someone, a man, had taken her.

Milly stubbed out her cigarette on a bin, threw it in the rubbish bag and looked around the street. The houses here were Victorian and grand.

She was in the Duchy Estate. A quick check on the Maps app confirmed the next street over was Kent Road. She had a vague idea of the town layout from memory.

She wanted to see Kent Road. If she wanted to find out what had happened to Susan, Kent Road was a good place to start.

The afternoon sun was hot on her skin. As Milly emerged onto the middle of Kent Road, she looked left and right to get her bearings. Hard to tell where she was exactly. She chose to walk right, looking for house numbers.

John's files had been detailed, and probably contained more information than it was good for him to record in private papers. Names, addresses, even some dates of birth.

The house that had captured that CCTV image of Susan was number fifty-eight. Milly passed number forty-two and kept walking. Next house was number forty. She was going in the wrong direction. She turned and walked back to the junction and kept on going.

The Simpsons lived in sixty-five.

According to John's notes, their daughter, Georgina, was the second person to go missing. At some stage, she would need to speak to them. As Milly had worked her way up the line as a journalist, first in small regional papers and then the dailies, and then the jump into TV news and broadcasting, she had done almost every job that journalists encounter. There was one job they all hated. Worse than court reporting, worse than live weather reports where you stand in the middle of a storm and try to do a piece to camera, worse than anything – talking to victims' families.

It was a tightrope. You needed to get the story, so your game face was firmly on, but at times, and even for long periods afterwards, it hurt. Hurt to be around so much pain and loss, and for that not to affect you. It's a stain, one senior reporter had told her; if you allow yourself to get too close it rubs off on you – keep your distance, emotionally. But Milly wasn't that kind of reporter. In order to write about someone, she had to know them; walk around in their shoes so she could understand how they felt. This was the skill that elevated her career, and no matter how hard it was on her psychologically, she knew it made her work so much better.

Seventeen-year-old Georgina Simpson had gone missing a year before Susan.

Georgina Simpson left her parents' house to meet her boyfriend, Declan. No one saw her again. For a time, Declan was a suspect, but John's notes revealed he never thought the young man responsible. He was too broken by her disappearance.

Milly passed the house with the CCTV, stopped and looked up the drive. The camera was still there, on the corner of the old Edwardian home, green moss covering the top. She turned, to mimic Susan's direction of travel. And then looked over her shoulder, back up the street, just as Susan had done.

Why had Susan looked back? Had someone been following her?

As Milly looked towards the direction from which Susan had come, she noticed a house further up the street. She turned and walked towards it, then stood on the pavement outside.

This was a Victorian home, and like most of the others on this road, it was Gothic in style and large. Unlike the others, the hedges bordering the property were not in good order. No lush green leaves. It was more like a tall barrier of thorn bushes and brambles, mostly brown and dead in the hot sun. The lawn was overgrown with weeds that crept onto the drive. More weeds sprouted from the broken tarmac. The house was old brick, blackened and mossy. The window frames looked to be original – rotten wood, flaking and broken. Yellowed lace curtains hung from the windows.

Then there was the smell. Something like smoke, and damp, and old meat.

A chill made the sweat on the back of Milly's neck suddenly feel very cold.

'Excuse me, luv,' said a voice behind her.

Startled, Milly jumped as she swung around.

Standing in front of her was a portly man who looked to be in his late sixties. A red and black Argyle sweater stretched over his stomach. A collared shirt beneath. What little hair he had left was ginger with streaks of white running through it. This colour scheme bled into his face, which was white with patches of red on his cheeks and nose. His grey trousers were stuffed into thick wellington boots and he had pruning scissors in one hand.

'I am sorry, I didn't mean to startle you,' he said, softly. 'It's just a friendly word of warning. The man in that house isn't the most pleasant. So if you're selling something or looking for charity donations, I wouldn't bother.'

'Oh, thanks for the warning. I'm not selling anything, I . . . I'm just having a look round the neighbourhood. I used to live in Harrogate,' said Milly.

The man turned away, waving a hand, 'Oh good, sorry to have bothered you. It's just I don't like seeing people upset and that man is more trouble than he's worth.'

'Do you know him?' asked Milly.

'Old Peculiar? No, luv. Nobody knows him. Keeps himself to himself mostly, but he's a right cantankerous git, pardon me for saying so. And that's not all. I wouldn't think it's safe for a young lady to be in his company, if you know what I mean.'

Milly glanced once more at the decrepit, creepy house, then turned back to the man.

'Thank you, I'm sorry, I didn't catch your name?'

'George,' said the man, stepping toward Milly with a smile and an open hand. He glanced at his palm and Milly saw some soil residue on his fingers. He wiped it on his trousers, and held it out again, 'George Simpson. I live across the road.'

At first, Milly tried not to let her recognition show in her features, then, as she took his hand, she decided it was better to be honest.

'I'm Milly Porter, Mr Simpson. I was meaning to come and see you,' she said.

'I don't recognise the name, I'm afraid. Did the wife arrange summat and not tell me? She's hell for doing that. Had a man come last week to re-tile the bathroom and I knew nothing about it. Course, Franny says she told me, but she didn't. I would've remembered an appointment for a tiler. You're not a decorator, are ya?'

George smiled and released Milly's hand.

'No, I'm afraid not. Is your wife at home? Maybe we could all have a chat together. My sister, Susan Porter, went missing many years ago. I came back to Harrogate to find out what happened to her. I met with the detective, John Asquith. He said maybe I should have a chat with you and your wife about your daughter. Susan went missing not long after your daughter disappeared.'

Milly forgave herself the lie, even when a flash of sorrow wiped the smile from his face and dulled his eyes. That's the way people live with loss. It creeps up on you, like a stranger in the street – it hits you when you least expect it.

'I'm very sorry to hear about your sister. I remember the story in the paper. They never found her. Just like our Georgina . . .' he said, his voice leaden, his throat tight with grief. 'You'd best come inside for a cuppa,' he said, forcing another smile, but one that he couldn't hold onto. 'These things are better discussed over a brew.'

Before he led Milly across the street, she noticed George looking behind her, casting a dark glance at the dark house that belonged to Old Peculiar.

Milly sat beneath an umbrella in the Simpsons' garden and sipped at her tea. Franny Simpson was a little younger than George, but not by much. She wore beige linen trousers, white half-inch heels and a floral blouse buttoned up to the neck, even in this heat. Sweat beaded her forehead and darkened some of the tight grey curls around her ears. Her small hands were bright pink and swollen with age, making her rings appear as if they were strangling her fingers.

Milly noticed Franny did everything with a great fuss and urgency. The good china tea-set had come out of her kitchen cupboard, a small plate was quickly filled with Mr Kipling's French Fancies, which George kept a close eye on, and a thick pink tea-cosy found its way onto the pot even though there was no danger of it going cold in this weather. She topped up Milly's teacup and asked if she wanted another fondant fancy.

George leant forward, gently waiting for her answer. Milly wasn't a fan of sweet things. She'd had one just for the sake of politeness. She said one was more than enough, and George's gaze then turned to Franny. Some subtle communication passed between them, something that only a long, close marriage could build, and with Franny's imperceptible blessing, George stuffed a fancy into his face with delight and Franny continued her story.

'The first we knew summat were up was when Declan phoned the house. Georgina was supposed to meet him at Valley Gardens. He said she was late and she weren't answering her mobile. I knew then summat bad had happened . . .'

Milly wanted to press for more, but experience told her to wait. This wasn't easy. Patience and kindness would give her more than firing out questions. She sipped her tea and looked out over their rear garden. It was large and well cared for. Manicured lawn, extensive flower-beds lining the boundaries and several patches dug for more. Milly noticed two dozen flowers sitting in plastic pots beside the churned earth, ready to be planted. A long receipt from B&Q sat beneath one of the pots. She must've interrupted George in the middle of his garden work.

She angled her gaze back to Franny, saw her staring over the hedge in the direction of Old Peculiar's house.

'If I'd only a known, I never would've let her go out. But that's it, you never do, do ya? You never know what the good Lord has in store for us. She were a lovely girl, our Georgina. Apple of his eye, you know?' she said, nodding at George, who took his eyes off the Mr Kipling plate just long enough to smile, sadly, at Franny.

'The detective, John Asquith, believed the last sighting of my sister was on this street,' said Milly. 'She was passing a house, and CCTV caught her looking back, over her shoulder, like she was being followed.'

George sighed. 'I remember John Asquith,' he began. 'Nice fella, couldn't have done more for our Georgina. All of them, the police, they were very kind. Funny you should mention that, about the CCTV. John asked us about *him*, you know? About Old Peculiar.'

'Dreadful, horrid man,' spat Franny.

'I don't know if he was officially a suspect but John had his suspicions. What do you know about him?' asked Milly.

George was about to speak, but Franny cut him off.

'He's not right. Harcourt, his name is. Martin Harcourt. But everyone round here calls him Old Peculiar. It has nowt to do with the beer, he's just old and very, very strange. George had terrible trouble with him when he was Chairman of the DRA, didn't you, George?'

'Terrible,' agreed George.

'What's the DRA?'

'Duchy Residents' Association,' said Franny. 'This is part of the Duchy Estate. Folk round here don't care for calling it an estate, but this whole area were owned by the Duchy of Lancaster before it were developed into housing. It were part of *that* estate. The DRA look after residents, deal with plan-ning problems with the local council, that sort of thing . . .'

'And,' added George, 'we encouraged residents to keep up the maintenance of their property. Keep the place nice, you know. Especially for Harrogate in Bloom. Make sure the place is spick and span and they don't make too many changes neither – this is a conservation area, after all. The character of the Duchy has to be preserved at all times. But of course, Old Peculiar never bothered his backside to look after that house, no matter how many letters we sent him.'

'So what's his story?'

Franny said, 'Oh, there are many a story about him. He's lived there for so long, but hardly ever comes out of the house, only at night. He frightens the young ones, shouts at them from his window if they ever go too close to his house. He wears that big black overcoat wherever he goes, has a long, dirty beard and a look in his eye. Doris Finkle says he threatened her with a knife when she called round to see me last Christmas. I opened the door and she were as white as a ghost and him standing in the road bletherin' at the top of his voice. Had to give her some of the Christmas brandy to calm her down.'

'Would Doris be willing to talk to me?'

'Oh ay, she'd talk the legs off a stool, that one,' said George, with a snigger, before a remonstrating stare from Franny silenced him. He coughed, then defiantly snatched another fondant fancy.

'And he only comes out of the house after dark?' asked Milly.

'Like a bloody vampire,' said George.

Milly checked her watch. It was coming up to four o'clock. She had a good sense of George and Franny, but she didn't have a picture in her mind of Georgina.

'Would you mind if I took a look at Georgina's room?' asked Milly.

They didn't mind at all. George showed her upstairs and Franny followed behind Milly.

As Milly followed George up the stairs she stopped halfway and looked at a framed photograph on the wall.

George and Franny were much younger in the photo, both slimmer. George had more hair that looked vibrant and not yet grey. They were at the seaside, sitting on a bench with the beach behind them. Ice creams in their hands. The girl who sat in the middle, flanked by her parents, was smiling widely and holding up her ninety-nine. She wore a sun hat and had to hold it in place with her other hand. It looked windy, the girl's long brown hair whipped around her face.

'Georgina had just gotten her braces off,' said Franny, standing at the bottom of the stairs. 'She had such a lovely smile . . .'

Milly nodded, said, 'She was beautiful.'

Franny pulled a handkerchief from her sleeve, sniffed and wiped her nose.

Milly didn't know what to say; she was bringing up old wounds. Part of her wished she hadn't come.

'It's all right,' said George, and then, as if sensing Milly's thoughts, 'we think about her every day. I'm sure you think about your sister a lot, too.'

'I do. That's why I'm here. I want to be able to deal with it. I suppose I just want closure. I think that'll help.'

George opened the second door at the top of the stairs, and said, 'We have done a bit of work in the room.'

Surprisingly, the bedroom was large. With a double bed, a sink in the corner, and what had probably once been a small dressing room had been converted into a toilet and shower.

There were fresh towels and clean sheets on the bed. A bedside table, chest of drawers and a wardrobe.

Two large bay windows offered a view.

Directly facing Old Peculiar's house.

'We moved Georgina's things to the garage. We've kept them all, mind,' said Franny, coming into the room behind Milly. 'It's been so long, we thought if she ever did come back she might not want a teenager's room. Plus, times have been hard recently, since George retired. What with the cost of living and the mortgage going through the roof, well, we rent it out now. George put it on t'internet, took pictures and everything.'

'Do you get many rentals?'

'Not too many. When there's conventions in town we some-times get a visitor, but no permanent lodgers.'

Milly looked at Old Peculiar's house. She could see the whole top floor. The yellowed curtains twitching in the breeze that crept through the rotten window frames.

'Would it be rude if I asked how much you charge? It's just, I'm going to be staying here a while and, well, I'm on sick-pay from work and . . .'

'Oh luv, we'd be delighted to have ya,' said Franny. 'We normally charge forty-five pound a night, and that includes a home-cooked breakfast. You have your own bathroom. We don't do dinner unless you request it a day in advance. I don't cook fish, mind. George doesn't like fish. We can't go much lower than forty . . .'

'I'll take it,' said Milly, 'At forty-five a night.'

After some creative excuses, Milly got away with only paying for one night at her hotel, and came back to the Simpsons' house with cash for the first week's stay and her luggage. Franny fussed over her, and George carried her case to the room.

George placed her suitcase on the floor of the room and said, 'I hope you find out what happened. For our sakes too. If you go out, be careful to stay clear of Old Peculiar. He's not right in the head. Now, let me know if you need anything. We're heading out this evening, back late. Probably after midnight. Captain's Night at the golf club. We'll try not to wake you.'

George left and closed the door after himself. Milly got settled in.

She unpacked her clothes into the wardrobe and the chest of drawers, put her toiletries in the bathroom and sat on the bed with John's notebooks, a pad and a pen. As the hours passed and the light faded, Milly lit the lamp on the bedside table and continued making her own notes on the disappearances. When she heard the front door slamming shut, about eight-thirty, she rose from the bed and looked outside. Franny and George, arm-in-arm, walked down the driveway and turned left – off out for the evening. They were a sweet old couple. United in love and grief. Loss can forge a bond or, in the case of her parents, tear people and marriages apart.

Milly looked around the street. Quiet. Peaceful. Dark. Lamplight throwing orange halos on the pavement.

A figure at the window of the old house.

Old Peculiar.

There was a faint light behind him. Casting his twisted figure in silhouette. A dark, hulking shape at the bedroom window.

Gooseflesh covered Milly's arms. Her chest tightened and it took everything not to duck and hide from view. Old Peculiar stood at the window like a golem of old. Still as stone.

The fear subsided in Milly. Replaced by something else. Her teeth squeaked as her jaw clamped down hard, and her fingers folded into fists so tight her hands shook. The man stood there for some time, then turned and disappeared from view.

Milly let out her breath and blinked. She went to the sink and splashed cold water on her face. It always helped to dispel the anger.

She was suddenly desperate for a cigarette.

She went downstairs, opened the back door and strode into the garden. She lit a Regal Kingsize and inhaled, deeply.

As she slowly blew out the smoke, she felt the tension leaving her body. She closed her eyes, took another drag. The only light in the garden came from the burning end of her cigarette. She thought of Susan. The last thing her sister saw could have been that huge figure in black, in the dark, coming up behind her.

'Bastard,' said Milly, shaking her head. John Asquith was right. The Simpsons were right. There was something very wrong about that man. Something . . . she hesitated to even think it . . . evil.

She had finished her cigarette and turned to find somewhere to put it out, when she saw him.

Old Peculiar stood in the garden.

His vast shoulders encased in a huge black coat.

His eyes were red and wild and fixed on Milly.

His arms rose, and as they did she saw the glint of metal beneath his coat. A long knife slung through his belt.

'Get AWAY!' he roared, and came at her.

Milly dropped the cigarette, screamed and stumbled backwards. He kept coming. His arms outstretched, reaching for her. Her heel touched something solid. Something metal. She reached down and lifted the spade with one hand. Soil still on it from George digging the earth for his new flowers that day.

Old Peculiar lunged towards her, hands outstretched and eyes wild.

Milly screamed.

She made a sound filled with all of her rage, her loss, her pain, her *issues* . . . as she swung the spade.

A sharp pain in her wrist made her flinch as the handle bucked in her grip.

And Old Peculiar fell.

She dropped the spade.

He wasn't moving. He was silent. Still.

Five minutes later, with her heart hammering through her chest, Milly took her fingers away from his neck, unable to find a pulse.

Panic.

Big panic.

She had come here looking for this man. Rented a room across the street. And now she'd killed him.

But he had attacked *her*, hadn't he?

She had no wounds.

She had sat in enough courtrooms with her reporter's pad filled with messy shorthand to know this wasn't good. It didn't look like self-defence.

His house.

There must be something in that house to tie him to Susan's murder. To Georgina's, to them all.

But that would take time to look. To search.

They couldn't find him here.

Not yet.

Milly paced the garden.

Her toe touched the spade.

Hide him. Bury him. For now. She had to give herself enough time to get a look inside that old house.

She dragged him by his ankles. He was big and heavy and she was sweating by the time she'd moved him five feet to the loose soil. Then the spade was in her hand. As her back muscles screamed, her arms burned and sweat rolled off her forehead, Milly dug a hole.

It was impossible to tell how long she laboured. Whenever she took a second to look at her work it just didn't look deep enough. He was so big.

The spade hit something solid.

Bugger, a stone.

Using the torch on her phone to see, Milly brushed away loose soil.

It wasn't a stone.

Looking back up at her was a smiley face. With Xs for eyes and a crooked smile.

Susan's Nirvana T-shirt.

She dropped the phone, tossed the spade aside and let out a wail. Digging her nails into the earth, the smell making her gag . . . there she was. Her sister.

Susan.

Her head swung to the side and she heard a loud noise, like the spade hitting another stone. That's strange, thought Milly. It felt like the back of her skull was on fire.

And then she felt nothing.

George stood over Milly's body, hauled the spade up high and let it come down again, hard, on the back of her head.

'Dearie me, what's gone on here?' asked Franny.

'Do you reckon Old Peculiar tried to warn her? Like he tried to warn her sister?' asked George.

'Must've done,' said Franny. 'Look, she's knocked over the flowers we bought yesterday.'

George tutted, said, 'They were lovely petunias. Never mind. Here, put the kettle on, will you luv? I'll be a while out here.'

'Will do. Make sure you change out of your good clothes before you start. Don't want those new trousers getting ruined. Marks and Spencer they are.'

'Will do.'

'Are you going to put her with her sister, or the others?'

'Her sister, I reckon. She's done some of the work already. Only seems right, doesn't it?'

Franny nodded, said, 'Don't let me keep you.'

Before she got to the back door, George called out, 'Oh, when you're bringing me tea, I'll have a couple more of those fondant fancies.'

PARKRUN

Ann Cleeves

They met up each Saturday for parkrun. Only Anna did any
real running, and even then it wasn't every week. She was on
the committee and sometimes she was Run Director, dishing
out the marshal's vests and instructions, or starting the runners
off, standing on a stepladder and shouting through a microphone. She would never have admitted it to the others, but
she quite liked that bit. She'd always preferred being in charge
and according to her friends she was a bit of a drama queen.
It did feel like a performance, standing in front of the crowd
of runners, welcoming the newbies and counting them down
to the start. She *could* run though and had done a half mara-
thon the year before. She'd been the person to get her friends
involved: 'It's a way to make sure we stay in touch, now we're
not working anymore. And it'll be good for us. We can go for
tea and cake afterwards and catch up properly.'

She, Clare and Sally had been teachers working in the same
authority, and they'd taken early retirement around the same
time. They'd been friends for years, despite their different
personalities. Sally had always liked animals more than people,
so her choice of career had been a mystery to Anna. Though,
Anna thought now, when they'd all left school, there hadn't
been much choice for young women who didn't consider that

university was for them. It was secretarial school or teacher training college.

Sally had fitted in to the primary school at first. She'd treated the children as if they were puppies, and her pupils had responded perfectly to her training, to the praise and disapproval. They'd always seemed well-behaved. Then there was a new headteacher who hadn't liked her methods, who hadn't really understood Sally at all. Clare had been the best support in the world, helping her through the trauma of the new regime, but in the end, Sally took the offered redundancy to spend more time with her dogs and her horse. She'd never married. Anna, who'd specialized in working with SEND kids, thought that Sally's brain worked a little differently. She was straightforward and honest and didn't see any need for pretence. She would have found the compromise needed to live with a partner hard to stomach.

Clare had started out in nursing and come into teaching once her own brood was at school. That way she'd be home to look after them in the holidays. She'd landed up in the same primary school as Anna, and they'd become firm friends. Clare had four daughters, they all lived within ten miles of Harrogate, and they fought over her for childcare. Anna thought they were taking the piss. They had good jobs and could afford to pay for a nursery or childminder, and Clare tore herself apart trying to please them all.

Clare's husband had retired at the same time as her. They'd looked forward to all the adventures they'd finally have time for: they planned to travel, to join a rambling club and explore his beloved Dales, and he'd helped her with the grandkids too. More importantly, he'd helped her set boundaries with the family.

'This is our time,' he'd said. 'Nobody helped us while our girls were growing up. Let *them* take responsibility.'

Then he'd gone to the doctor feeling ropey, been diagnosed with pancreatic cancer and two months later he was dead.

Anna thought their weekly post-run chat over coffee and cake was more important to Clare than it was to Sally or her, and Clare always turned up to parkrun, whatever emotional blackmail she was subjected to by her daughters.

Clare was a little overweight and couldn't *run* more than a hundred yards without getting out of breath, but she loved the exercise, so whenever she was Run Director, Anna made her the Tail Walker. It was an important role, walking behind the slowest participant, making sure that they all got back to the finish line. The fast runners would have finished ages before, filing through the rope funnel to collect their tokens, checking their times on the parkrun app. But the philosophy of the run was that every participant mattered, no matter how slow they were, and Clare was the most encouraging member of the team.

Anna had become a teacher out of a sense of vocation. She'd loved it, especially working with the special educational needs kids and their parents. Then local authority cuts, and a regime that valued academic success over a child's happiness, turned every day into a battle, and she'd bailed out, racked with guilt.

The day she'd resigned, she'd discovered that her live-in lover had been having an affair with a student – he was a university lecturer – and that he was leaving her. In tears, she'd called Clare, who'd dumped whichever kid she was minding that day with a neighbour and turned up on Anna's doorstep. Anna had got very drunk, and the next day she'd applied to train to be a play therapist. That had been Clare's idea: 'You'd be bloody brilliant! Nobody understands screwed-up kids as well as you.'

Now Anna was self-employed in the role, fulfilled and enjoying every minute. She missed the sex but, she told herself, she revelled in living on her own.

'I am,' she said to her friends every time they met in the Lavender Tea Rooms for their post-race gossip (they never went to Bettys, which was really only for tourists), 'living my best life.'

And she almost believed it.

It was the first Saturday in March, sunny, with little gusts of wind that brought the smell of spring and made the daffodils on the Stray dance. There was that light that made all the colours seem sharp and bright. Harrogate looked its welcoming best, and the respectable Yorkshire ladies hitting the shops were already in their spring outfits. Here on the Stray, everything was green. It was as if the countryside had been brought right to the edge of the town.

Anna always got to the run first. She dressed carefully in Lycra, with a running club sweatshirt to look the part. There were a lot of single older men in the club and some of them were surprisingly fit. She hadn't given up all hope of finding a new bloke. For fun, of course. Not for any sort of commitment.

Today she was in charge, which she liked best. The teacher coming out in her, she supposed. She took it in turns to be Run Director with Gordon Biggs but felt that she suited the role better. She was more approachable. More welcoming. Gordon looked after the group's finances and could be very petty when it came to volunteers' expenses. Clare knew the family quite well because she'd taught their son, Jonathan, and Anna knew that the Biggs had sometimes given her a hard time at parents' evening. Anna despised anyone who gave Clare a hard time.

Sally walked up soon after, looking (and smelling) as if she'd just mucked out her horse. She was happy to fill in the marshalling gaps. She was a great marshal, reliable and jolly, cheering on the runners as they went past her, especially if they were accompanied by a dog on a lead.

Clare arrived ten minutes before start time, looking exhausted and wearing a tracksuit that she'd probably had since her teaching days, embellished with baby sick.

She must have seen Anna looking at the stain.

'I had Abbie overnight and I didn't have time to change. But it doesn't matter, does it? And it'll be covered by the vest.'

The vest was orange and had 'tail walker' on the front. Clare wore it like a badge of honour.

The Stray was full of runners now, with latecomers still gathering outside Wedderburn House, ready for the start. This was a green space, surrounded by substantial houses, but not all the participants came from the affluent part of town. The run brought them together, strangers and friends, waiting to get going. They were like hounds, ranging, waiting for the start of a hunt. Sally went hunting, and once Anna had gone with her to the meet to watch the horses and hounds set off. Never again!

Some Saturdays there were five hundred people of all strengths and abilities gathered there. Anna recognised lots of the locals – the blind woman with her guide runner, an army veteran in combat gear, the middle-aged woman who'd started coming as a new year's resolution and who had got hooked – but there were strangers too. Parkrun tourists who liked to visit a new venue every month, or who were working their way through the alphabet, starting with Aberdeen and ending with Zeebrugge. These were often elite athletes in the first group to finish.

Anna looked at her watch. Five minutes to go. Gordon Biggs bustled towards her, full of his own importance as he always was. He'd worked in the bank in town before the branch closed and he was made redundant. Anna was sorry for him, of course she was, but she thought now he was greedy for power. He'd managed the bank and now he wanted to manage the run.

'I wanted to talk to you about Clare.' His accent was nasal Yorkshire. 'There are other people who'd like to do the tail walking. I think we should set up a rota.'

Anna made a point of looking at her watch. 'I can't discuss this now, Gordon. I need to set them off.' Because she knew that these Saturday mornings were the only break Clare had, and tail walking made her feel important, good about herself. She wouldn't turn up if she were given any other role.

Besides, Anna knew that Gordon had an ulterior motive. His wife, Rosemary, was a blustering woman, a local councillor and a bully. She'd decided that involvement in parkrun would help her meet potential voters and it would soon be election time. Last time the vote had been very close, and her rival was a popular man, the leader of a local charity. She'd decided that she needed to prove that she could take part in community activity too. She couldn't run to save her life and marshalling bored her. Too much standing and cheering on the runners. Too much focus on other people. Tail walking, she'd decided, would suit her very well.

'Rosemary is here.' There was a touch of desperation in his voice. 'I've told her she could be tail walker. I discussed it with the senior team. They all know she's taking over today.'

'Sorry Gordon, Clare was here a while ago and she's all set.'

A pause. 'But Rosemary would *like* to help.'

'Great! I'm sure she would. We need a marshal at that far corner. Can you give her a vest, Gordon, and show her where to stand?' She expected some sort of argument, but it was nearly nine o'clock and even Gordon knew that the start time was set and couldn't be delayed.

Anna climbed the step ladder and looked out at the expectant runners, knowing it was ridiculous but enjoying her moment of glory. She made out Clare in her orange vest. Rosemary Biggs was fighting her way through the crowd to confront her. There seemed to be some sort of altercation and for one moment, Anna thought the councillor would rip the tail-walking vest from her friend's back. Although there was still a minute to go, she lifted the microphone and announced the start of the run. When she looked again Rosemary had disappeared, presumably to take up her position as marshal.

She held the microphone to her mouth and counted them down. 'Three, two, one, go!'

The serious runners were at the front of the crowd. They could run the whole course in twenty minutes. Anna loved to watch the power of their movement, the long loping strides, the determination to get a personal best. This was supposed to be a relaxed event without a hint of competition, but the good runners took the whole business seriously. Occasionally, there was a scuffle as people jostled to be first into the finishing funnel, and some problems when the other users of the Stray, the dog walkers and families with their skates and their scooters, resented the runners and stood their ground on the paths. Generally, however, it was a good-natured event. The start of Anna's weekend.

Soon the fastest runners had done their three laps of the course, and the scanners and the token collectors were busy registering their times. Anna waited as the slow ones came in, red-faced and panting, followed by the walkers and buggy-pushers. She was looking out for Clare, ready now for a decent coffee and one of the Lavender Tea Rooms' famous cheese scones. And for a gossip about Gordon and Rosemary. They needed to plan a strategy.

By now, all the regulars had come through. People were drifting away, wandering back into town through the spring sunshine, their shadows long and thin in the low light. There was no sign of Sally or Clare. Anna walked the route, anxious now that there might be a problem. She took her responsibilities seriously. Perhaps someone had tripped, and Clare was helping them back. Once, there'd even been a heart attack on the route. Because of her nursing experience, Clare had been very useful then.

Anna realized that she hadn't seen Gordon or Rosemary either. She hoped they weren't causing a fuss again. She was always protective of Clare, who was a gentle soul, not given to standing up for herself.

She saw Sally first. There was a dip in the landscape here, with the path hidden by trees, so Anna came upon her suddenly. She was crouched by the side of the path, and straightened when Anna approached.

'I've called an ambulance.' Her voice was shaky, which wasn't like Sally at all. 'They're on their way.'

On the ground at her feet lay Clare, unconscious, her clothes soaked in blood.

'She's still alive,' Sally said, 'but only just, I think.' She looked across at Anna. 'Someone stabbed her!' Her face was as white and still as marble. It was as if all the blood had drained from her body too.

Anna crouched and took her friend's hand. The feud with Gordon and Rosemary now seemed remarkably trivial.

In the Lavender Tea Rooms, Anna was pleased to see that their usual table in the window was empty. The café sat between an antique shop and a vintage clothes boutique. Usually, the three of them liked watching the shoppers go by, the students looking at the sixties dresses, the loons and the punk T-shirts and the smart elderly couples, who'd watched too many episodes of *Antiques Roadshow* and were convinced that they'd spot a bargain. Now, after the drama at parkrun, she felt that she and Sally needed familiarity, and she bagged the table before anyone else could get it.

The ambulance had arrived very quickly. The incident had happened where the Stray was close to the Knaresborough Road, so they hadn't had far to carry Clare. The police turned up soon after, first a young woman in uniform, then a male detective who looked close to retirement. He was carrying too much weight and could have done, Anna thought, with taking up parkrun himself. She would have suggested it, but he seemed harassed enough. He interspersed their conversation with comments about the shortage of staff.

'If the poor woman dies, we'll be turning it over to the Murder Investigation Team.'

It was almost, Anna thought now, as if he didn't want Clare to survive, so he could pass on the responsibility.

He'd chatted briefly to Sally and to Anna, and she'd explained about parkrun, and that most of the participants had already dispersed.

'We'll put out a call for witnesses,' he'd said. 'With so many people about, someone must have seen something.' He'd looked at them, across the dip in the ground where Clare had been lying, squinting against the sunlight. 'She doesn't seem the sort to have had any enemies.' As if that was a bad thing. 'I don't understand this running obsession. It doesn't seem natural. My old mate Gordon turns out every week to take charge, but he's got more sense than to take part himself.'

Anna had just been about to suggest that Gordon and Rosemary had a motive but stopped just in time. If the detective was friends with the Biggs family, he'd hardly want to consider them as possible suspects. Besides, who would believe that a retired bank manager and a respectable councillor would stab an older woman just so they could have a particular role in the Harrogate parkrun? That would make her a laughing stock. She couldn't really believe it herself.

The detective had wandered away muttering under his breath about homeless people, incomers and nutters, and how once Harrogate had been a lovely town. Anna had decided in that moment that if there was to be justice for Clare, she and Sally would have to be the people to find the attacker.

In the tearoom, the owner came to take their order. Anna liked that. She'd felt that the only good thing about Covid had been mandatory table service.

'No Clare today?' The woman spoke brightly.

Anna jumped in before Sally could go into detail about the incident. 'Not today. She's feeling poorly.' It didn't feel right to be gossiping about their friend, here, where they'd discussed so many other people's business. Not with the owner, who could chat for Yorkshire. 'Two cappuccinos and two cheese scones please.' Their regular choice. No need for discussion.

Now, Sally did pipe up. 'And a salted caramel brownie.' That was Clare's favourite. She had a very sweet tooth.

Anna smiled across to her. 'And two forks. We'll share the brownie.'

When the coffees had been delivered and the owner had left them in peace, they could review what had happened.

'Did you see anything?' Anna asked, because Sally's marshalling spot had been very close to where Clare was found.

Sally shook her head. 'You know what it's like. So many people bunched together as they run, and I do love to cheer them on, I get so caught up in the moment.' A pause. 'When Clare didn't walk past after the slowest ones, I went to look for her. Usually, we walk back together and come to find you.'

Anna nodded. She knew the routine. 'That part of the Stray was quiet by then. It's a bit out of the way there and all the runners had gone through. And there she was.'

'The police didn't find the knife that stabbed her.' Anna was thinking out loud now. 'Did you see anyone at all?'

'There was a couple walking away from me towards the finish,' Sally said, 'but they were a long way off and I only saw their backs.'

'Was the woman wearing a marshal's pink vest?'

'Yes! And the man was small, dumpy.'

They looked at each other. 'Gordon and Rosemary Biggs.' The words came out in unison.

Anna's phone rang. It was Emily, one of Clare's daughters. Anna had texted her, asking for an update. Emily ran her own business. Something to do with advertising. She was the oldest daughter and the one Clare found most intimidating.

'She's awake.' The woman could have come from a smart London suburb. You'd never have known from her speech that she was Yorkshire through and through. Anna thought that Dennis, Clare's husband and a proud Yorkshireman, would be turning in his grave. 'And out of ICU. According to the doctor, she was very lucky.' Her voice was accusatory, as if it was Anna's fault that Clare had been stabbed. 'She'll be out of action for a while.' A pause. 'Really, it couldn't have happened at a more inconvenient time. I was hoping to get to a conference in Frankfurt next week and mother was going to have the children. Now, a colleague will have to go in my place.'

'Have the police spoken to her? Did she see anything?'

'Apparently not. The coward came up behind her, and then she lost consciousness. All that blood loss, I suppose.'

'Does she remember being stabbed?'

'She doesn't seem to remember anything.' Again, the daughter seemed more irritated than concerned.

'It was just as well Sally found her when she did.'

'Humph. Much better if mother hadn't been there at all, alone and vulnerable.'

Anna was about to reply that Clare had hardly been alone, surrounded by 500 runners, but Emily had already ended the call. If it had been a landline, Anna thought she would have slammed down the receiver, but Emily was of a generation that could hardly remember landlines.

'At least she's OK,' Anna said to Sally when the conversation was over. 'Out of danger, it seems. But she can't remember what happened to her, so we'll have to sort it out, won't we? We can't trust that detective to do anything useful.'

'Oh!' Sally just seemed bewildered now. Anna supposed she'd be the person who'd be most affected. She'd found the body after all.

She couldn't quite think what they *could* do to find the culprit, and stared out of the window, an attempt to find inspiration. At that moment, Gordon and Rosemary walked by on the opposite pavement, deep in conversation. For once, Gordon appeared to be in charge. He was laying down the law, and Rosemary was almost having to run to catch up with him. Neither glanced towards the Lavender Tea Rooms.

Anna grabbed her coat, threw money onto the table and got to her feet. 'Come on! Let's see what they're up to.' She thought nothing this exciting had happened since she'd landed the lead in a production of *Joan of Arc* in college.

Sally muttered something about not being able to leave the dogs on their own for too long but all the same, she pulled on her jacket and scrambled after.

By the time they were outside, there was no sign of the Biggses. The two women ran to the end of the street and saw the couple heading back towards the Stray. Gordon was marching ahead, and Rosemary followed with her tiny, trotting steps.

'Returning to the scene of the crime!' Anna was triumphant. Her guilty pleasure was reruns of traditional detective dramas on the TV.

But the couple walked on past the place where Clare had been found and turned into one of the nearby streets.

'I think they're just going home.' Sally might not be as toned as Anna, but she wasn't out of breath. All those long walks with the dogs and country rides must have made her very fit. 'Honestly, I'm not quite sure what you hope to find out.'

It seemed that Sally was right, because the couple paused outside one of the larger Victorian houses in the street. They were still arguing though and stopped for a moment before going inside.

Anna pulled up the hood of her coat to cover most of her face and they both hid in a bus shelter on the corner of the road. The Biggses seemed entirely unaware that anyone was listening, and they spoke so loudly that Anna could hear every word.

'At least now,' Rosemary said, 'I can be Tail Walker for the parkrun. For a few months at least, until the woman is well enough to walk again. Until after the election.'

'Don't be stupid!' Gordon was so exasperated that he was shouting. 'If the police go digging into our affairs, they'll see we have more to gain from that woman's death than a more important role in a Saturday morning community event.' He paused for a moment. 'It might be best if we resign altogether. Keep our heads down, until the police forget all about it.'

He fidgeted in his pocket for a key and let them into the house.

'Well!' Anna's mind was racing. 'What do you think all that was about?'

Sally shook her head. She seemed lost in a world of her own, self-absorbed as only Sally could be. Anna thought that her mind was probably on her dogs, on their food and need for a run, so she didn't press for an answer. This was an investigation she might have to follow on her own.

At home, Anna checked the internet for the visiting times of Harrogate District Hospital and turned up in the ward later that afternoon with a box of chocolates and a bunch of tulips from her garden. Clare was sitting up, reading a book. One eye was swollen where she must have fallen, but she looked remarkably well. Anna thought she was probably enjoying being waited on for a change. There was a mug of tea on the table beside her.

'I was very lucky,' she said. 'The doctors reckon the knife slid across the nylon Tail Walker's tabard and it caught the fleshy part of my thigh, rather than any vital organs.'

'Did you see who did it?'

Clare shook her head. 'They must have come up behind me.'

'*They*! So, there were two of them?'

'No, *they*, as in non-specific gender. You know, like the pronouns. I couldn't tell if it was a man or a woman. Though I suppose there might have been more than one of them. The ground's a bit squelchy where I was standing. I didn't hear any footsteps. I just felt a sharp pain and then I fainted.' A pause. 'I used to faint all the time when I was a girl.'

'I think Gordon and Rosemary Biggs had something to do with it.' Anna relayed the conversation she'd heard outside their house.

'Don't be daft!' Clare gave a little chuckle that made Anna think she might still be on some strong painkillers. 'Those two wouldn't try to kill me. They wouldn't have the nerve.'

'They might try to scare you off. Do you have any inside knowledge about what they might have been up to? Didn't you teach one of their kids?'

'Yeah, not long before I retired. Jonathan. A dreamy little thing. He was a late arrival, born after their other kids were almost grown-up. Given to strange fancies.'

'What sort of fancies?'

'He made up stories. You know, he was one of those kids who believes their own fantasies. Once, he made out that his parents were big-shot criminals, about to flee the country with their ill-gotten gains. Of course, I didn't take him seriously. The week before, he'd told us all that he'd been chased past Harrogate train station by a dinosaur. He needed the attention. I got the impression that he didn't get much at home.'

Anna thought about that. Gordon had worked in a bank, but these days security would make it impossible for an employee to steal, wouldn't it? There might be other forms of theft though. Maybe the haul wouldn't be big enough to run away to the Costa Del Crime, but it might provide a bit extra for Rosemary's original election campaign. She remembered there'd been an issue with the parkrun finances, regular sums apparently disappearing. Jonathan might have overheard the couple discussing that and turned it into a tale of mystery and intrigue. Gordon had been one of the signatures on the Harrogate parkrun's bank account. When the discrepancies had come to light, he'd blamed another group member, who'd been forced to resign, and had taken credit for sorting out the mess. But what if he'd been the thief all along?

'Did you ever talk to Gordon and Rosemary about Jonathan's story?'

'Yeah, just before the run this morning. Rosemary came up to me, ranting about nepotism and dishonesty, and how it was her turn to be Tail Walker. I hate aggro, so I was wittering on about Jonathan, asking how he was getting on at high school, praising his fertile imagination. Remembering that story of his about them both being master criminals. Just to diffuse the situation.'

'And then you were stabbed!' At the other end of the ward, Anna could see two of Clare's daughters approaching. She decided that she didn't need the aggro either, so she picked up her bag, said a quick goodbye to her friend and headed off.

She could hear Clare shouting after her. 'Honestly, you can't really believe it was them.'

Clare always thought the best of everyone.

Outside the hospital, Anna sat for a moment in her car. She was tempted to drive straight to the Biggses' house to confront Gordon and Rosemary about her suspicions, but even she could tell that would hardly be sensible. If they'd stabbed Clare, they must be desperate. She needed to sort out her thoughts first, to discuss things with someone who viewed the world objectively. Sally.

Sally lived fifteen miles outside the town, on the edge of the Dales, in the cottage where she'd been born. It had been her home even when she'd been teaching. In winter, she'd battled through floods and snow to get to school, only staying overnight with Anna when the weather made it impossible to get home.

Anna found her next to the paddock where she kept Misty. She was leaning over the gate, stroking the horse's head. There were two black labs at her feet. The sun was low in the sky now. Soon it would be dusk.

'We need to decide what to do about Gordon and Rosemary Biggs. Should we go to that detective and tell him what we know?'

Sally turned away from the horse. The sun was behind her, so her face was in shadow. 'Really, I don't think that would be a good idea.'

'So, we should investigate ourselves?' That was what Anna had been hoping for all along.

'No! I think we should let it drop. The detective believes Clare was stabbed by some random homeless person and won't put a lot of effort into finding them, especially as Clare wasn't seriously hurt.' Sally paused. 'If he does find someone and charges them, we can go to him then.'

'I don't understand what you're saying.' The sun had almost disappeared behind the fell.

'I stabbed Clare.' Sally felt in her pocket and pulled out a knife, one of those complicated Swiss ones with loads of attachments. It even had a bottle opener, which had come in very useful when the three of them had taken kids away on a residential school trip and they'd needed to relax with a beer at the end of a long day. The knife was very sharp, and Anna thought she could make out a blood stain at the hilt.

'I don't understand.' In this strange light, it felt to Anna as if the world was spinning around her, out of control.

'It was her idea. She asked me to do it. Showed me what to do. She trained as a nurse. She knew exactly where there'd be most blood, but I'd do very little harm.' A pause. 'And she knew that she'd faint. She always did when she felt any pain. When she came round, I think she just pretended to be unconscious.'

'But why would she want you to hurt her?'

'Because she was exhausted!' Sally was angry now and the words spilt out. 'Her daughters were making all those demands, fighting over her as if her only role in life was to look after their children. Pretending that she enjoyed being an unpaid nanny, that they were doing her a favour. She tried to discuss it with them, but they wouldn't listen. She couldn't see any other way of getting a break. She'll be off her feet for several weeks. If she was out of action for a while, she thought they'd have to make alternative arrangements.' Sally looked up at Anna. 'I know it sounds crazy, but she was desperate. And I love her, just as I love you. I'd do anything either of you asked.' There was a pause. 'But there was so much blood. I really thought I might have killed her. It was horrible and I've never been so scared in my life.'

A week later, they were back at parkrun. Anna was Run Director again, because Rosemary and Gordon had resigned from the organising team. To concentrate, they said, on Rosemary's political ambitions. Anna thought it was because they didn't want anyone looking too closely into the run's accounts. Clare was back tail walking, though she was being pushed in a wheelchair by Sally. All the runners cheered as they made their way to the back of the crowd. They hadn't heard any more from the detective. Anna supposed Clare would be just another crime statistic.

After the run, they went to the Lavender Tea Rooms. The owner had saved the window table for them, because that was the only place with room for the chair. It seemed that Clare's daughters had miraculously discovered that there were nursery places available for their offspring. The friends drank coffee, and ate cheese scones, and they each had a caramel brownie to celebrate.

PATHWAYS THROUGH THE SECRET DOOR

M.W. Craven

Bettys Café Tea Rooms.
Harrogate.

'He has that thing soldiers get.'

'What, crabs?'

'No, the other one. The social anxiety one.'

Detective Sergeant Washington Poe's eye-roll could have powered Harrogate's lights for a week. He sighed and said, 'I'm sitting right here. And it's not social anxiety; it's post-traumatic stress disorder. PTSD. I certainly don't have crabs.'

Poe was in Bettys and wishing he wasn't. Harrogate was full of nice pubs. He didn't know why his fiancée had wanted to eat here. It didn't look like his kind of place at all. Also, he'd made a flippant remark to Karen the waitress and she'd gone all hyper-offended Gen Z on him and called over her manager, a bruiser of a woman called Miss Coates.

'Your PTSD is why you yelled at Karen?' Miss Coates asked.

'I didn't *yell* at Karen,' Poe replied. 'I merely answered her question.'

Miss Coates turned to the waitress. 'Karen?'

'I asked if he wanted to see the wine list and he said he was driving. So I asked if he wanted one of our alcohol-free drinks instead, which was when he raised his voice and said he'd rather listen to a Jimmy Nail album. I assume that's a bad thing.'

'It is,' Miss Coates and Poe said at the same time.

'Then he apologised and explained that he has PTSD – which I already knew – and has been snapping at people lately.'

'But I definitely didn't yell,' Poe said.

Karen was a bony thing, all protruding elbows and pointy knuckles. Maroon hair and more rings in her ears than a curtain pole. Her fingers were heavily tattooed. Poe missed the days when finger tatts were considered a bad thing. A Borstal tag. Now it seemed like everyone had them. Poe didn't understand the modern world. He thought it was stupid. He thought it was stupid that you could buy jewels to cover your cat's arse-hole and he thought it was stupid that books could run out of batteries. There were even things called 'digital detox retreats'. When did that happen? When had people got so addicted to their smartphones that they had to pay for time away from them? It wasn't even a London thing. They had digital detox retreats up north now. There was one nearby. He'd seen the flyer on a lamp-post.

'If I've offended you, Karen, I'm sorry,' Poe said. He *didn't* say that if she thought the Jimmy Nail quip was offensive, she should try listening to *Crocodile Shoes*. That album was an offence against nature and God.

Miss Coates nodded, as if the matter was resolved. She seemed like an old-fashioned, rock-solid, unoffendable, no-frills Yorkshire woman. You'd never catch Miss Coates at a digital detox retreat. 'Thank you for your service, sir,' she said. 'What regiment are you in?'

'I'm not in the army. I'm a police officer.'

'I didn't know police officers *could* get PTSD,' Karen said.

Poe shrugged. 'Neither did I.'

'Anyone can get PTSD,' Miss Coates said softly. *'Anyone.'*

Which kind of killed the ebb and flow. Poe wasn't going to volunteer *why* he had PTSD and he thought Miss Coates would rather wear the Red Rose of Lancaster than ask.

Instead, she said, 'Why has the gentleman been seated at a table for three, Karen? There's a window seat for one over by the . . .'

'Window?' Poe said helpfully.

'He was with a woman earlier,' Karen said. 'Kind of looked like a goth Elizabeth Taylor. She's the one who said he had PTSD. She told me as she was leaving. It sounded like a pre-emptive excuse.'

'She's called Estelle and she's my fiancée,' Poe said. 'She's putting more money on the car. And it wasn't a pre-emptive excuse; she tells people I have PTSD as she knows I don't like it.'

'She said you need to open up about it.'

Miss Coates nodded. 'Talking is healing,' she said.

'I have a trauma therapist for yakking. I've just been to see her. It's why we're in North Yorkshire. And Estelle will be back soon. We'll order when she arrives.'

Karen and Miss Coates drifted off. Poe relaxed and watched Karen take the order from a nearby table. It seemed to pass without incident. He replayed his encounter with her. Decided he hadn't done anything wrong. That although comparing Generation Z to the Greatest Generation – the guys and gals who grew up during WW1, lived through the Great Depression and fought in WW2 – wasn't fair, Gen Z really were a whiny bunch.

While he waited for Estelle to return, he picked up the menu. She was buying him afternoon tea. Said that he'd been through the wringer recently and he deserved something nice. Poe thought 'nice' was an ambitious word for afternoon tea at Bettys. There was no black pudding. No pies or massive slabs of meat. And although kedgeree was on the menu, Poe didn't consider that a proper curry. A *proper* curry caused your eyes to sweat and your ears to leak. Afternoon tea at Bettys seemed to be a selection of dainty sandwiches and even daintier cakes, of teas and speciality coffees. The menu proudly stated that the sandwiches were crustless, the cakes were miniature, and the scones were packed with plump sultanas. Like plump sultanas was a selling point instead of a reason to avoid them.

Estelle entered Bettys and slipped into the seat opposite. Poe's heart melted a little. She was a beautiful woman. A *brilliant* woman. A goth Elizabeth Taylor, Karen the waitress had said, and she was right. And for some reason Estelle wanted to marry him. A two-bit loser with an anger-management problem. She was a member of the aristocracy and could trace her family tree all the way back to the Norman Conquest. Poe couldn't trace *his* family tree past his grandad, who, ironically, was called Norman.

Estelle picked up the menu and smiled. 'Have you seen something you like?'

'They put sultanas in everything. I don't like sultanas.'

'Of course they put sultanas in everything, Poe. It's a tearoom.'

Poe shrugged. 'This is fine, Estelle,' he said. 'Honestly. Anyway, I'm so hungry I could eat a scabby dog between two pissed mattresses.'

'Is something you'll never be saying again. Agreed?'

'Sorry.'

'Anyway, this is supposed to be a treat so cheer the fuck up.'

'Sorry,' he said again.

79

'And I have a surprise for you. One I think you'll like.'

'You've been to that lingerie shop we walked past?'

Estelle grinned. 'Actually, I have. But that'll have to wait. This surprise can't.'

'What is it?'

'Tilly's joining us. She's running late but she'll be here soon.'

Tilly!

Now that really *did* cheer him the fuck up.

Tilly Bradshaw walked into Bettys the same way Frank Spencer would walk into a china shop. She clipped an old dear around the ear with one of her laptop bags. Hit another as she turned to apologise. She saw Poe at the back of the tearoom and started waving madly, like she was stranded on a desert island and he was a low-flying aeroplane. She yelled, 'Poe! Poe!'

Poe returned her wave, then ducked behind his menu while Tilly bumped her way through Bettys like a pinball. When she took her seat, the tearoom gradually went back to normal. It was as if a very small, very concentrated whirlwind had entered, then taken a seat next to the grumpy man at the back of the room.

'Did you know I was coming, Poe?'

'Not until two minutes ago, Tilly.'

'It's been *ages* since I've seen you. Did you get my email?'

'I did. I'm still reading it. It was quite . . . detailed.'

'Four thousand, three hundred and two words.'

'Really? Seems like it was longer.'

Karen the waitress came and took their order.

'Three afternoon teas, please,' Estelle said. 'Extra meat in one of them, the most vegan thing the chef knows how to make in another.'

'And what do you want in the third?'

'Nothing extra for me, thanks. I'm normal.'

Karen tapped her tablet then disappeared into the kitchen.

'Do you still hate the training unit, Poe?' Tilly asked. 'I heard you had another argument with the chief instructor last week. What happened?'

Poe, as well as having questionable lineage, couldn't even call himself a police officer these days. Not really. He certainly wasn't allowed to arrest anyone. His last case, actually *their* last case, hadn't gone the way anyone had expected. He'd almost died and the Serious Crime Analysis Section, the unit responsible for catching serial killers and solving apparently motiveless murders, had effectively been disbanded. Tilly had been seconded to something she wasn't allowed to talk about, their boss, Steph Flynn, had been promoted to the anti-modern slavery unit and he'd been sent to the training wing until the National Crime Agency quack said he was fit for service.

'Who told you that, Tilly?' Poe asked. 'I haven't even told Estelle.'

Tilly didn't answer him.

'Where *do* you work, Tilly?'

'I'm not supposed to talk about it. Even though my phoney baloney colleagues talk about it *all* the time. One of them was even sacked for putting a photograph on Instagram. What a nitwit. Anyway, I asked you a question – what did you say to the chief instructor?'

Poe sighed. Tilly was like a dog with a bone when it came to his career. She wasn't going to let it go. 'One of my students asked a stupid question,' he said. 'Some grizzled old sergeant from the Forest of Dean asked if it was possible to extract DNA from urine. He was literally taking the piss. I told him to leave my mock crime scene.'

Estelle tried unsuccessfully to hide her smile.

'What?'

'Hey, I'm a forensic pathologist,' she said. 'I'll go round for round with you when it comes to stupid questions from cops. I was once asked if it was possible to saw off your own head.'

Poe waited a beat. 'And is it?'

She winked. 'I'll lend you one if you want to try it later.'

'Tilly, make a note, next time we're called to a beheading we can immediately rule out suicide.'

'I will, Poe.'

'And the chief instructor told you to let the Forest of Dean sergeant resume his training?' Estelle said.

'He did.'

'And what did you say?'

'That I'd rather get filmed seal clubbing.'

Tilly opened one of her laptops and started typing. She shook her head and said, 'Classic Poe.'

'I was joking about making a note on sawing off your own head.'

'I know, Poe. But I keep a list of all the things you say you'd rather do instead of the things you're *supposed* to do.' She spun the laptop so he could see the screen. 'See, I've put seal clubbing under S. It's just before the one about how you'd rather have a verruca than eat a pear.'

Poe glanced at the screen. 'Crikey, that's a big list.'

Tilly nodded.

'You seem to be picking fights with a lot of people recently, Poe,' Estelle said.

Karen arrived. Poe made sure he was extra polite when the three-tiered plate of afternoon tea was put in front of him. Made sure he said it looked delicious. He didn't want Karen raising the Jimmy Nail incident. After they'd filled their china cups with tea – Yorkshire for Poe and Estelle, green for Tilly – they tucked in.

Poe watched his fiancée and his best friend eating their afternoon teas with gusto. He was missing something. Bettys was a lovely place, a national institution, but it wasn't him. They could have gone somewhere that did beer flights and pie platters. There were Indian and Chinese and Thai restaurants in Harrogate. But Estelle had chosen Bettys. A tearoom. He felt something stir. Something he hadn't felt in a while.

Curiosity.

'I don't know why you've brought me to a tearoom full of posh ladies in bobble hats, Estelle. It won't cure my PTSD. In fact, it's likely to make it worse. I mean, look at this.' He held up a sandwich. It was white bread, cut the size of a fish finger. 'It's a cucumber sandwich. An *actual* cucumber sandwich. Look, the crusts have been cut off and everything. I didn't think they existed outside of jokes about the royal family.'

'This isn't about curing your PTSD, Poe,' Estelle said. 'It's about getting you to think about something else for a bit.'

'Well, mission accomplished,' he said. 'I'll be thinking about this sandwich for years.'

She didn't respond. Just put down the knife she'd been using to cut her scone in half. Tilly did the same. They waited for him to say something.

'What is this, an intervention?'

They waited.

After a moment he said, 'I don't sleep anymore.'

'I know,' Estelle replied. 'I lie awake next to you.'

'I mean, I *want* to sleep, but I'm scared to close my eyes, if that makes sense.'

'Of course, it makes sense.'

'What do you see, Poe?' Tilly asked.

'I've told my trauma therapist what I see,' he said.

'But you haven't told me.'

'I see *her*, Tilly.'

Tilly nodded. That was all he needed to say. She knew who he meant. They all did.

'Sometimes the flashbacks seem so real, so vivid, I can't tell if I'm awake or dreaming. I think I'm back . . . there. And then I wake up screaming and shaking, drenched in sweat. It feels as though I can't breathe, like I'm drowning in the shit I went through.'

'We'll walk this path together, Poe,' Estelle said. 'Every step of the fucking way.'

He put his hands across the table and held hers. 'I know we will.'

'I'm here for you too, Poe,' Tilly said. 'Whatever you need.'

Poe smiled at his friend. 'I know that too, Tilly,' he said.

'After a traumatic event, the body goes into self-preservation mode, Poe. It's so you're ready if the danger returns. It's why you're hypervigilant. On permanent alert. PTSD is the rational response to what you went through. But permanent hypervigilance isn't sustainable. It's why the brain gets confused. It wants to drop its guard and get some rest, but it's also worried the danger isn't over. It's like an overloaded computer memory. Eventually everything shuts down.'

'So I've been told. And Estelle's the doctor; when did *you* become an expert in it?'

'One hour after your diagnosis.'

Poe nodded. That sounded about right. It didn't take someone with Tilly's intellect long to become an expert in anything. She was a true polymath. A once-in-a-generation mind.

'And it's worth repeating what Dr Lang told you in your first session, Poe,' Estelle said. 'You have everything you need to get better. A good support network. You're not denying there's anything wrong with you. You're attending counselling.

And as painful as you find it, you talk about what happened. You're doing fine, Poe. Better than fine. But recovering from PTSD takes time. You won't see overnight results. You need to be patient. And until then, the world will just have to put up with you getting angry about Jimmy Nail's singing.'

Poe said, 'You heard about that, huh?'

'The waitress told me when I came back in.'

'I think I'll eat my cucumber sandwich now,' he said.

Intervention over.

He poured himself another cup of tea and nibbled on a pink macaron. He grimaced. It was sweeter than candied sugar. Poe looked around Bettys. It was almost like Estelle had deliberately chosen somewhere outside his comfort zone. Which didn't really make sense. Why would she? It wasn't thoughtlessness. Estelle wasn't thoughtless. If they were at a tearoom instead of a pub, it was by design. As if the location was as important as meeting up with Tilly. He realised he hadn't picked up on something Estelle had said earlier. Something about bringing him to Bettys so he could think about something other than his PTSD.

'We're not here by accident, are we?'

Estelle put down her scone and dabbed her lips with the luxurious white napkin. 'No, we are not,' she said. 'You're here to work, Poe.'

'Work?'

'Yes, work. You haven't exercised that brain of yours since the mercy chair case. Tilly and I thought it was high time you got back in the saddle.'

'Not an actual saddle, Poe,' Tilly said. 'It's an idiom. It means to return to an activity you were previously involved in.'

'Thanks for clearing that up, Tilly,' Poe said. 'For a moment I thought you wanted me to join the Mounties.'

'You're welcome, Poe.'

'And sorry, Estelle, but I don't even want to *think* about work at the minute. It was work that turned me into a wibble-head.'

'That's OK, Poe,' Estelle said. 'I won't ask you to do something you aren't comfortable with.'

'Thank you.'

'We'll talk about the wedding instead,' she said. 'What type of flowers do you want? I'm thinking dahlias. The Black Narcissus is particularly lovely.'

'And I've finished the seventh draft of my best man speech,' Tilly said. 'Do you want to hear it? I've added an interesting anecdote about the mole on my bottom and what you said when I asked you to measure it.'

Estelle nodded. 'Yes, that bit's particularly funny.'

Poe frowned. He felt like a cork in a stream when it came to planning their wedding. He was sure he was consulted on the major stuff, but he never seemed to have any say on the decisions. Tilly and Estelle were in charge. They said it was so he could concentrate on his recovery, although he suspected it was so that suggestions like ten Herdwick sheep roasting on a spit for the wedding breakfast could be politely ignored. And he was dreading, absolutely *dreading*, Tilly's best man speech. He'd been in the room when Estelle read the first draft and she'd laughed so hard she'd had to go and change her underwear.

'Tell me how I can get back in the saddle,' he said.

'Attaboy,' Estelle said.

Tilly opened her laptop and went straight to a news site. She turned the screen so Poe could see it.

'What do you know about the Jessica South case, Poe?'

'The movie actress?' he said. 'Just what was in the papers. A stalker broke into her hotel room and bundled her away in a laundry trolley. Took her to a remote farmhouse and handcuffed her to a radiator. He thought she'd been sending him secret declarations of love through those stupid superhero movies she starred in. She ended up cutting off her own thumb to get out of the handcuffs. Managed to escape to a neighbouring farm and call the police.'

Tilly nodded. 'The man who abducted her is a nasty pasty called Andrew Mills. The judge gave him a Section 37 Hospital Order instead of prison as he believed he was—'

'A wibble-head?'

'I was going to say mentally ill.'

'He gamed the system?'

'He did, Poe. I read the transcribed notes of the two court-appointed psychiatrists and Andrew Mills had clearly rehearsed his answers. Some of them were taken directly from the *Diagnostic and Statistical Manual of Mental Disorders, Fifth Edition, Text Revision*.'

Poe nodded. 'Personally, I prefer the fourth edition.'

'Are you crazy?'

'I think we've already established I'm nuttier than squirrel shit.'

'But the fourth edition is so flaw— oh, you're joking.'

Poe grinned. 'I was. Sorry. How did you access the psychiatrists' notes, Tilly?'

She coloured. 'That's not important right now,' she said. 'What *is* important is that Andrew Mills escaped from the secure hospital last week.'

'Ah.'

'And Jessica South is missing again . . .'

'Okaaay,' Poe said carefully. 'That's bad. In fact, it's bloody awful. That poor woman. I assume the Met are leading on it?'

'They were the first time,' Tilly said. 'But it's a joint investigation with North Yorkshire Police now.'

'North Yorkshire? Why?' He took in Estelle's unusual location choice again. 'And why are we here? What's Jessica South got to do with Bettys?'

'Jessica is originally from Harrogate and Bettys is the last place she was seen, Poe,' Estelle said. 'According to witnesses, she got a message on her phone and immediately got up and left. She didn't even finish her coffee.'

'She left voluntarily?'

'It seems so.'

'Where did she go?'

'She was outside for less than a minute before a car pulled up. She got into the back seat and that's the last time anyone saw her.'

'Registration plates?'

'They were unreadable. Covered in mud.'

'Deliberately?'

'Muddy cars aren't unusual up here, Poe, but yes, it looks deliberate.'

'Working theories?'

'The police are playing it low key as they don't want Andrew Mills to panic,' Tilly said. 'But they believe he coerced her into getting into the car with him. Jessica has a younger sister she dotes on, and the police think Mills threatened to hurt her unless she went with him.'

Poe nodded. It was certainly plausible. He said, 'I sense a "but" coming up.'

'I don't think the timing works, Poe. When Jessica got in the car, Andrew Mills had only just escaped.'

'Would he have had time to get up here?'

'Technically, yes.'

'What's the margin?'

'No margin at all. From the moment he escaped, there are only five hours unaccounted for.'

'Where was he being held?'

'A secure hospital on the outskirts of London.'

'And the alarm wasn't raised late? He didn't have a head start?'

Tilly shook her head. 'No. I've checked.'

'So, in five hours he travelled up to North Yorkshire, located Jessica and coerced her into getting into a car. He then completely disappears. That's a pretty big "but", Tilly.'

'It is. But the police are insisting the two things are connected.'

'OK,' he said. 'This *is* a three-pipe problem.'

'As a result of the Health Act 2006, smoking indoors has been banned since July 2007, Poe. And I didn't know you smoked a pipe.'

'It's an idiom, Tilly. You know, like getting back in the saddle.'

'Actually, it's a noun,' she muttered.

'Whatever,' he said. He raised his hand and caught Miss Coates's attention. 'Another pot of tea, please.'

When it arrived, he poured himself a cup and broke the three-pipe problem into one-pipe pieces.

Andrew Mills had absconded from hospital.

Andrew Mills was a danger to women in general and Jessica South specifically.

Jessica South got into a car outside Bettys.

These were the facts. Everything else was guesswork.

Poe blew on his tea and thought it through. He decided that Andrew Mills was a red herring. He hadn't had time to do the things the police thought he had. He'd be holed up in a shithole bedsit somewhere. He might have fooled the court-appointed psychiatrists but in all other aspects of the Jessica South abduction, he was an unsophisticated criminal. Poe dismissed Andrew Mills. It wouldn't take long for him to be caught.

Jessica South disappearing again was interesting though, particularly when Andrew Mills was no longer in the equation. She had been through an horrific ordeal. A *mercy chair*-level ordeal. She'd been abducted and handcuffed to a radiator. She'd thought she was going to die. But she hadn't been passive when it came to surviving. She hadn't relied on others. She'd cut off her own thumb with a kitchen knife like she had been jointing a chicken. That took serious balls.

Poe remembered the media's feeding frenzy when she was found. It was almost as bad as when Princess Diana was dating Dodi. He remembered Jessica's pale face and wide eyes. The scared looks. Not understanding why she wasn't being left alone to heal. And because she hadn't agreed to any interviews, or even to release anything beyond the statement her agent had written for her, parts of the press turned on her. Suggested, but didn't directly state, that maybe the whole thing had been an elaborate publicity stunt. That her career was waning, and this had been a way to get back in the spotlight, figuratively and literally.

Poe remembered thinking it was shameful, even for the British tabloids. And these were the same tabloids that used headlines like *Gotcha* and *Shoots you, Sir*.

Then he remembered how *he* had been in the aftermath of the mercy chair case. As soon as he had been discharged from hospital, his immediate instinct was to run. To go to his isolated shepherd's cottage on Shap Fell and shut out the world. To get into the foetal position and close his eyes. That was what he'd wanted to do. Instead, the people he cared about had cared about him right back. Estelle had taken a month off work and taken him to Highwood, her ancestral home. Tilly had put off starting her new job to ensure he had everything he needed. Even then he had wanted to hide away. Estelle had once found him in Highwood's old game larder, sitting on the stone floor, clutching his knees, rocking backward and forward. Crying.

He had just wanted to be left alone.

And he was a forty-five-year-old detective. He was no stranger to violence. He had Tilly and Estelle guarding him like rottweilers. Estelle faced off the National Crime Agency human resources machine and wouldn't let them near him. Tilly monitored the internet and took down anything to do with the case. And he didn't have a plague of press arseholes with intrusive tactics and long-range lenses pounding him to dust.

Still the PTSD had got him.

Jessica South had none of the advantages he'd had. She was half his age. It was her first experience of violence. She'd had no one protecting her from the press, no one watching her back. Even her agent had turned on her. Sold his story to one of the tabloids.

Poe reckoned that when Jessica's PTSD had struck, it had struck *hard*.

But she wasn't a wilting willow. She had dealt with the Andrew Mills abduction on her own. And she would have dealt with the PTSD on her own. She'd have had no choice.

'She's not a victim,' Poe said eventually. 'She's Agatha fucking Christie.'

Estelle and Tilly stared at him in astonishment.

'Er . . . would you care to elaborate, Poe?' Estelle said.

Poe *did* elaborate.

And when he'd finished, they asked him what he planned to do about it.

'I want to lend Jessica one of my rottweilers,' he said. He turned to Bradshaw. 'I need you to check some things for me, Tilly.'

Bradshaw and Estelle shared a look. They both smiled. Bradshaw opened one of her laptops.

Ready to work.

'How far is the Old Swan Hotel from here, Miss Coates?' Poe asked.

'A ten-minute walk down the hill,' she replied. 'Is that where you're staying? It's very nice. Sort of timeless, but in a good way.'

'We're thinking of staying there tonight. We're Agatha Christie fans, you see?'

Miss Coates didn't respond.

'I'm not an Agatha Christie fan, Poe,' Tilly said. 'I read *The Murder of Roger Ackroyd* because you said that I should at least try them. I thought it was balderdash.'

'Do you know the story about Agatha Christie and the Old Swan, Miss Coates?' Poe said, ignoring Tilly.

'Of course. Everyone in Harrogate knows it.'

'She disappeared in 1926,' Poe continued anyway. 'Ditched her car near Guildford and checked into the Old Swan under the assumed name Mrs Teresa Neele. She stayed there eleven days, and until she was identified as a guest, it was as if she'd evaporated into thin air.'

Miss Coates folded her arms like she was Nora Batty. 'Why are you telling me this?'

Poe ignored her question. He said, 'There's been a lot of speculation about *why* Agatha Christie did this. Some people said it was a PR stunt, while others thought she wanted her husband arrested for her murder. Personally, I think her reasoning is a lot more straightforward. She had just found out her husband wanted a divorce. That he wanted to be with his mistress. I think the fact that the surname she used to check in at the Old Swan – Neele – was the same as that of her husband's mistress is telling, don't you? It hints at what she was going through. That her husband's infidelity had caused her some mental distress and she wanted to be left alone.'

'I really must be getting along,' Miss Coates said. 'Can I get you anything else?'

'I'm told you were the last person to see Jessica South before she disappeared again, Miss Coates?' Poe said.

Miss Coates stiffened. 'I was,' she said carefully. 'Why do you ask? I've given my statement to the woman from North Yorkshire Police.' She gestured around the tea room. 'We've *all* given our statements.'

Poe drained his tea. Theatrically wiped his lips.

'It's an interesting surname, Coates,' he said. 'Do you want to know why?'

'I don't think I do.'

'It's interesting because Jessica South's best friend from school has an aunt called Christine Coates.'

Miss Coates said nothing.

'I assume you knew Jessica?'

'I did,' she said after a pause. 'I haven't seen her for years though.'

'Except the day she disappeared, you mean?'

'Yes.'

'You see, earlier this year, after I'd Forrest Gumped my way into something my brain wasn't equipped to deal with, I just wanted to disappear. To hide away from the world. Just like Agatha Christie did in 1926.' He picked up a cucumber sandwich, said, 'Nope,' and threw it back on the plate. He stared at Miss Coates and added, 'And just like Jessica did last week.'

'If you know something, I suggest you call the pol—'

'But where to hide when the world's press is hounding you in person and online? When they climb ladders to get pictures of you in your bedroom. Where can someone truly get away from the idiot press and the idiot internet trolls these days?'

'The Old Swan, perhaps? Is that why you want to stay there?'

'Where does your niece work, Miss Coates?'

'My niece?'

'Yes. Jessica's childhood friend.'

'I'm sure I don't know.'

'And we think you do,' Poe said. 'Tell me where she works, or I'll call North Yorkshire Police right now.'

She mumbled something they didn't catch.

'I'm sorry?' Estelle said. 'I don't think anyone heard that.'

'I said the Faraday Retreat and Wellness Centre.'

'The digital detox place, near Harrogate?' Poe said.

'I assume you already know that it is,' Miss Coates said.

Poe nodded. 'Yes, we do. Just like we know that when the press intrusion got too much for Jessica, she turned to her best friend from school, a friend who happened to work at a place where no one is allowed a phone or a tablet or a computer. In fact, it's named after Michael Faraday, the guy who invented the Faraday cage, which Tilly tells me is an enclosure that blocks electromagnetic fields. What better place to get away from it all for a few days? No press. No online bile. Just peace and rest. And as your niece no doubt squirrelled her into the Faraday Retreat and Wellness Centre under an assumed name, no one even knows she's there.'

'And now you've found her,' Miss Coates said. She looked sad. Disappointed in him. 'How very clever of you.'

Poe didn't respond.

'I thought you of all people might understand why Jessica did what she did.'

'Oh, I do,' Poe said.

'Are you going to arrest me?'

'Have you broken the law?'

'I don't think so.'

'Then I'm not going to arrest you.'

Miss Coates held his eyes.

Poe said, 'But I am going to give you something.'

'What, advice? Tell Jessica to hand herself in to the police?'

'No, I'm giving you Tilly,' Poe said. 'She was my rott-weiler when I got hurt and she's now Jessica's. Tilly will make sure that no one on the internet even mentions the Faraday Retreat and Wellness Centre and Jessica South in the same sentence. Internet trolls are going to wish they lived during the Stone Age, which to all intents and purposes, they will be. They certainly won't be able to use any of their devices for a long time. The press who went after Jessica are going to have significant website problems. The paparazzi will find they can't access any of their cloud accounts, whatever the fu . . . heck that means.'

'Why would you do this?' Miss Coates said. 'You don't even know Jessica.'

'Because it was done for me, and it works. I'll also call the senior investigating officer in charge of her high-risk missing persons case and tell them they can stand down. That Jessica is safe.'

'They'll take your word for it?'

'Yes.'

Poe handed her his police business card. It was ratty and stained and had been in his wallet for almost five years.

'If Jessica wants to talk to someone going through the same thing, I'll be at the end of that mobile number. And if she ever feels threatened by Andrew Mills, or any other misogynistic arsehole, you tell her she has three rottweilers watching out for her from now on. We have her back, Miss Coates.'

Miss Coates leant forward, put her hands on their table and breathed out a huge sigh of relief. 'Thank you,' she said. 'How can I ever repay you?'

'Another pot of tea?'

'Oh, I think we can do better than that.'

She disappeared into the kitchen, returning a minute later with a fully loaded plate. She put it in the middle of their table. It was a mountain of sconey-looking things.

'On the house,' she said proudly.

'What are these?' Poe asked, eyeing them suspiciously.

'They're called fat rascals. Half rock cake, half scone, all goodness. It's one of the things Bettys is best known for.'

Poe prodded one with his butter knife. He thought the fat rascal looked like a pastry toad. It was all squat and beige. Sultanas bulged out like warts. He looked at Tilly. He looked at Estelle. He looked at Miss Coates.

'I'm not eating that,' he said.

THE HARROGATE HOARD
Elly Griffiths

Hi! I'm Jennie and this is *Unsolved Mysteries*. Today, we're looking at a crime that has puzzled both police and archaeologists for almost twenty years. When metal detectorists discovered a hoard of Viking treasure in a remote Yorkshire field, experts greeted the discovery with excitement. But two days after the objects had been examined and removed, the body of local landowner, Lord Alastair Fishbourne, was found lying dead in the trench, a hammer on his chest. Despite years of conjecture and rumour, the killer has never been found. It's a very special case for me because my family has lived in the area for generations. In fact, my dad used to farm the land where the hoard was discovered. I was only eighteen when the murder happened. I vividly remember the atmosphere afterwards – shock and terror, and, amongst some members of the community, a certain sense of . . . *satisfaction* would be too strong a word . . . but a feeling that this death was not unexpected.

To set the scene. Yorkshire is an old county. These days, it's really four counties: North, West and South Yorkshire and the East Riding. But anyone who lives here will tell you the same thing: it's different from other places. The earliest inhabitants were the Celts, who formed several tribes including the Brigantes, who lived in the north and west, and the Parisi, who settled in the East Riding. After the Roman Conquest, the Brigantes ruled the area but under Roman control. I never liked the idea of this as a child. Yorkshire as a client state. I did like Queen Cartimandua, who left her husband for her armour-bearer and created a whole lot of trouble. After the Romans left, the area was divided between small Celtic tribes. In 866 the Vikings, also known as the Great Heathen Army, invaded Northumberland, on the Yorkshire border. They renamed the area Jorvik. The Vikings were expelled from the north in the reign of King Athelstan, the grandson of Alfred the Great, although there was a resurgence of Viking rule after Athelstan's death. That ended with the death of Erik Bloodaxe in 954.

I say it ended, but recent DNA studies have found a high preponderance of Scandinavian ancestry in the inhabitants of Yorkshire. Even our names – Richardson, Atkinson, Hodgson, Neilson, etc. – follow the Icelandic tradition of the patronymic, son of Richard and so on. Or 'dottir' for daughter. You only have to look at sheep farmers in the Dales, or drinkers in any local pub, to know that the Vikings still walk among us.

The Harrogate Hoard – also known as the Vale of York Hoard – probably belonged to a chieftain in the service of Erik Bloodaxe. The field where it was discovered is a peaceful place, a forgotten corner of farming land, home only to the curlews and myriad burrowing creatures. There's no evidence that there was ever a structure there, or even a building nearby. Yet it was here that our Viking chose to bury his most precious possessions.

And it was here that Alastair, Lord Fishbourne, met his death. These are the facts. On the January night in question, Alastair Fishbourne dined with his wife, Caroline, and his son, George, at Fishbourne Hall, near Harrogate. Also present were George's friend, Hugo Challoner, a recent archaeology graduate, and Derwent McGrew, a wealthy American on holiday in the area. At eleven o'clock, Alastair said good night to his wife and son. Sometime after that, he set out on a night-time walk. His body was found at 6 a.m. the next day by Hugo Challoner. Alastair had been struck several times about the head with a hammer. The police called it a frenzied attack. The murder weapon was lying on his chest, his hands clasped over it.

In my opinion, this is a story that needs to be told because it's not just about the demise of one wealthy man, it's the story of Yorkshire itself and the descendants of Erik Bloodaxe. I've spent several months interviewing the people concerned with the case. Here are their accounts.

Professor Hugo Challoner

The Harrogate Hoard was a very significant find. Yes, I suppose you could say it was the start of my career. I wouldn't say 'illustrious' exactly, although that's very kind of you. I've certainly written several books about the Vikings. And I still think the hoard was a wonderful discovery; great for archaeology and great for Yorkshire. Despite what came next.

You want to know more about the objects themselves? Well, we've traced some of them back to Russia, Afghanistan and Scandinavia. It shows how widely the Viking people travelled – they weren't just looters and pillagers. The coins date from the late ninth and early tenth centuries and include Anglo-Saxon, Anglo-Viking, Carolingian and Islamic types, typical of early tenth-century Viking hoards. But what made this collection special was the cup. At first the detectorists simply thought it was a lump of clay. Then they saw the coins sticking out. Upon excavation, it was revealed to be a silver gilt chalice – only the second of its kind to be found in Britain. The decoration was quite extraordinary, fantastical animals being chased by lions. The cup itself was filled with coins and jewellery, including a gold arm ring. There was also a pewter hammer, possibly ceremonial in use. There was a small inscription on it: *'Hmar X is'*.

It means 'This is a hammer'. No, it wasn't the hammer that killed him. That was a common or garden thing. The type found in any DIY shop.

These sorts of troves are often called 'escape hoards'. It's likely that the treasure was buried by a Viking warlord, fleeing Athelstan's men and planning to come back when the coast was clear. My conjecture is that the items were buried shortly after the most recent coin was minted, around AD 928. The fact that it wasn't reclaimed suggests that some harm befell the original owner. No, of course I wouldn't say that the hoard was cursed. What utter nonsense.

The detectorists reported the find, very properly, to the Finds Liaison Officer. She, in turn, consulted the Portable Antiquities Officer. I wasn't officially involved but I was staying with Lord Fishbourne at the time. I was at school with Fishy, Lord Fishbourne's son. I know the area quite well because I'd often been to Fishbourne Hall for hunt balls and the like. The usual stuff. I'd known the family for years although this was the first time I'd met Caroline, Alastair's new wife. They'd only been married a few months at the time. She was a lot younger than him. Only a bit older than me, in fact. No, I didn't go to the wedding. It was a very private affair.

I was still staying at Fishbourne Hall when . . . when the tragedy happened. In fact, I was the one who discovered the body. I went for an early morning walk. I love the countryside at that time of day. Anyway, I went to look at the excavation site and there was Alastair, lying dead in the trench. I'll never forget it. I ran back to the house and called the police. Later, I was the one who took the woman officer to examine the scene. She was very young and I think the sight of the body – really, it was too horrible – upset her a great deal. She was professional, though, called for back-up and, when it came, escorted me back to the Hall. She asked us all a lot of questions. Over the next few days we were asked the same questions over and over again by many different people. Fishy – George – got quite angry about it all. But the police were only doing their job.

I still think about it sometimes. Poor Alastair. Well, I suppose he could have had a worse resting place. A sky burial, the Tibetan people call it.

George, Lord Fishbourne

I don't know why you're dragging all this stuff up again. Let sleeping dogs lie. That's my motto. But Annabelle, my wife, says that a podcast will be good publicity. We need it now that we've opened the Hall to the public. We've made big changes to the old place. There's a children's adventure trail in the woods, croquet on the lawn, a café in the old orangery. There's even a Harrogate Hoard room. No, I don't think it's in bad taste at all.

Hugo was staying with us when the treasure was found. Clever chap, Hugo. He'd just graduated from Oxford with a degree in archaeology. We were at school together. He was a scholarship boy, of course. Hugo's father was from the north somewhere. He'd been a miner, I believe. I never met him. Hugo had a bit of an accent sometimes but mostly you couldn't tell. Pa was fond of Hugo too. I remember once, when Hugo came to stay, he made some gaffe about calling hunting coats red instead of pink. Pa used to tease him about it, call him a pinko. Hugo always knew how to laugh at himself.

It still seems extraordinary to me that all this treasure was just lying in a field, waiting to be found by one of those metal detector thingummies. Hugo says some Viking chappie must have buried the stuff, planning to come back for it. He didn't – maybe he was murdered, like Pa – so it just stayed in the ground for over a thousand years.

I went with Hugo to see the stuff when it was first found. To be honest, it was a bit of an anticlimax. Just a lot of dirty-looking coins. Even the famous cup was all covered in mud and cow shit. An archaeologist girl was brushing the dirt off it. What a job! We stood there for a while and Hugo asked all sorts of questions, then we went back to the Hall for a much-needed drink.

Caroline didn't come with us. She didn't seem interested at all. Hard to know what she *was* interested in, except for clothes and jewellery. Well, she's got plenty of both now. She inherited all of Dad's money and now she's married to an Italian fashion designer. Loaded, of course. Did I resent her? I suppose I did, in a way. Ma hadn't been dead long and then Pa comes home with this floozy, half his age. Ma was a strong woman – she threw the hammer for England – but Caroline looked as though a puff of wind would blow her away. Pretty though, I'll grant you that. Still is, from what I see on the internet. Annabelle says she's had plastic surgery but I wouldn't know.

It was Hugo who found Pa's body. Hugo liked to take these early morning walks and, of course, he went to have a look at the place where his beloved hoard was found. Pa was lying in the ditch with a hammer on his chest. It was the same hammer that had been used to kill him. Horrible. I had to identify the body because Caroline was in hysterics. Pretty grim.

What happened that night? Honestly, I've been asked these questions so many times that it's started to seem unreal, as if it never really happened. OK. We ate in the small dining room, just the five of us. Me, Caroline, Pa, Hugo and the American chap, Derwent McGrew. I never really worked out who he was or why he was there. Pa liked him, said he was a rough diamond, but I remember thinking that he could be a dangerous character if roused. Caroline didn't like him either. I could tell.

Caroline said she had a headache and went to bed early, about nine-thirty. Hugo and I went to play billiards. Pa stayed drinking with this McGrew character. At around eleven, Pa put his head round the door of the billiard room to say good night. McGrew had gone home by that time. Hugo and I carried on with our game and then we had a nightcap. We went to bed at midnight; I remember the grandfather clock striking. I fell asleep immediately and, the next thing I knew, Hugo was shaking me awake, saying something had happened to Pa. He went to tell Caroline next. She hadn't even noticed that Pa was missing. They were already sleeping in separate beds. That tells you something, in my opinion.

What do I think happened? I think Pa went for a midnight stroll, met some madman and was horribly murdered. Much as I dislike Caroline, I can't quite see her bashing someone's head in with a hammer. Have you seen her? She's the size of a matchstick. Of course, Pa's death made her a rich woman. I only got the Hall because that was entailed on the heir. And, as I say, it's a struggle to keep the place going these days. Hence the open house and all that.

Who does the hoard belong to? Well, it was discovered on our land but the case went to court and the objects were found to be Treasure Trove, belonging to the Crown. So you could say that the Harrogate Hoard belongs to the British people. They're welcome to it, that's all I can say.

Caroline Strangolagalli

Don't worry about the pronunciation. No one gets it right. It actually means 'strangle the French'. Wild, right? There's a place called Strangolagalli in Lazio, where apparently they did a lot of that sort of thing.

It's hard to remember. I was only married to Alastair for a few weeks. I've been married to Gianpiero for fifteen years. But I was in love with Alastair, whatever anyone says. He was fifty-five when we met, thirty years older than me, but he still seemed like a young man. He'd been in the army and was very fit. He swam fifty lengths in the indoor pool every day, rode horses, skied like a demon. I couldn't keep up with him, to be honest.

What do I remember about the day he died? We'd all had dinner together, me and Alastair, George and his rather stuffy friend, Hugo. Oh and the American. Something McGrew. Odd name and rather an odd character. I didn't take to him. One way and another, it was rather a sticky evening. McGrew kept talking about his ancestor, a local nutcase who used to dress up like a Viking. I could tell Alastair didn't like it. I tried to change the subject but, of course, Hugo took the opportunity to bore on about coins and chalices and the like. The whole thing gave me a headache so I excused myself as soon as we'd finished eating. The men stayed downstairs drinking. I've always hated that habit, the women retiring so that the men can drink themselves into a stupor. According to George, 'Ma' was fine with it, but I've got a bit more respect for myself, thank you.

I went to sleep in one of the spare bedrooms. Alastair came in to say good night an hour or so later. He seemed his usual self. No, he didn't seem drunk. Alastair could hold his booze. He didn't say anything about going out again but that wasn't out of character for him. Alastair loved walking in the dark, 'night manoeuvres' he called it. Said it reminded him of his days in the SAS. I was woken at about seven in the morning by Hugo banging on my door saying that something terrible had happened. By the time I got downstairs, a police officer had arrived. It was a young woman detective. To be honest, I wasn't very impressed with her at the time, but she's gone on to great things.

I couldn't see Alastair's body. Not when I knew how he'd died. George went to identify him and I was grateful. No, I don't suspect George of anything. He might not have got on with his dad – he was furious about our marriage – but he'd never do anything like that. It was obviously just a random psychopath. They do exist, you know. The police thought the same. Eventually.

Derwent McGrew

A podcast, eh? I've got a company that makes them. I assume you'll let me listen to the tape before the episode goes out? Smart girl. I've got lawyers, you know.

It was a hell of a long time ago. I was staying in Harrogate because that's where my ancestors were from. In fact, they used to live on Fishbourne's land. That's how we met. I just marched up to his front door and asked to see his archives. That's the American way, sweetheart. There's no nonsense about class here. If a man is rich, he's got class. And I've got plenty of money. Made it all myself too, not like some aristo who inherited it all from mummy and daddy.

Fishbourne was quite helpful to me, I have to admit. He found me some press cuttings about my ancestor. He was known as Old McGrew and it turns out that he was quite the local character. He used to dress up as a Viking and scare local children. What a card. He's buried in the local church-yard but he was a pauper so they couldn't afford a tombstone. Sad story, huh?

Yeah, I had dinner at the Hall that evening. I think Alastair liked my company. Some people do, you know. I think he liked that I told it to him straight. I didn't toady like that archaeologist guy, Hugo. Fishbourne wasn't one of your effete aristos, not like his son. He was a hard man, he'd been in the army. Special forces no less. He was an interesting fella. Also I like my bourbon and he had a fine liquor selection.

It was the first time I'd met his wife, Caroline. I remember thinking: she's trouble. It wasn't just that she was so much younger than him. It was the fact that she had a roving eye. It even roved in my direction but I told her, without actually using the words, that I wasn't interested. Yes, she was pretty, if you like 'em skinny, which I don't. But I wasn't about to seduce another man's wife. I'm not so sure about the archaeologist, Hugo. He avoided talking to Caroline but I saw him looking. A man can't miss that. I don't think even Fishbourne's son was immune.

So the evening was tough going, you could say. Caroline claimed she had a headache and went to bed early. The son and the archaeologist went off to play pool. Or billiards, as they called it. Alastair and I stayed at the table, drinking brandy and bourbon, according to taste. What did we talk about? Oh, this and that. The state of the world. I remember one thing: we were talking about the Viking, the one who buried his treasure in the field. I said, joking, of course, 'What if he comes back from the dead and demands the return of his land?' Alastair said, without missing a beat, 'I'd bash his head in.'

I went home shortly after that. I'd had too much liquor to drive so I left my car at the Hall and walked. It wasn't that far and it was a fine night. I got back to my hotel, The Swan, at about midnight. The first thing I heard about the murder was when the police turned up to interview me. I was having breakfast at the time. Gave the staff quite a shock, I can tell you.

Of course the police didn't suspect me. What motive would I have? I hardly knew the man. Oh no, you're not going to get me to speculate. I'm too old a hand for that. And I've got lawyers, remember? I'll just say one thing. Did you study French at school, sweetheart? I bet you did. *Cherchez la femme.*

Chief Superintendent Clare Atkinson

Of course I remember the case. I was only a DS then. My boss, DI Clive Hodgson, was the Chief Investigating Officer but I was the officer sent to the Hall when the body was discovered. I was nervous. I'm a local girl and the Fishbourne family were famous. Infamous, I should say. Lord Fishbourne was always buying up land and then selling it again at a profit to developers. There had been a recent case involving a local farmer, Steve Neilson, who subsequently killed himself. So feelings were running high. But I knew I had to keep an open mind, be professional at all times.

It was Hugo Challoner who called us in. He's quite a famous archaeologist these days, always on TV, but he was just a young man then, fresh out of university. I went with Hugo to the site and I saw Lord Fishbourne lying in a deep ditch with straight sides. Mr Challoner said it was a trench that had been dug by the archaeologists excavating the hoard. The victim's skull showed the impact of blunt force trauma but the body had clearly been laid out post-mortem; the hands were crossed on the chest and a hammer placed between them. On later inspection, this proved to be the murder weapon. No prints were found on it. I didn't disturb the scene at the time. I called SOCO – sorry, scene-of-the-crime, although some people say CSI these days – and secured the site. Then I went back to the Hall and interviewed the residents. None of them had an alibi for the time of the murder, which was later estimated to be between midnight and 3 a.m.

There are three questions an investigating officer must ask at the beginning of a murder inquiry. Why this person? Why here? Why now? So yes, initially our investigations did centre on the family. Both Caroline and George stood to inherit from Lord Fishbourne's death. But there was no real evidence against either of them. We also looked at Hugo Challoner and Derwent McGrew. Neither of them had any obvious motive but DI Hodgson used to say, 'motive comes at the end'. McGrew had left the Hall at around 11 p.m. and the night receptionist at The Swan saw him returning to the hotel at midnight. It's not impossible that he could have killed Lord Fishbourne on the way – coroners' timings are never a hundred per cent accurate – but it seems unlikely. The receptionist would surely have noticed if a guest turned up covered in blood and there would have been plenty of blood, believe me. Besides, Derwent McGrew hardly knew Lord Fishbourne. Hugo Challoner found the body, which is sometimes suspicious, but it's hard to see why he'd kill his best friend's father.

The other possibility was that the killing – a truly frenzied attack – was the work of a psychopath unrelated to the victim. We investigated known criminals in the area but there was no one with a suitable profile. Our only lead was a civilian sighting of a person dressed in Viking clothes, spotted near the crime scene a couple of days earlier. We never traced this individual. Yes, I have heard of the legend of Old McGrew but I don't think it's relevant to this case.

What do I think? Well, it's an unsolved murder and the police hate those. So I have pondered it over the years and I have to say I've come to the conclusion that it was the work of a random killer. No, there were no similar attacks in the area but that sometimes happens. Even murderers can catch trains.

Jennie

So, who killed Alastair Fishbourne? Was it his son, George, the man who inherited the title and the historic mansion? Was it Caroline Strangolagalli, who got everything else? Or perhaps it was Hugo Challoner, the scholarship boy mocked by the Fishbournes for not knowing red from pink. And what about Derwent McGrew, whose ancestor used to dress up as a Viking? Remember what Lord Fishbourne said about being visited by the ghost of the man who had buried the hoard? 'I'd bash his head in.' Almost the same words his son used to describe the murder.

Or maybe it was Caroline acting in collaboration with one of the men? Derwent thought that both George and Hugo were attracted to her. George admits to following her on social media, even now. Did Derwent himself protest too much about evading her 'roving eye'?

Or was it, as Chief Superintendent Atkinson would have you believe, the work of a random psychopath? This, despite the fact that there were no similar attacks in the area before or after the murder.

For me, there are a few unanswered questions.

Why would a random attacker take the trouble to lay out Lord Fishbourne's body with a hammer on his chest? It's interesting to note that the Vikings believed a warrior could not enter Valhalla unless he had his weapon in his hand.

A lot of people seem to have been taking night-time or early morning walks. Yorkshire in January is not the place for strolling in the dark.

Is it significant that the late Lady Fishbourne once threw the hammer for England?

Who was the person dressed as a Viking and why did the police not follow up on this lead?

To my mind, it's a tale of revenge.

Thank you for listening to *Unsolved Mysteries*. If you've enjoyed this podcast, please leave a rating or review or, better still, tell a friend about it. *Unsolved Mysteries* is produced by me, Jennie Stefansdottir, and is a Thor's Hammer production.

Author's note

The Harrogate Hoard is real, as was Erik Bloodaxe. Everything else in this story is fictional. You can visit the hoard at the Yorkshire Museum in York.

EG 2024

WHY HARROGATE?

Janice Hallett

'Why Harrogate?' I said to the surgeon when he mentioned the town. It seemed a rather unusual choice.

'It is just far enough away,' the surgeon replied. 'London is too . . .' and he paused, as if anyone could find themselves in want of a word for the capital. 'Hectic.'

'I understand this operation is . . .' now *I* found myself in want of a word. 'Controversial.'

He stared at me. I caught a certain emptiness in his eyes. An absence of judgement over me, which I appreciated, but also a dearth of emotion . . . which I found unnerving.

'You want it, do you not, this operation?' And I did.

The lovely Clara Wigmore and I have been on speaking terms for two years. Now, each time we meet, our knees pressed together beneath the table at Fortnums, she delivers news of another female friend in receipt of a proposal from their beau. Last week, no fewer than two friends were considering the same question. I wish with all my heart that Clara should be the next lucky friend, yet there is an obstruction that prevents me and I *must* remove it. She will not wait forever, and nor should she, having lost her first fiancé in the Great War.

Thus, I found myself nervously boarding a train at King's

Cross, a fat overnight bag stuffed with enough supplies for four nights. Just in case.

My First Class carriage fellows, of whom there were six, settled into their seats as we pulled away. A city gent with a silver band on his cane and a gold signet ring. An elegant young woman balancing her own overnight bag on a silk-covered knee. An army officer who disappeared into his overcoat as soon as he became seated. A young bounder who wore no hat on his shocking red hair, and two older ladies who might have been chattering gayly to each other had they not been clad in sombre mourning.

The city gent unfolded his newspaper. *The Times*. I could read the front and back pages quite clearly from my seat opposite. I find it helps my nerves to concentrate on such inconsequential things.

A baronet's son takes to the air in a flying machine. His masters at Cambridge are baffled. A dowager's gloves are stolen from Claridge's. The maître d' is baffled. An antiquarian suffers the loss of jewels and his ankle joint in a burglary. The police are baffled. Three horses escape their stable and disappear, leaving an entire Cotswolds village baffled. A venerated member of parliament is in debt to a gambling establishment. At last! No one is baffled.

The crowded carriage lurched and rumbled. It shook me back to the present moment and my maddening, confounded, *baffling* body. I placed a hand over my lower right abdomen and breathed away the imaginary pain that seemed worse with each passing sunset. Appendicitis. The family curse.

'He's an accommodating sort of chap. Got a friend out of trouble,' Jack Davies said of the surgeon.

'How much might he charge?' I asked.

'A pretty penny.'

'Is he safe? Skilled, I mean. Will he do a good job?'

'My friend lived to tell the tale.' It was scarcely heartening. There could be a hundred who did not and who would be the wiser?

Still, had it not been for Jack's common sense and shrewd guidance, I would be buried now beneath the bloody soil at Sarrebourg. I saw no reason, at this moment, to doubt my trust in him.

'Please Jack, summon the fellow for me.' And he did.

On first meeting the surgeon, one weekday afternoon, I was curious. Baffled, some might say. The front door yawned open and there he was, a figure planted on the doorstep, unsmiling, but not unfriendly in the light, undecided drizzle. He then loitered, damp and silent, in the drawing room as he cast his emotionless eyes over the paintings and ceramics on display.

'My late parents were collectors, as am I.' My nervous urge to explain was a matter of immediate regret. I excused myself for what I assured him would be the briefest time.

He nodded. I sidled through the door. A light rain patted the glass, filled the silence.

Some minutes later I peered through the chink. If possible, I like to observe a man's behaviour when he considers himself unwatched.

The doctor's gaze was, for the most part, deadpan, but a brief few paces to the fireplace saw him alight at random on a particular vase. A gaudy Egyptian design from the last century. His back to me, I watched the doctor extend his stance to a tiptoe, as he answered a natural compulsion to peer inside. I smiled at this simple evidence of a healthy curiosity and enquiring mind.

On any given day, I find members of the medical profession to have a rambunctious confidence, a dismissive attitude, fine clothes and clipped speech. This surgeon was unprepossessing and reserved, his suit at least a decade out of fashion and his flat, unfamiliar vowels hailed from the sort of place I probably would not care to visit alone. But then, the war had seen men not born to the profession encouraged, by necessity, to take it up.

'What can a gentleman like yourself want with a gentleman like *myself*?' His manner was quiet and straightforward. His words reassured me he knew his place.

'I am in dire need of an operation that no surgeon in London will perform.'

'Why do they refuse you?'

'They will not remove a diseased organ before its disease takes hold. I'm informed that a code of ethics dictates their moment of engagement with malady, however fatal that malady will inevitably be.'

The surgeon scowled. 'And you are confident the malady is in you?'

'My father, my uncle and my brother. All dead because of the appendix. Its inflammation, its disease. And for months now, I lie in bed and feel it there, awaiting its moment. I am in a state of constant . . . dis-ease with myself.'

'Pain?'

'Pain to come. I fear the malady has transferred silently to me.'

'You want to cure the malady or the fear?'

'I understand the Great War saw your profession gain much practice in the art of abdominal surgery and I hope to hear that you yourself have performed this operation . . . many times.'

Of my words I had more hope than confidence. My eyes pleaded with him, as they had with every doctor of medicine I had found myself in the disapproving shadow of.

'It is not the operation gentlemen usually seek from me. That is
. . . a particular procedure involving the women of their acquaint-
ance. However, your assumption that I have performed extensive
surgery to the abdomen is correct and I believe that if I perform
this for you, it will cure both the malady and the fear of it.
However, the risk of dying as an outcome of the mechanics is
somewhat higher than the risk you will develop the disease that
has blighted your family. That decision is for you to make.'

'This . . . dis-ease prevents me taking the next, natural step in
my life. I must make it,' I said. 'I make that decision.'

I've since discovered the water in Harrogate is considered
optimum for health, recovery and convalescence. I hope that is
why I am on this train now, in the company of strangers. What
other possible reason could the surgeon have for choosing this
location? While our little agreement is *controversial* it is not, to
the best of my knowledge, illegal. I must trust that drawing me
so far from home betrays the simple desire to protect a professional reputation and not a need to hide from the suspicious
gaze of London's many eyes.

The officer takes a paper parcel from his coat and unwraps
two hearty slices of bread, pulls them apart, ripping the butter
between them into jagged shards. His teeth tear at the crisp
crust and he chews, oblivious to the paroxysms of hunger the
sight throws me into.

'Eat and drink nothing from six the night before,' the surgeon
had said, his quiet voice firm on this point.

'May I take a pot of tea for breakfast?'

'The anaesthesia causes sickness.' A note of irritation had
entered it. 'The more you eat, the more sickness you will endure.
I suggest you drink water and *only* water from six the previous
evening. Remember, you will be alone after the operation.'

To distract my stomach from the soldier's bread, I imagine my appendix. I imagine that it senses the rocking carriage, my shifting travel companions, the change in air as we head north. I imagine the sudden realisation that its life will be cut short, just as its blood relatives cut short the lives of pa, Uncle William and brother Albie, only 16 when it snatched him away.

Does my knowledge that this operation will soon be performed transmit itself through the circulation of my blood, like telephone wires carry our voices? Will the organ sense its fate and make a final attempt to erupt in a burgeoning tidal wave of pain and toxicity, to sweep me away before I can do the same to it?

I am shaken awake by the elegant woman, who curtly informs me 'we are there', and clips her way from the compartment before I can correct grammar that ill befits her class. As I bend to rise from my seat, I feel my appendix calm and quiet, the pain in my imagination still.

I am residing at a dour boarding establishment – of the surgeon's choosing, I assure you – and currently sit behind the closed door to my room. I notice the only window has been bricked up and papered over. A simple fan-light remains, but it is opaque with grime. Unsurprisingly, at barely four o'clock in the afternoon, it is dark in here. He said 'wait and I will send for you,' so wait I will.

A day ago – or is it two now? – I sat in my room, expecting a message to meet the surgeon wherever it is he does his work. Instead, there was a knock on the door and there he was, black bag in hand, hat down over his eyes and scarf up to his nose.

He unwrapped himself, threw his overcoat down and rolled his shirtsleeves up to the elbow before I mustered enough voice to say 'You'll do it here?'

He gave me a look of indeterminate disdain. 'It is safest. I know the people and have already requested the maids leave you alone for the duration of your stay.' That quiet, steady voice again.

'Will you come back to . . .?'

'No need. Now, lie on the bed.'

The surgeon lifted a roll of cloth from his bag and as I lay back, I watched it fall open. My eye caught the glint of silver, of polished steel and hard, sharp edges. I looked to the ceiling and winced. *Did my appendix spasm just then? Aware its time is up? There it goes again. I swear I might seize the sharpest edge in the room – my shaving razor - and perform the dratted operation myself!*

'When you awake, there will be a bucket beside you for the sickness and a cup of water on the bedside table.'

The surgeon smeared dark-yellow iodine over his hands and forearms. Its acrid smell turned to dread in my nostrils.

'Harrogate water,' I whispered, 'I hear it is good for recovery. This is why you chose this place, is that so?' It was my attempt to fish for conversation, but my bait alighted on dry land.

'As soon as agreeable, move around to stimulate your blood. When you feel able to travel, leave here and go directly home. After ten days, cut the stitches with care and gently pull them free.'

The surgeon loomed above me. In one hand a bottle of clear liquid and in the other a kerchief folded into squares. He deposited a dash of one on the other.

'Now, breathe as usual.'

'Wait, wait . . . I want . . .'

What did I want? Perhaps to delay the moment. Not for lack of desire to see my appendix gone, but a sudden fear of that leap into the unknown. Either way, the surgeon was of no mind to converse further. Before I could conjure a final question – before the chloroform and its mysterious power of oblivion overtook me – I witnessed a dark shadow fall across his face. In that tiny, unguarded moment I glimpsed a very different man.

The surgeon's hands seized my head and forced the sweet-smelling cloth over my nose and mouth. I resisted, suddenly all the more desirous to postpone the inevitable, but the surgeon was silently adamant. One breath, two, and that was that.

Once back in the room, the bucket and water both availed of, I dared not look beneath the sheets. I could feel a rough bandage and a gentle discomfort, but where the offending organ was, deep inside, all was silent. Not even my imagination could goad a response from a knot of gristle that is no longer there.

The fourth day saw me feeling better and, rising early, I decided to tread a slow and careful path back to London. The train was my greatest hurdle. The waters in Harrogate may be sympathetic to the invalid, but its train line certainly is not. I opted for the slow train in the hope it would be gentler.

Through all this time, how did I feel? Glad to have conquered my nemesis, yet, strangely, peace evaded me.

When my eyes closed at night, I saw the surgeon's face as he forced me under his chemical spell. Surely my hesitation was something he saw and dealt with all the time? It was my fault. No wonder he was exasperated with me. Surely, he did not look as if he just wanted to get the procedure over with . . .

Days and weeks passed. Gingerly, I made my way to the club again and ordered a glass of port, an indulgence I had not allowed myself for fear its distilled state was detrimental to the appendix. I had no such fear now.

After my third glass and as many hours later, I found Sir Thomas Colquhoun in the chair beside mine.

'Been abroad, old boy?'

I considered answering in the affirmative, but wasn't convinced in my pleasant state of inebriation I could maintain the deception beyond the original question.

'Under the weather, old boy.'

'Sorry to hear it. Gout?'

'No.'

'Pneumonia?'

'No.'

He lowered his voice. 'The *pox*?'

'Most certainly not!' But his expression betrayed the fact my most vehement answer carried with it the greatest likelihood of truth.

'I underwent a preventative extraction of the appendix.'

'You were not *unwell*, yet underwent a *surgery*?'

I nodded. Sir Thomas was silent as his own pickled brain searched itself for a comparative experience to share. He must have drawn a blank.

'I hope it went well.'

'It did. Thank you, Sir Thomas.'

The old man shifted in his seat, his red brow furrowed with thought.

'How fascinating,' he went on and leant towards me as if requesting access to a secret. 'Can you describe to me the *appearance* of the appendix?'

'What do you mean, its *appearance*?'

'Was it large or small? Did it appear bloody or . . . dry? I have heard much about the mischievous organ since the Great War and yet have no picture in my mind to represent it. Surely you were curious yourself?'

'I cannot say I was,' I was most certainly curious as to why Sir Thomas would describe the brutal murderer of my entire family as 'mischievous', but did not trust myself to phrase that distaste in a manner that meant I was not asked to leave the club at once.

'You didn't *see* it? You did not ask the doctor to keep it for you?'

'Why would I wish to set eyes on a thing so foul? And anyway, the surgeon . . .' I stopped myself recounting that the man was gone when I awoke, along with all trace of my flesh and blood. 'The surgeon didn't find it necessary.'

'But he found it necessary to charge you a fee for his work?'

'Eight guineas.'

Sir Thomas shifted in his seat.

'And you are confident he fulfilled his contract?'

'Of course. Why would he not?' But Sir Thomas simply gazed at me over the rim of his spectacles.

'Why would he not? Let me tell you. Not long ago I employed a fellow to scrub my chimney pots. Up he went with bucket and brush, and up he stayed, on my roof, for an hour. Then down he came and off he went with my thruppence in his pocket. No sooner had he vanished when my neighbour, who lives across the street, knocked on my door in a bate and said her maid had seen the scoundrel from the upstairs window, his back to my filthy chimney pot, cap over his eyes, fast asleep for the entire hour. I had to borrow a ladder to check with my own sorry eyes and yes, she was right. The pots were still black as night up there and I was thruppence poorer.'

It was a cautionary tale indeed. I couldn't help but chuckle at the thought of Sir Thomas edging his corpulent form up a ladder to inspect his own roof.

'I say, Sir Thomas, the vagabond fooled you for certain! You could easily have checked the colour of the water in his bucket, without having to ascend to the rafters yourself.'

Sir Thomas took another sip of his brandy and pointed a fat finger in my direction.

'The water in the man's bucket was black. I watched him pour it into the gutter, the coin ready in my palm to reward him for his hard work. The idle wastrel had scraped a handful of soot and ash from the rim of the chimney pot and dyed his water. Evidently, it takes considerable effort and ingenuity to be so lazy! I hope your surgeon was not thus.'

Sir Thomas and I chuckled our way back to our glasses. I found myself vastly amused at the very idea the surgeon could have fooled *me* into thinking he had removed my appendix!

I lay awake. My bed somehow a hard, flat board, the sheets thin and cold. My fingers found the scar left by the surgeon's knife, every ripple echoed a stitch. I had followed his instructions to the letter. Clipping and unpicking those black spiders' legs exactly ten days after our meeting in Harrogate. The skin had healed into a puckered red line, no hint of infection or gangrene. The surface remained a little sore, but I could touch the area without consequence.

Had the surgeon removed my appendix as bidden? Or had he made a simple cut in the skin, stitched it together and wrapped a bandage around my middle, knowing I would not dare to look for the prescribed ten days?

My mind's eye conjured the fraudster on Sir Thomas's roof, scraping soot from the chimney to tint his bucket water and charm thruppence from his target. Who would go to such effort?

The surgeon was surely an honourable man. Jack Davies would not have cast me into the clutches of one who was not. The prevailing opinion is that his profession is not given to dishonesty. Yet his first thought on meeting me was that I wished to obtain his usual service – a procedure contrary to the law.

He carried every item I expected to see. A doctor's bag, bundle of knives, tongs and scalpels, iodine, chloroform. Yet all are as available to those of poor character as they are to the good.

I awoke from the operation feeling nauseous, my belly sore, and with the feeling, deep down, that something troubling had been cut away. Yet the sickness was thanks to the anaesthetic, the soreness from a cut whose depth I had no evidence of, and the feeling of emptiness, freedom from tyranny? My imagination had been conjuring a personality and motivation for the malicious organ for so long, could it simply be conjuring this new emptiness too? But whether the man was honourable or a scoundrel, there was nothing to be done about it now. Time and time alone would see my questions answered.

As my scar continued to heal, so too did my dis-ease. I began to feel lightness of heart at last. A joyful outlook I had not entertained for some years. If the surgeon had indeed left my appendix *in situ*, then he had scared it into submission, for I felt no twinges or pain in the region.

My new buoyant spirit saw me, finally, ask Clara to be my wife, and in due course we were married. You can imagine my surprise when she suggested we honeymoon in Harrogate. Her reason being the waters there might be favourable to her producing an heir, which, at nearly 40 years old, she was not confident of.

Thus, we set off on the same train journey I had taken some six months earlier, only this time with joy and optimism. As if in agreement, the sun shone and the town that greeted us as we alighted was bright and welcoming. The very air infused us with vital energy and a sense that all things that lay in wait would be good.

Without a word of concurrence, we strode past the loitering hansoms and motor taxis on Station Square and onwards, upwards, past ladies and gentlemen similarly at promenade. We cleaved through the fashionable centre of town, all the way to Valley Gardens where Clara squealed with schoolgirl delight at the sight of hydrangeas in hues of blue, white and red, apparently all colours she had never before dreamt. I had not the heart to tell her these shades are manmade – a common trick reflecting the soil in which they grow.

I was careful to book a more prestigious hotel than the establishment favoured by the surgeon, but otherwise I thought no more about that dark day. My new wife and I availed ourselves of the town's famous spa waters, its delightful afternoon teas and a most agreeable balance of novelty and timelessness. Our honeymoon there saw Harrogate itself reborn in my eyes. On our final day we took a stroll along Parliament Terrace and Clara gazed into the windows of the jewellers that lined the passage.

'William, look! A moonstone!'

The bauble was a pearly trinket in pendant form, pleasant to the eye, but quite lacking in real value, which I explained to her. But she would not be discouraged and lowered her voice, her eyes shining with simple excitement.

'I've heard the moonstone is *conducive*.'

'Conducive to what, my dear?'

'Conducive to a *male* heir.'

The shop bell shook the downcast and lame proprietor out of his chair. As he and Clara discussed the merits of that and other, incrementally more expensive moonstone fripperies, I wandered the shop, pleased to note its contents demonstrated a good eye for the antique as well as the novel.

I was careful to make regular observations to demonstrate the fact I knew more about the value of artefacts than the proprietor's average clientele, and that my eyes were impervious to any wool he might seek to pull over them.

As I returned to her, my wife expressed an interest in seeing an item at the upper reaches of the window. The proprietor gave three insistent raps on the floor.

'My boy will have to reach that,' he muttered, and to fill the silence while a weary stirring could be heard from below, he continued, misty-eyed. 'Had a blue moonstone not so long ago. Set in pure gold and edged with diamonds. It was lost along with other fine gems.'

'Lost?' my wife trilled brightly. 'How careless of you!'

It is fair to say the proprietor did not share Clara's amusement. He sniffed, scowled and pulled out a local news sheet, its date some six months prior. It landed with a slap on the counter. Clara and I peered closer. An article had been circled many times with a lead point. 'Gem Robbers Strike'.

'A robbery! How exciting.'

'They did *this*,' the downcast fellow held aloft his lame foot, wrapped in bandages and set at a tricky angle. 'Took whatever they laid hands on and scarpered.'

'My goodness, and were they found?'

The fellow's rueful grunt told us the miscreants had not been caught.

'Nor were the gems they took,' he scowled. 'I don't need to tell *you*, sir, this is a small world and items as distinct as these do not stay lost, but bob to the surface sooner or later like a dead and bloated body washed into the sea. No, treasures like these do not stay hidden for long.'

A door to the cellar clicked and a 'boy' sidled through the gap, as if unwilling to open the sesame further than he had to.

Reader, my soul leapt from my skin. There, with his back against the closed door, his emotionless eyes level with mine, was none other than the surgeon! His shirtsleeves were rolled up still, much as they had been while I lay on the bed, moments before oblivion. Quite possibly the very same shirt. It occurs to me now, those unfamiliar vowels . . . they are from *here*, this place. Harrogate. He chose it not for its spa waters or its remoteness from scrutiny, but because *this* is where he resides. The soil in which he had been planted.

His demeanour was sullen with none of the shock or surprise of my own reaction. It occurred to me he had been watching and listening behind that door, an advantage for certain. I did not hear the proprietor's instruction to retrieve the item from the window, but the surgeon cast his head down and set about the task, disappearing into the window cabinet whose door fell closed in his wake.

Clara meanwhile busied herself with a hat pin that seemed to gain in beauty the longer it remained before her eyes.

'I say, rather old to be a boy?' I whispered to the proprietor and nodded my head towards the surgeon.

'Indeed,' the man confided and lowered his voice. 'My greatnephew, disgraced and turned out by closer kin.'

'Why?' I gasped, my heart pounding. 'Why disgraced?'

The proprietor fixed me with glowering eyes, his voice a whisper, heavy with menace.

'After the war. He went to London.'

His words hung in the air like the city fog.

'And that is all?'

'To practise medicine. An idea quite above his station in life. The Great War broke some, but left others with delusions of grandeur.' At this, he tapped the side of his head. 'Inevitably, he transgressed. Then came legal expenses. Bankruptcy. Finally . . . the bottle.'

'I'm sorry,' I whispered, 'but he is . . . he *is* a doctor of medicine? He is *qualified*?'

'*Was*. They de-frocked him of his apron. He scrapes a living here now.'

'Kind of you.'

The proprietor grunted. 'Indeed. And he repaid me with abandonment in my hour of need. That day vagabonds came, hessian over their faces and a hammer to break any bone they chose, *he* was at large,' the proprietor gestured towards the window where the surgeon's form could be seen teetering on a ladder. 'Doing the Devil knows what!'

'I am sure he was . . .'

'He was up to no good! It is in his nature. Still, he languishes in daily misery, of that I make sure.'

Clara decided upon a moonstone hat pin of such ornate design and with a silver stem so long and tapering it could not possibly be sold for less than eleven guineas. I kept my eyes away from the lurking surgeon as I paid and ushered my delighted wife from the shop, determined that would be the last we'd see of him.

There was a thought in my mind that squirmed like a maggot, one that gradually devours its surroundings until, fat and immobile, it pupates in its own juices. The date on that newspaper. It was six months ago. Had *my* rotten appendix meant the surgeon abandoned his uncle that day, leaving him to the savagery of callous robbers? I loathed that demonic organ even more for trying to claim a final victim before its own demise. Or was the robbery divine vengeance for the surgeon's medical 'transgressions'? For every action, there is a reaction.

No. I chased those thoughts away. It was a mere coincidence.

'He was up to no good! It is in his nature. Still, he languishes in daily misery, of that I make sure.'

I would later turn the proprietor's words this way and that. One voice would assure me. Despite his 'transgressions', why should I doubt the surgeon? I was, after all, a walking example of his skill, honesty and good character. But another voice would insist on drawing for me his face as he held the chloroform firmly over mine to mute my protestations. I would dream I was Sir Thomas, balanced on a ladder at my own crumbling eaves. Legs weak at the sight of my soot-black chimney pots, the cold ground looming three floors below . . .

Over the coming months, time and tide again saw my dis-ease ebb, in daylight at any rate. Awake in the small hours or alone in my drawing room while Clara rested upstairs, her confinement imminent, my mind would find its way back. Likewise, whenever the rain patted the glass, just as on that first day when the sordid business was set in motion, the maggot would suddenly writhe and my hand would creep to the scar as I tried to sense the former turmoil there. Yet all seemed quiet. In truth, my dis-ease was only resting in metamorphosis, as does the maggot in its pupa.

For my son (Clara is convinced) is about to be born. Should he too have the operation? And when, given brother Albie was struck at 16? Dare I trust the surgeon a second time, and with the life of my child? Knowing what I now know about him? Yet who else would perform such a procedure? He is the devil I know.

'He's one of those you don't see 'less you need 'im and then poof! There he is,' Jack Davies assured me, as he finished buffing the front step. Clara had taken Master Will to the park where he liked to run about, so there was no danger she would overhear us.

His second birthday imminent, Will's future health, not my own, was the nagging fear that kept me awake. I found myself unable to discuss my concerns with more orthodox medical men, for the subject of my own operation would be sure to arise.

'I can put the word out, if you need.' Jack's eyes looked me up and down. He seemed cheerful, but did he judge? I find it hard to tell with those whose living depends on one's good humour.

Within a week, the front door opened and there, again, stood the surgeon. In the same suit he wore three years ago. Had I replied with a 'yes' or had Jack had taken it upon himself to summon the devil from his lair . . .?

'Ah,' I said. 'Thank you for coming. I have a question for you.'

Once more he stood by my hearth, his eyes wandering over the artefacts, eyes I now knew to have more knowledge in them of such things than I had previously assumed.

'Oh. You feel discomfort in the abdomen?' he asked.

'No. Quite the opposite. Since you . . . since I visited you in Harrogate, my abdomen has been quite obedient. No, it is for my son I wish to enquire.'

'*You* wanted to speak with *me*?'

'Well, yes, that's why you're here, is it not?'

'Go on.'

'The fear has returned. I wish my son's appendix gone, lest it take him from us. I seek your advice on *when*, at what age, would be safest to remove it.'

The surgeon looked at me long and hard. His eyes lifeless, eerie, his face without expression.

'I did not come here for that.'

'Why? What did Jack Davies say to . . . summon you?'

'No one summoned me. I am here of my own volition.'

Those dead eyes. Why did my flesh creep and my heart leap?

'I have booked a passage to America and will start afresh there.' I swear he spoke as if to my absent organ. Or was it? Was it absent or still there?

'Your uncle is quite recovered?' My squeal of a voice betrayed me.

'My uncle is quite dead.'

'I am sorry.'

'I am not. The shop is closed, the stock sold to pay his debts. I am finally free of the old tyrant.'

His eyes met mine for the first time that day. In them, my mind flashed back. Back to my room in the boarding house. No, before. The train. In the train carriage, the gent opposite. *The Times*. 'An antiquarian suffers the loss of jewels and his ankle joint in a violent burglary'.

I had suspected the surgeon left his uncle alone to perform my operation. But the robbery took place before then. Long enough before to have been reported to the police and then the newspaper prior to my leaving London. The proprietor's voice whispered in my ears, back from the dead . . .

Items as distinct as these do not stay lost, but bob to the surface sooner or later like a dead and bloated body washed into the sea.

'I need something,' the surgeon whispered. 'And you have it.'

'I assure you I have nothing of value, sir! But if you left my appendix where it will surely murder me before my son is of age, I swear I will . . . I will . . .'

'You will not,' he said, a new confidence in his voice. 'For I removed your appendix, healthy as it was.' I stopped in confusion. My mind wound itself back to the day he stood, damp and dour in my drawing room. His eyes wandering over my parents' artefacts like a snail drags itself across a stone.

'Three items: a moonstone and diamond pendant, a ring and an amulet. All pure gold. I have come for them.'

The Egyptian vase. That moment I observed when he peered inside. It would have taken a split-second for him to drop his loot there and, if wrapped in cloth, the move would have been noiseless.

It was the perfect hiding place. He could be sure I would not part with my beloved parents' collection. He knew I, in my ignorance, would keep his loot safe. When he was ready, all he had to do was knock on my door and inveigle his way back to that corner of the drawing room, distract me, dip his hand in . . . only, of course, the vase was not where it had been that day. One of many items banished upstairs when my son began to crawl. His plan was thwarted!

'I see. And now you are back to retrieve what you secreted about my house.'

'It could be said.'

'You took a chance, did you not?'

'I did. But then, so did you in asking me such a favour.'

'A favour? I paid you, sir!'

The doctor sighed. He spoke as if about to deliver an obvious and reasonable request.

'I desire to realise my investment and set up a business in the New World. Let me have my stake and you will not hear from me again.'

'A few stolen gems shoved into the neck of an old vase is barely an investment!'

He stopped, his eyes as dead as ever, but if surprise could cross them, cross them it did at that moment.

'A vase? No, sir.'

And with that, my eyes fell to his hand. To the knife in it. And in the other, a folded wad of cloth, a sight that had filled me with dread and loathing the first time.

I took a step back.

'I recall the vase. A pretty piece. But my investment is not in any pottery,' the doctor's voice seemed louder now, commanding, confident. My mind raced in surprise.

'It is not? Then where else in this room did you hide your loot, stolen most disgracefully from your own kin?'

Our eyes met; mine, wild with horror, were compelled to follow his as they crawled down my body and lingered at my lower abdomen.

I took another step away. My hand raced to my scar and pressed it, gingerly as always, then firmer, firmer still. What is that in there? A mass. Deep. Unyielding. Painless. But there.

'It should be no worse than before,' the doctor advanced on me until my back found the wall. 'As soon as agreeable, move around to stimulate your circulation. After ten days, cut the stitches and gently pull them free.'

'No,' I stammered. 'No, I refuse to undergo . . .'

'Do not give me those eyes, sir,' the doctor spat out his growing irritation. 'The package is quite sterile. You have had no ill effects these past two years and more.'

I thought back to the last time I tried saying 'no' to the doctor, and a memory struck me from that day. A straw appeared before me and clutch I did!

'I . . . I . . . have not fasted, as before.' How long could I hold off the inevitable? His knife as dead and unfeeling as his eyes, chloroform dripping from the cloth.

'I will leave you face down. When you regurgitate, you will not choke to death. It is how I leave patients who are, like you were then, all alone.'

The doctor lunged at me, his smaller stature somehow compensated for by determination to overpower me, and years' experience of the same. I felt the cloth smother my mouth and nose. As I gasped the awful fumes I caught a glint from the corner of my eye. The knife? That blade? Something . . .

As I sank into oblivion, did I hear my Clara's voice drift through the fog?

'But he is not alone this time.'

I awoke to see a large blue bat hanging from my drawing room ceiling. On gaining further consciousness, I saw it was a police constable, his cape askew, leering down at me as I lay on the rug.

'He is altogether too stupefied to speak,' Clara trilled. From the glint in her eye, even in my fugue state, I knew her words to be as much an instruction as a statement.

'I arrived from upstairs where I had been settling my son, and there was the intruder, poised to assail my husband with a knife. I had to act, Constable, else I would be a widow and our son fatherless before his third birthday.'

Clara crouched beside me, lifted me up on her knee.

'He is still quite *dumb*,' she stated, firmly. 'If I had not seized the element of surprise with my own hands and killed the assailant, the scene here would be very different. Distressed as I am to have taken a life.'

I glanced to my right. To a pair of dead eyes, trained directly on me. The doctor was quite lifeless, his mouth agape, the knife still in his grip and through his neck, Clara's hat pin, its milky moonstone slowly dripping with fast congealing blood.

Clara would repeat her story, of deterring my attacker by thrusting her hat pin through his jugular vein, several times before the matter was filed away and forgotten about by Scotland Yard. The doctor had no living relatives, or at least none that cared to clear his bad name, and at our last meeting the Inspector waved us away.

We took our usual route through St James's, the three of us. Clara held William's perfect little hand. My arm linked through hers but my other hand came to rest where it always did at times like this . . . on my scar.

Since I realised my body is a trinket box for a criminal's loot, I spend my days trying to forget it, and my nights prodding the scar for any hint of the cold stones within. For that little part of the story was never imparted to the police.

'You can forget it,' Clara said, glancing to my hand. 'Your appendix is gone and whatever the doctor replaced it with has caused no grief these last three years.'

She sought only to comfort me, but as she knows so very little about matters of medicine I could only smile thinly. Quite aside from that, there is now no devil to trust with my son's future health. Lacking words in which to couch my feelings, they made themselves apparent on my face.

'William Senior!' she said, in that brightly admonishing tone she adopts. 'I can see you are worrying about the doctor's criminal cohorts. You imagine them hunting you down and ripping those gems from your belly with as little finesse as they would gut a herring. Well, the police inspector was adamant the doctor acted quite, quite alone. The only soul who knew of those gems inside you is dead himself. You have nothing to fear, my darling. Now, let's walk, take lunch, play with little William in the parlour and dress for dinner.'

I smiled. Of course, she is right about most things.

I hung back as Clara stepped ahead. Our son tottered, shrieked and stamped with delight as she parroted him gaily, her hat pinned firmly over her fair curls. That lucky Harrogate moonstone glinted in the sun, as it glinted that day in our drawing room, and it occurred to me she was wrong on one point: there *is* someone who knows my secret. As we made our way home I kept my eyes on her and my hand on my scar, as I contemplated a new, and, I fear, unending state of dis-ease.

MURDER IN MASHAM

Vaseem Khan

'Come again?'

'There's been a murder. Richard Crannigan.'

'And who's he when he's at home?'

'An actor. With the Masham Shakespeareans. He was killed last night. At the Masham Town Hall.'

Detective Chief Inspector Tiberius March gave his junior officer a blank look. And then belched loudly. 'Sorry. Had a curry last night. Touch of the Delhi belly. By the way, the *h* in Masham is silent.' He scratched his nose. 'Probably can't say "Delhi belly" anymore, can I? Your lot will be up in arms, for starters.'

Detective Constable Zeenat Rasheed bit her tongue.

'So what have we got?' March reached for his morning plate of Greggs delicacies. Sausage roll. Pasty. Doughnut. Washed down by half a litre of Coke. Nothing like a balanced breakfast.

Rasheed eyed the plate queasily. 'Autopsy is scheduled first thing. Forensics have gone over the scene. Crannigan was murdered in his room. The Shakespeareans – five of them plus their manager and his PA – were all staying at the same bed and breakfast and they were the only guests. The owners and staff don't stay there overnight. Estimated time of death is between 2 and 4 a.m. The alarm system says no one else entered during the night.'

'So you're saying it had to be one of them?'

'Seems likely. Unless we can show how someone else got in without triggering the alarm. Plus, the murder weapon was the same dagger they used in the play. They use a real dagger. Don't ask me why.'

Rasheed knew that the Masham Shakespeareans – an offshoot troupe of the renowned Masham Players – had been established earlier that year with the backing of a local brewery tycoon turned patron of the arts. The tycoon's cheque-book had coaxed a group of respected actors to the small English town whose close neighbour – Harrogate – had been made infamous by mystery writer Agatha Christie back in the 1920s. Harrogate was where the 'Queen of Crime' had reappeared, having vanished for eleven days, resulting in a nationwide hunt and endless speculation ever since.

Rasheed knew all this because her last Tinder date had been a maven for the theatre *and* crime fiction. He'd also been a pompous arse. Nevertheless, when she'd heard that the Shakespeareans' leading man had been found stabbed in the chest following the opening night of *Macbeth*, she'd had the strangest feeling that she'd been here already.

'Never liked actors,' said March. 'Did I tell you about the time I met Sir? Absolute tosser. I was called in on a domestic. He'd smacked his girlfriend around. Claimed she'd accidentally fallen onto his knuckles.'

'I've set up some interviews. First one's in about three hours, right after the autopsy. Which is in thirty minutes.'

'Thirty minutes? Christ, how about giving me some warning?'

'The case was handed to us this morning. The on-call DS went out to the scene last night, but the Chief Super wants us to take over. And I did give you warning. I sent you a WhatsApp.'

'I don't do social media. Social media is for saddos.'

'I also texted you. And emailed. And tried calling you three times.'

'I was doing my yoga.'

Rasheed looked at her superior officer. March was a big man, troll-shaped, massively overweight, with whiskery jowls, scraped-back dark hair, and a scar running down one side of his face. He wore clothes rescued from the late seventies. Shoes – currently up on the table – that looked as if a tramp had spent years breaking them in for him.

And this was the man they'd chosen to mentor her.

She had known the DCI less than a fortnight, and her initial assessment was anything but promising. She could practically feel her nascent career as a detective flatlining. As if it wasn't bad enough dealing with Neanderthals like Len Martin, the other DCI at the station house. She'd heard him when he'd thought she was out of earshot. *Bad enough she's a woman. And then, one of* that *lot. Fatwa incoming! It's positive discrimination gone mad.*

'May I suggest you bring your breakfast with you, Sir?'

The body lay on the autopsy table, washed out by the overhead lighting.

The coroner, Miles Abell, a ghoul-thin elderly man, as pallid as the corpse he'd just finished with, ran his hands under a tap at the sink. 'Death was caused by the stab wound. Entry wound through the mid-left sternal border; knife struck the left ventricle. Massive internal trauma and blood loss. He died quickly.'

DC Rasheed continued to look at the body. Crannigan had been a tall man, imposing, with a head of bright red hair and a sculpted hipster beard.

'Don't think I've ever seen a ginge Macbeth before,' remarked DCI March. 'Which is strange, given that it's a Scottish play.' He was chewing on a taco he'd bought from a van parked outside the coroner's office. The smell clashed with the lingering smell of formaldehyde. Rasheed had watched as he'd breezed by a sign prohibiting food and drink in the autopsy suite. The pathologist was clearly used to March, as he'd simply peered disapprovingly at him then got on with the job.

'Were there any defensive wounds?' asked Rasheed.

Abell finished washing his hands, walked back towards them. 'None that I could find.'

'So Crannigan knew his killer.'

'Gold star for you, detective,' said March. 'Bet you didn't think binge-watching *CSI: Yorkshire* would pay off so spectacularly?' He winked at Abell, who looked at him coldly.

Rasheed ignored March. She knew he was only doing it to wind her up. 'Anything else you can tell us?'

'He was in his forties, in relatively good health. That's about it.'

March waved the stump of his taco in Rasheed's direction. 'Where's the murder weapon?'

'In the evidence room, back at the station.'

'Ah. Evidence room. By which you mean the cupboard labelled "Crap We Are Not Allowed To Throw Out".' He scratched his jaw. 'How did the killer get hold of the knife?'

'It was used during the performance and then put into the props room. Anyone could have taken it, then smuggled it back to the B&B.'

Abell glanced at the clock on the wall. 'My report will be with you in due course. Now, if you don't mind, my next customer is waiting.'

*

138

Leonard Ruff sat with his boots up on a desk. Cowboy boots. With spurs.

Above the boots he wore a three piece suit, fitting snugly around a heavy frame. A garish tie and yellow-framed, tinted spectacles completed the ensemble.

He was a pink-faced man in his early fifties, with a bald dome surrounded by a hula skirt of peppery hair that fell to his shoulders.

He was also a man who enjoyed shouting.

March and Rasheed entered the tiny first floor office on Masham's market square to find Ruff hollering at someone on the phone. 'It's a contract. That means you do what you said you would do or I come down there and drill you a new bumhole. How does that sound?' He listened for a minute, holding up a beringed finger at them. 'I'm glad we got that sorted. Thank you, Reverend.'

He put down the phone. 'Never work with animals or priests. They're all bloody paedos anyway. The priests, not the animals. Can I offer you a cup of something?'

'Whisky?' said March.

Rasheed frowned at her senior officer. 'Some water would be great.'

Ruff leered at March. 'I thought you lot weren't allowed to drink on duty?'

'She can't drink full stop. She's a Muslim. They're a bit funny about that sort of thing. I, on the other hand, joined the force before they changed the rules about not getting plastered while in uniform.'

Rasheed glared at the DCI, as Ruff grinned. 'Vicky!' His bellow startled a slim young woman in her mid-twenties sitting in the next-door office. She stumbled in and looked at them. Her face was red below dark hair scraped back into a limp ponytail. A trace of acne hinted at teenage cruelties.

'Get some glasses and the Glenfiddich. The real one, not the knockoff shite. And some water for Lady Fuzz here.'

Ruff watched her go. 'Nice enough arse but not the brains God gave geese. Now . . . I expect this is about Richard. Poor bastard.'

'What was your relationship to Richard Crannigan?' asked Rasheed, as Vicky returned and handed the men glasses filled with a murky amber liquid. March threw his back in one go, then returned the glass. 'Refill, bartender. He's paying.'

The girl held a small bottle of water out to Rasheed. 'Is still water OK?'

'Yes, that's fine.' Rasheed watched the girl leave, then turned back to Ruff.

'Relationship?' said Ruff. 'Well, we weren't shagging, if that's what you mean.' He maintained a straight face for two seconds, then burst out laughing. It sounded like a donkey being drowned. Rasheed looked at him stony-faced. 'Fine. Pardon me for trying to cope with my friend's murder with a spot of gallows humour.' He sipped from his glass. 'I was Richard's agent. I'm also the tour manager for the Masham Shakespeareans.'

'What exactly does a tour manager do?'

'What it says on the tin, my darling. I book tours. I manage. I go along on said tours and make sure they don't take a dump on their own careers. I'm basically a glorified roadie, but without the sex and drugs. Well, maybe without the sex.'

Rasheed stiffened. 'Please don't call me darling. My name is Detective Constable Rasheed.'

Ruff looked at March, who shrugged. 'She's sensitive.'

Rasheed ignored the exchange, focused on her next question. 'Why did they need a tour manager? I thought they were playing in Masham throughout the season?'

'Not enough money in it. We don't do daily shows. So I book gigs elsewhere. A payday here, payday there. Edinburgh. London. Grimsby.'

'Grimsby?' March raised an eyebrow.

'Massive arts scene in Grimsby these days. It's all that drugs cash sloshing about.'

'Can you tell us what happened yesterday?' said Rasheed, raising her voice a notch. 'At the theatre, I mean.'

'Well, we had a full house, for starters. This lot were on top of their game – rare for a first nighter. The critics actually looked like they were enjoying the show. I mean, none of them fell asleep or got their phones out or started playing with themselves in their seats.'

'And after the performance?'

'Well, there was the afterparty. Drinks. Crap canapés. Sign a few autographs. Chat up a few groupies. The usual drill.'

'Where was that?'

'Also at the town hall. They've got this lovely little space round the back. You could swing at least two cats around, if you tied them together by the tails.'

'And what happened next?'

'We all went out for a curry. Quaffed a few beers. Then back to the B&B and off to bed.'

'What time was that?'

'Around midnight, I reckon. Can't be too sure. I was totally wrecked by then.'

'Why were you staying at a B&B?' said March. 'A-list celebs like you. Might have sprung for a Premier Inn, I'd have thought.'

'Easier keeping an eye on them in a small place rather than a great big hotel.'

Rasheed leant in. 'Did anything untoward happen yesterday evening?'

'Yeah. My leading man was murdered. With a great big knife. That untoward enough for you?'

'I meant before the murder,' said Rasheed. 'At the afterparty or the restaurant.'

'Not that I can remember.'

Rasheed was silent a moment. 'And how did Richard seem through all this?'

'He was his usual self. By which I mean he was full of it. The man was a fine actor, but he was an absolute arsehole.'

'I thought you said he was your friend.'

'He was, sweetcakes. That doesn't mean he couldn't be a complete shite. But that's actors for you.'

Rasheed's cheek twitched. 'Don't call me sweetcakes.'

'When you say "full of it",' said March, 'what are we talking here?'

'I meant he had a bit of a complex. Reckoned he was carrying the show. Kept going on about it. Put everyone's backs up.'

'So you're saying he upset his co-stars?' said Rasheed.

'Par for the course, love. Don't read anything into it. They're all massive narcissists. Make Genghis Khan look like Mother Teresa.'

'Don't call me love.'

Ruff eyed her coolly. 'Let me take a wild guess. You're single, right?'

Rasheed breathed in through her nostrils. For an instant, she was back at the academy, in a mock-up interview room, sitting through Interviewing 101. *Don't react. No matter how combative, no matter how much of an arse, never let your interviewee know what you're thinking. Or feeling.* 'One last question. Where were you between 2 a.m. and 4 a.m. last night?'

Ruff frowned. 'Well, let me think. 2 a.m.? I was in bed. Out like a light.'

'And you never left your room?'

'Not unless I was sleep-wanking in the corridor. It's a real thing. I saw it in a documentary.'

She continued to stare at him. There was something about Ruff's cavalier manner that was unconvincing . . .

'Oh, for God's sake . . . Vicky, get in here!'

The girl came running.

'The cops want to know where I was last night.'

Her eyes wobbled behind her spectacles.

'Just tell them.'

'He was in his room. With me. We were – ah – together.' A furious blush turned her cheeks scarlet.

'You and Mr Ruff?' said Rasheed.

'Yes.'

'*This* Mr Ruff?' said March, pointing at the impresario.

'Hey, I'm sitting right here!'

'No accounting for taste, I suppose,' said March, as they made their way to their second interview. 'I mean, what *did* he see in her?'

'Young impressionable girl. Powerful older man. It happens.'

'You're not about to wrestle me to the floor and tear my clothes off, are you?'

They found their next interviewee, James Wang, in a reading room at the back of the B&B where the troupe had been lodged.

'Wang? You've got to be kidding me,' muttered March.

James Wang was a ball of nervous energy. He ricocheted off the walls, a book in his hand. Rasheed noted that it was a copy of one of her own favourites: *Moby Dick*.

'So, Mr Wang,' said March, 'what role did you play in *Macbeth*? I mean, last I checked, there weren't any Japanese characters.'

'I'm not Japanese. I'm Chinese. *British*-Chinese.'

'My bad. Haven't really had the pleasure of a lot of Wangs before.'

James looked at him coldly. 'It's the most common surname in China. In the world, in fact.'

'Well, knock me down with a rubber cosh.'

'To answer your question, I played the witches.'

March looked at him blankly. 'The witches? You mean, the three women with the black hats? And the cauldron? Double, double, toil and trouble? Those witches?'

'It's a gender-neutral production. And colour-blind casting.'

'Well, someone certainly had to be optically challenged casting *you* in a female role.'

'Roles.'

'Come again?'

'I played all three witches.'

March stuck a finger in his ear, wriggled it around. 'How does that work, then? And they're called warlocks. Male witches. Chinese or otherwise.'

'We didn't have the budget for three witches. And I can do voices.'

'In that case, perhaps you'd do the voice of a sane person and tell us where you were last night when Richard Crannigan was being stabbed to death?'

'I was asleep. In my room.'

Rasheed spoke up. 'Can anyone vouch for that?'

'I was alone, if that's what you mean.'

'How did you get on with him?' Rasheed continued.

A slight hesitation. 'We were friends.'

'Strange,' said March. 'We were told Crannigan got on everyone's tits.'

'He could be abrasive. But we got on fine.'

144

'So no urge to shove a knife into him, then?'

Wang said nothing.

Rasheed chimed in again. 'Here's our problem. We know one of you killed him. No one else had the opportunity.'

Wang pulled out a pack of cigarettes, lit one. 'Look, I had nothing to do with it. Why would I? If you're looking for motive, then go talk to Ben Duggan. If anyone had a reason to kill Richard, it was him.'

Rasheed glanced at March, then said, 'And what motive would that be?'

Wang hesitated, then told them.

Ben Duggan turned out to be a small, dark-haired white man with a wispy beard, twin earrings and a thick sweater.

They were sitting in the B&B's kitchen, Duggan cradling a cup of something warm.

'Mr Duggan,' said Rasheed, 'we have been informed that you and Richard both auditioned for the lead role in the play. When Richard got it, you were, shall we say, less than pleased?'

'Not bloody impressed was how we heard it,' said March. 'The pair of you almost came to blows. Apparently, you had the idea Richard stole the part out from under you.'

Duggan blinked rapidly. 'I don't know what you've been told, but it wasn't like that.'

'You threatened to kill the man. In front of witnesses.'

'It was a heat of the moment thing.'

'These things usually are. Next thing you know there's a ruddy great knife sticking out of someone's chest.'

Duggan reared back. 'You're out of order.' He glared at March, then seemed to regain control over himself. 'Look, I admit, when Richard got the part I was pissed. I thought he'd been a bit underhand.'

'How so?' asked Rasheed.

'What does it matter now?'

'How about we get to the part where you tell us what we want to know and I can stop growing older and more handsome sitting in this kitchen?' said March.

Duggan licked his lips. 'Fine. I was told I had the part. Or as good as. And then Richard brought his wife in. To audition for Lady Macbeth. And *then* he said the chemistry between Macbeth and Lady Macbeth would work a lot better if *he* played the lead. How could the producers argue with that?' His expression became bitter. 'Of course, it didn't hurt that she was—' He stopped, cut his eyes at Rasheed.

'Was what?' said the detective constable.

'Never mind. My point is that, yes, I had a grudge, but then I got over it. They gave me the part of Banquo. I needed the work.'

'Not quite the same, is it?' said March. 'From leading man to embittered ghost.'

'I had nothing to do with Richard's death.' Duggan's voice became high-pitched. 'If you really want to put someone in the frame for his murder, then maybe you should go back and ask James why he wouldn't ever be left alone in the same room as Richard.'

'I'm sorry?' said Rasheed.

'Do I have to spell it out? Richard assaulted him. Sexually. Groped him.'

'Richard groped . . . Wang?' March's grin was wide enough to swallow a cat.

'Yes. Richard occasionally went both ways.'

'Now that's what I call a proper plot twist,' said March.

'So you're saying you think James Wang killed Richard?' said Rasheed.

He was silent a moment. 'Not really. It was only the one time and Richard was stoned out of his mind – to hear James tell it. He could have complained, but what was the point? No one would have believed him. And even if they had, there was no payday to be had. Richard was hardly Harvey Weinstein.'

'That's highly offensive,' said Rasheed. 'Suggesting that victims of sexual assault only come forward so that they can sue for damages.'

'Quite right,' said March. 'They usually only come forward for the free publicity to bolster their flagging careers.' He registered his colleague's glare. 'Down with the patriarchy!'

Rasheed resisted the urge to respond, directed herself back to Duggan. 'So if it wasn't you and it wasn't James Wang, then who?'

Duggan cracked his jaw. 'I suggest you go talk to his wife.'

They tracked Adele Ambrose, Richard Crannigan's wife, to her room, where she had retired after a terrible morning dealing with her husband's murder.

'Let's go easy, shall we?' said Rasheed, knocking on the door. 'She's probably had a rough time of it.'

'Of course,' said March. 'I shall be the very soul of sensitivity.'

Rasheed raised an eyebrow, but forbore from comment.

The door swung back to reveal Adele, dressed in jeans and a turtleneck.

'So,' said March, holding up his warrant card, 'word on the street is you might have murdered your husband.'

The woman jerked back. 'What the hell are you talking about?'

'Ben Duggan tells us you and Richard were having problems. Apparently, he couldn't keep his wang where nature intended, i.e., in his pants. Richard's wang, I mean. Not James Wang.'

She stared at him, then turned to Rasheed. 'He can't speak to me like that.'

Rasheed began an apology for her superior officer's crassness, but was cut off by March: 'Oh, I assure you I can. Unless you'd rather do this down at the station. You can even get a lawyer to hold your hand if you like.'

Seconds ticked by, then Adele seemed to compose herself.

She walked to the room's only desk, sat down on the accompanying chair. 'I have just lost my husband in the most terrible circumstances. I have no idea what you've been told, but I had nothing to do with his death.'

'Can you explain why you and your husband were staying in separate rooms last night?' said Rasheed.

'We always stay in separate rooms. Even at home. Richard is – *was* – a restless sleeper. A lifelong insomniac. He'd keep me up half the night, until we got a place big enough for us to have our own bedrooms.'

'How long were you married?'

'Two years.'

'Ah. The two-year itch,' said March. 'That explains why he was out shagging anything that moved.'

The woman looked furious, then her shoulders slumped. 'No point denying it. Richard had a wandering eye. It's my own fault. He was always going on about wanting an open marriage.'

'An open marriage. Fancy that,' said March.

'Are you married, Detective?'

'Perish the thought. If I wanted to have strips torn off me every day by my social and intellectual inferior I'd just shack up with my landlady.' He took out a Mars Bar, unwrapped it, then shoved the entire thing into his mouth.

Adele stared at him.

'They call it shrinkflation,' he mumbled. 'Back in my day a Mars Bar was the size of your arm.'

'Ms Ambrose, where were you last night between two and four?' said Rasheed.

'I was here, in my room. Watching TV. I couldn't sleep.'

'Did you hear anything? What I mean is, Richard's room is next door to yours.'

'No. When I say I was watching TV, I mean I was watching Netflix on my laptop. And I had my headphones on.'

'We understand you and Richard had words at the afterparty?'

'Who told you that?'

'Banquo's ghost,' said March. 'I mean, Ben Duggan. I'm beginning to get those two mixed up.'

Adele looked suddenly angry. 'Ben? What did he tell you?'

'He said you walked in on your husband pawing a groupie. In an alley round the back of the theatre.'

'She wasn't a groupie. She was some housewife from Harrogate. They'd both gone into the alley for a cigarette. I went out to ask Richard something and saw him—'

'With his pants down, bending the old dear over the bins?' March grinned.

Adele's gaze dropped to her hands.

'What did Richard say about it?' Rasheed's tone was sympathetic.

'What *could* he say? This wasn't the first time.'

'Expect you were furious,' said March. 'Hell hath no fury and all that.'

'Richard didn't scorn me, detective. He wanted to have his cake and eat it too. Like most men.'

'Not me,' said March, patting his stomach. 'Can't stand cake. Now, a bag of Tesco's value donuts. Can't go wrong.'

'I know how it looks. But I didn't kill my husband. I loved him. In spite of everything, I loved the stupid bastard.' Tears hovered in the corners of her eyes.

'Well, *someone* murdered him,' said Rasheed. 'And we know it had to be someone staying in this building last night.'

Adele shook her head, then stopped. 'Have you spoken to Orson, yet?'

Rasheed looked quizzical. 'Do you mean Orson Drake?'

'Yes. He—' She hesitated.

'Well, don't stop now,' said March. 'You were about to dish the dirt.'

Adele's eyes became cold. 'I only mention Orson because I sensed a genuine frostiness from him towards Richard. And this was in spite of Richard worshipping the man. I mean, Orson had a proper Hollywood career. God knows why he agreed to do *this* gig.'

'Isn't he knocking on a bit now?' said March. 'Last time I heard his name my nan was young enough to enjoy a knee trembler behind the bike sheds. Rather like your late husband.'

Adele stood up. 'I would really like to have some privacy, Detectives. So that I might grieve.'

'You do that,' said March, lifting himself to his feet from the bed. 'Just don't go too far, hey? You'd be amazed how many people grieving their partners' murders suddenly feel the need to hop on a flight to a non-extradition country.'

'You know, it wouldn't hurt for you to show a little empathy,' said Rasheed, as they tracked across the road to a pub where they had been told they might find Orson Drake. 'The woman *has* just lost her husband.'

'That *was* me showing empathy. I mean, I didn't once mention that I thought she was a shit actress – oh, pardon me, act*or*. Did you see those tears? She was practically biting her lip to squeeze them out. Nor did I mention that she probably got the part because her dead husband pulled some strings. And possibly because she was black.'

She stopped and squared up to him. 'Sir, I—' words banged at the inside of her mouth, but she couldn't get them out.

'Is this the part where you tell me you're wildly attracted to me but cannot possibly act on your raging desires because you value your career and/or the higher calling of justice too much? Well, there's no need to fret. I'm perfectly happy to keep this a friends-without-benefits deal.'

She stared at him, then spun on her heel and walked into the pub.

They found Orson Drake in the corner, beer in hand, hunched over a newspaper and a plate of fish and chips.

'Spare a chip?'

Drake glared up at them over the top of half-moon spectacles. 'If you want an autograph you can come back later. This is my me time.'

'Charming,' said March. 'And here I was telling my fellow detective that my nan would practically have an orgasm at the thought of me meeting the great Orson Drake. Course, she can't actually do that on account of being dead. Meet you, I mean. Not the orgasming. I've heard stuff about corpses that'd make your hair stand on end.'

Drake frowned. 'Detectives?'

Rasheed held up her warrant card. 'We'd like to talk to you about Richard Crannigan. Sir.'

Drake cursed under his breath, then got to his feet. 'Fine, but the beer goes with me. And keep your hands off my chips.'

They found a room at the back of the pub.

Drake fell into a tiny sofa. A big man, robust despite being in his seventies, with a wild beard and a corrugated brow. 'So, what is it you want to know?'

The actor's baritone bounced off the floral wallpaper. The detectives knew that Drake played King Duncan in the play.

'As you know, Richard Crannigan was murdered last night,' Rasheed began. 'We know that it could only have been one of the people staying at your B&B.'

'Sounds like an Agatha Christie plot. I hate Agatha Christie.'

'I'm sure the feeling is mutual,' said March. 'Your turn as Poirot in that *Murder on the Orient Express* remake was savaged by the critics, as I recall.'

Drake turned scarlet. 'I tried to take the franchise in a new direction.'

'Well, technically, into the shitter *is* a direction.'

'*Sir*,' interjected Rasheed, 'we understand that you and Richard had a somewhat cool relationship.'

'Who told you that?'

'His wife.'

'Richard and I were professionals.'

'But you didn't get on?'

'One doesn't have to get on with one's co-stars.'

'Well, one doesn't have to murder them either, but one did,' said March. 'Or one of you did, I should say.'

'It wasn't me.'

'What exactly was your problem with Richard?' persisted Rasheed.

Drake looked at her over his beer. 'The man was a sycophantic leech. Mr Drake this, Mr Drake that. Christ, he made my stomach turn.'

'Crannigan fawning over you can't be the only reason you didn't get on,' said Rasheed. 'I mean, I'm sure you get plenty of adulation from younger actors. What was it about Richard that made you dislike him?'

Drake breathed in through his nose, as if debating with himself. 'About fifteen years ago, Crannigan said something, a throwaway comment that was picked up in a blog piece. Something not very complimentary about a performance I gave in *The Donkey of Bethlehem*.'

'Ah. That all time Christmas classic,' said March. 'You spent half the film talking to the donkey, as I recall.'

'I didn't write the script,' muttered Drake. 'But I needed the money. I was going through a messy divorce. I had debts. Sometimes, one takes a payday, eats a bucket of shit, and swallows one's pride.'

'Sounds like every day in the police force. Without the payday.'

'Look, the point is, Richard said something nasty and so I was less than kindly disposed towards him.'

'Then why did you agree to work with him?' asked Rasheed.

'I only found out about the comment when I was Googling my co-stars after I'd signed the contract. It was too late to pull out.'

March snorted. 'By which you mean you were skint again and needed the money.'

Drake looked furious. 'If you weren't a policeman I'd kick your teeth in.'

'And if you weren't a sozzled old has-been I'd ask for your autograph. Just so I could wipe my arse with it.'

'That went well,' said Rasheed as they stepped out of the pub.

'If he was any more pompous he'd vanish up his own bum.'

'Be that as it may, we need to rein in our tempers if we're going to get anywhere.'

'By we, I suppose you mean me?'

'I wasn't the one a seventy-year-old threatened to beat the shit out of. Sir.'

March pulled a pack of cigarillos from his pocket and lit one. He blew a smoke ring into the air. 'Fancy a cheeky Nando's? I'm ravenous.'

The restaurant was bustling with a decent lunchtime crowd.

They found a table. Rasheed ordered for them both via the Nando's app.

Fifteen minutes later, she watched as March took a bite out of a drumstick. A whole grilled chicken sat before him, with side orders of chips, fully loaded chips, peri-salted chips and creamy mashed potato.

'Tastes just like chicken,' said the DCI. He picked up his plastic pint glass of Coke, slurped at it like a camel. It was his third glass.

She looked down at her own chaste salad. Perhaps she should have ordered more.

'So, this is the bit where you tell me more about yourself,' said March. 'That's how this whole mentor–mentee thing works.'

'There's not much to tell. I joined the force because I believe in the idea of policing by consent.'

'Oh, goody. An idealist. It's so rare to see one in the wild.'

'What would the world be without law and order?'

'Because, of course, it's such a utopia today.'

'You know what I mean.'

March took another gulp of his Coke. 'How are you settling in at the station?'

She hesitated. The first rule of policework: never rat on your colleagues. She'd seen *Serpico* enough times to have learnt that lesson. 'Fine.'

'Really? I heard you were fitting in like a nun in a brothel.'

She coloured.

'No need to blush. At least, I'm assuming you're blushing. Bit hard to tell, what with you being brown.'

She gaped at him.

He shoved a chip into his mouth. 'I hear DCI Martin calls you Constable Curry.'

Her jaw throbbed. 'And what if I were to call you a big fat ignorant bastard? Sir.'

He raised an eyebrow. 'Now I never said *I* called you that.'

She took a deep breath. 'Perhaps we could focus on the case?'

'Suit yourself.' He picked up an extra hot chilli sauce bottle and emptied half of the contents over his chicken. 'Enlighten me.'

'Well, I thought we might go over what we know so far. Perhaps try to find out who actually killed Richard Crannigan?'

'Knock yourself out.'

She resisted the urge to hurl her fork at him. 'OK. Well, let's look at what we know. Crannigan was killed between 2 and 4 a.m. last night. He was murdered with a dagger taken from the theatre. He was murdered by someone he knew, one of the other individuals staying at the B&B. We know that James Wang may have been sexually assaulted by Crannigan in the past. We know that Ben Duggan thought Crannigan stole the lead role from him. We know that his wife caught him with another woman yesterday evening. We know that Orson Drake bore a grudge against Crannigan for an offensive remark he'd made about Drake. On the face of it, none of these seem serious enough motives to murder a man in cold blood.'

'You'd be surprised the things people kill for. I once caught a case where a thirty-five-year-old man murdered his mother because she hadn't ironed his shirt that morning.' March waved a fork around. 'Detective work really isn't complicated. Means, motive and opportunity.' He pushed his plate aside and turned over the paper table mat below.

She watched him pat at his pockets.

'I seem to find myself without a pen.'

'I've got one.'

'Of course you have.'

She looked on as he drew two overlapping circles on the sheet. 'Now, watch carefully. This is where the magic happens.' He wrote a legend above each circle, then pushed the sheet towards her.

The detective constable looked at the sheet. She knew that March was testing her. 'Do *you* know who killed Crannigan?' she said.

'I have a fair idea.'

'Why don't you just tell me?'

'I wouldn't make a very good mentor if I just *told* you now, would I?' March's face became serious. 'Besides, you were almost there. You just need to think a little broader.'

Rasheed looked back down at the sheet. The faces of the various suspects cycled through her thoughts. Means. Motive. And opportunity . . . they all had motive. They all had access to the means. Which left . . . opportunity. Who *genuinely* had the opportunity?

And what had March meant by thinking a little broader?

And then, she had it.

She told March her conjecture.

March picked up a chip, grinned. 'I knew you'd get there in the end.'

'Well, are we all sitting comfortably? So glad you could make it.'

They were gathered in the dining room of the B&B. The two detectives, the four actors and the impresario Leonard Ruff, together with his assistant, Vicky.

'What are we doing here?' growled Orson Drake.

'Well, being an aficionado of Poirot, I thought you might recognise a denouement when you saw one,' said March.

'Are you saying you know who killed Richard?' asked James Wang.

'A gold star for Mr Wang!' March looked at Rasheed. 'Detective Constable?'

Rasheed pulled the sheet from her pocket, unfolded it, held it up.

On the sheet were two overlapping circles. Inside one, the words: PEOPLE WHO WANTED TO VISIT RICHARD IN HIS ROOM AT 2 A.M. And inside the other: PEOPLE WHO RICHARD WOULD LET IN IF THEY CAME KNOCKING ON HIS DOOR AT 2 A.M.

In the middle, where they overlapped, were two words: THE KILLER.

'Is this a joke?' said Ben Duggan.

'Premeditated murder is no joke, Mr Duggan,' said Rasheed.

'Why don't you both stop fannying about and tell us what you think you know?' said Orson Drake.

'Richard Crannigan was a weak man,' said Rasheed, ignoring the actor's outburst. 'Vain, egocentric, unfaithful, unkind. A hard man to like. Not the sort of man many would think of visiting in the middle of the night. Bear in mind that most of you were already out of it after your post-opening-night celebration.' She paused. 'Let's consider each of you . . . James Wang – you were intimidated by Richard. He assaulted you. You weren't about to go near him, let alone wander over to his room, alone, at 2 a.m. Ben Duggan. Perhaps you might have gone to his room, but Richard would have given you a short shrift. He knew how you felt about him "stealing" the lead part from you. He wasn't about to let you in. Orson Drake. You'd already made it clear to Richard how *you* felt, by treating him like a leper. You had no need or desire to go to his room, to sort him out or otherwise.' Rasheed turned finally to Adele. 'Which leaves you. The grieving widow. Who admits to being awake at the time of the murder. You were upset – more than you made out earlier. I imagine it's no easy thing catching your husband in the very act of infidelity. It ate away at you, expanded inside you until it choked off all reason. And, of course, Richard would have let you into his room – you were his wife, after all.'

'I didn't kill Richard,' said Adele, voice barely a whisper.

Suddenly, March was looming over her, eyes glittering.

The silence stretched.

And then he burst into a grin. 'No. Of course you didn't. Because the actual killer was young Vicky here.'

He turned to face Ruff's assistant, who had frozen in her seat. 'Richard was a tomcat. He simply couldn't keep it to himself. And a young woman as impressionable as you – impressionable enough to sleep with an old warthog like Mr Ruff here . . . well, I can only imagine how you might have felt when Richard – the play's leading man – turned his attentions your way.'

Rasheed took up the story. 'But what for Richard was just another disposable liaison, became something more for you. And yesterday evening, after he was caught out by his wife, you finally came to your senses. Adele obviously shared what had gone on – I mean, Ben Duggan knew, so I'm assuming everyone else did too.'

Duggan started, looked around guiltily. No one met his eye.

Rasheed continued. 'And while you had no problem with Richard cheating on his wife *with* you, you couldn't live with the idea of him cheating *on* you. Treating you as just another notch on his bedpost.'

Vicky was staring at the detective constable, transfixed.

'Now wait a minute—' began Ruff, rising to his feet.

'Shut up and sit down,' growled March, turning to him. Ruff blinked, and then his legs seemed to give way and he crashed back onto his seat.

Rasheed held up the sheet again, tapped it, addressed Vicky once more. 'You were the only person who had a reason to go to Richard's room at 2 a.m. *and* a person Richard would have willingly let in. You told us you were with Ruff that night. He told us he was "totally wrecked" after dinner. I suspect he was dead to the world when you slipped out, went to Richard's room along the corridor, stabbed him and then came back and slipped into bed again. The whole thing wouldn't have taken more than a few minutes.'

March looked down at his shoes, watching the stream of piss hit the urinal cake.

The door opened behind him.

DCI Len Martin walked over to the sink, began running a tap.

March shook himself off, zipped up, and went over to the sink.

Standing beside Martin he turned on the tap and washed his hands.

'Tiberius.'

'Len.'

'Nice work on that fag actor's murder.'

'Didn't you get the memo? You can't say that sort of thing anymore.'

Martin grinned. 'I know what you mean. If it was up to Rasheed, we'd all be woker than Wokeasaurus Rex the Woke Dinosaur.'

'Did you just make that up?'

'Yeah.'

'It's shit.'

Martin's grin slowly faded.

March straightened, looked at Martin in the mirror.

Then, moving surprisingly quickly for a big man, he turned, shoved Martin against the wall, pinned him with one arm across his throat and grabbed his testicles with the other hand.

Martin yelped.

'Now listen to me, you slimy toad. Detective Constable Rasheed is the best thing that's come into this place in ages. And she's one of mine . . . do you understand?'

Martin's eyes were watering. 'Get . . . off . . . me.'

March yanked. Martin let out a low scream. 'Please . . . God . . .'

'Tell me you understand.'

'I . . . understand.'

March let go and stepped back.

He watched as Martin slid down the wall, then curled into a ball on the floor, clutching his genitals.

'I'm so glad we had this little chat.'

He turned, straightened his tie in the mirror, then walked out, whistling a tune.

THE PERFECT SMILE

Clare Mackintosh

The launch party was standing room only. Brianna spotted the mayor talking to the owner of the new dress exchange that had just opened in Albert Street, a well-turned-out woman wearing vintage Dior. Brianna could spot a designer label at a hundred paces, as her bulging wardrobes could testify. She would have to pop in and see what they had in stock.

The local police commander was in attendance too, along with several councillors and a man Brianna assumed was a journalist (there was no other excuse for that monstrosity of a vest, its khaki pockets stuffed with notebooks). In short, the great and the good of Harrogate had come for the networking, for the canapés, and – above all – for the gossip. Everyone wanted the scoop on this blow-in from London; everyone was wondering if the interior of the newly refurbished North Park Mews house would live up to the expensive hand-lettered sign that hung above the door.

The Vestry Dental Clinic.

It didn't disappoint. Brianna would have picked up on the Harley Street vibes even if she hadn't read Dr Cleveland's impressive bio, which filled a whole page of the clinic's elegant website. The waiting room in which the launch party was being hosted was furnished not with a perimeter of plastic-coated chairs, but with two velvet sofas facing each other. Between them was a glass coffee table topped with cloth-bound books on gardening and interior design. A walnut chiffonier held a bowl of shiny apples and a tray of cut-glass tumblers for the bottles of Perrier in the glass-fronted fridge beneath it. A huge painting hung above a fireplace in which half a dozen fat church candles were flickering.

'It looks stunning, doesn't it?' Brianna turned back to her friends. The four women had arrived together, skipping their usual book club discussion in favour of a few free glasses of bubbly and a snoop at Harrogate's new arrival.

'But I've already made notes on this week's book,' Olivia had moaned, after Brianna suggested they attend the launch party instead. 'I thought the ending was so romantic and sweet.'

Brianna had folded her arms disapprovingly. 'You watched the film instead, didn't you?'

'I didn't!'

'In the book, she ends the relationship because she thinks he's too young to be tied down. In the film, she tells him to come back in five years' time, and they get their happy ever after.'

'Dammit.' Olivia grinned. 'Once a lawyer, always a lawyer, right?'

'Nothing gets past me.' Brianna had been pushing for *Tess of the D'Urbervilles* for next week's read, but was being met by complaints from the others.

'You only ever pick old books,' said Alexis, who had been outvoted on Emily Henry's *Happy Place*, largely because Megan refused to read anything that hadn't been reviewed in the broadsheets.

'The classics are timeless,' Brianna retorted.

'The classics are boring.' Megan pulled a paperback of *Lessons in Chemistry* from her Mulberry tote. 'How about this one?

The *Telegraph* called it a "triumphant feminist fable", and it's supposed to be very funny.'

Damn, but Megan was good, Brianna thought, as she saw Alexis's eyes light up at 'funny', just as Brianna's had lit up at 'feminist.'

'And . . .' Megan delivered her *pièce de résistance*, 'there's a TV adaptation.'

'Sold,' Olivia said, immediately opening her library app to reserve a copy.

Their weekly book club discussions were fun, but Brianna was enjoying being 'out out' for a change, and it was clear she wasn't the only one. All around them, people were knocking back champagne and swooping up the delectable canapés displayed on silver platters around the room.

'The place certainly looks a bit different to when Dr Adler was here,' Olivia said. 'Bless him.'

The previous dentist, Dennis Adler, had tried to find someone to take over his shabby but thriving practice in the centre of town when he'd wanted to retire.

'Don't worry,' he'd said, when his patients asked about his plans. 'I won't leave you in the lurch.' There were several other dentists in the area, but all were oversubscribed and getting an appointment was impossible. One receptionist had laughed in Brianna's face when she'd enquired about transferring; another clinic had resorted to hanging a vast banner above their door. *Not accepting new patients*. Even Olivia, whose job in PR enabled her to talk her way in to practically anywhere, had drawn a blank.

When Dr Adler finally admitted defeat and hung up his drill, his patients had mixed feelings. On the one hand, the dentist's increasingly shaky hands had been a little disconcerting (Megan and her husband had once played a four-ball with the Adlers, and reported that the dentist handled a putter as though he were beating an egg). On the other hand, hundreds of Harrogate residents were no longer registered with a dental practice.

'People will just have to go private,' Alexis had said, in that *let them eat cake* way the others liked to tease her about. Brianna, Olivia and Megan were far from the breadline, but Alexis was in another league entirely. The former wife of a start-up millionaire, Alexis had never done a day's work in her life.

'No one can get a private appointment either,' Megan had explained. 'It's a national crisis.'

Horror stories began to emerge. Impacted wisdom teeth; broken crowns; kids with ill-fitting braces and no one to adjust them.

'Those poor kids,' said Olivia, whose eyes always filled up at the thought of a child in distress, despite – or perhaps because – she had never been able to have children of her own. 'A whole generation growing up in a dental crisis.'

The *Harrogate Advertiser* ran a double-page spread – complete with colour photos – about a man who had pulled out three of his own teeth in desperation. His bloodied mouth had prompted several letters of complaint to the editor.

All of which meant that the Vestry was welcomed with open arms (and, for those who had been nursing nagging toothache for several months, open mouths).

'Has anyone seen a price list?' Olivia asked. 'With a set-up like this, even a check-up won't be cheap.' She was wearing one of her linen tunics over wide trousers, and as she swiped another glass of champagne from a passing tray, a pair of chunky earrings swung out from beneath her silver bob.

'There's a list of treatments on their website,' Brianna said, 'but no prices.'

Megan raised a single, perfectly plucked eyebrow. Not a single crease appeared above it. She'd overdone the Botox, Brianna thought, but there was no telling some people. 'You know what they say: if you have to ask how much it is, you can't afford it.'

'I'm past caring about the cost.' Alexis put a hand to her jaw and winced. 'I just want this tooth sorted.' Alexis's mass of auburn hair and huge smoky eyes had turned heads when the women had arrived. She was dressed in a vivid green wrap dress, teamed with heels which made Brianna feel underdressed in her skinny jeans and navy blazer.

There was a sudden clink of cutlery on crystal, and a buzz from the guests around them as everyone turned to find the source of the sound.

'If I might have a moment of your time?'

Although couched as a question, Dr Anthony Cleveland did not look like a man who ever needed to wait for permission. Indeed, his guests fell instantly silent before a ripple of applause made its way across the room.

'You're too kind.' Dr Cleveland smiled.

'Holy crap,' Olivia breathed.

Brianna let out an appreciative murmur. 'I wouldn't mind *him* filling my—'

'Brianna!'

'What? He's *hot*.' Brianna used to have a hot husband. Then his blossoming legal career had trumped Brianna's own to the extent that she had never gone into practice and instead hosted extravagant dinner parties for him and his partners, and somehow it had taken the edge off his hotness.

'So's his wife.' Megan nodded towards the onyx-topped reception desk, from where a willowy brunette was gazing at her husband adoringly. She wore a crisp white belted tunic dress and her glossy hair was twisted into a chignon. Her left hand was holding a champagne flute, and from her fourth finger glinted the largest diamond Brianna had ever seen.

Alexis sighed. 'Bet she's got lovely teeth.'

'Ladies and gentlemen.' Dr Cleveland looked around the room, nodding as his eyes fell on special guests. 'Mr Mayor, Chief Superintendent. It's wonderful to see so many of you here tonight. Tell me, friends: do your teeth reflect the person you want to be?' He didn't wait for an answer, which was perhaps for the best, as people were clamping their lips tight or running their tongues self-consciously around their teeth.

'You *deserve* straight teeth,' Dr Cleveland declared. Brianna was reminded of a preacher she once saw on American TV. Just as she had been transfixed by the preacher's sermon, despite having no strong faith herself, she now found herself nodding enthusiastically at Dr Cleveland's proclamation. She *did* deserve straight teeth.

'You *deserve* white teeth.'

Brianna thought of the red wine stains on her lower incisors and nodded fervently.

'You *deserve* to be pain-free.'

'Hell yes!' Alexis shouted, then winced and clutched her jaw. There was a murmur of agreement from the other guests.

'And at the Vestry,' Dr Cleveland waited for a beat, 'my wife and I want to give you the smile you deserve.' He raised his voice above the applause. 'I'm delighted to be able to offer a ten per cent discount *for life* for anyone who signs up to our monthly direct debit plan tonight, *and* discounted aesthetic treatments for our first ten customers. The Vestry is more than a dental practice. It is an oasis. A place of transformation, where our expertise will ensure your outward appearance reflects the beautiful person you are inside.' He waved an arm towards his wife, who had exchanged her champagne flute for a leather-bound book embossed with the clinic's logo. 'Please, enjoy another drink while you wait to speak with Cassandra. Our diary is officially open!'

The following Wednesday, Olivia was due to meet the others for their weekly brunch at The Ivy Brasserie on Parliament Street. She had contemplated cancelling, but she couldn't hide away forever, and hanging out with the girls always cheered her up. For once, Olivia was glad of the dim lighting, keeping her head low as she made her way to their usual table at the back. Her cheeks were swollen, and the corners of her lips were cracked from the hours she'd spent in the dentist's chair with her mouth clamped open.

'Oh my God, Olivia!' Megan's eyes were saucers.

'I'm fine,' Olivia said, except that it sounded more like *mime mine*. A tiny bubble of drool escaped from the side of her mouth and she snatched up a napkin. God, how mortifying.

'Let me order you a coffee.' Alexis clicked her fingers at a passing waiter.

Olivia shook her head. 'Just water.' Her lips barely moved. It was better that way. 'And a straw.'

'What—' Brianna dropped her voice. 'What happened?'

'Let's just say Dr Adler must have been well and truly past his sell-by date by the time he retired.' Olivia took a sip of water and winced as the ice clinked against her jaw. 'You wouldn't believe how much he'd missed. I needed twelve fillings.'

'*Twelve?*' Alexis said incredulously.

'Dr Cleveland said it was lucky I came in when I did, otherwise I'd be looking at . . .' Olivia sobbed. '*Dentures.*'

The other three women looked at each other in horror.

'Have you made an appointment already?' Brianna asked Alexis, who was rubbing her sore jaw again.

'A week next Friday. Maybe I'll call and bring it forward.'

'I was going to wait until after my holiday,' Megan said. 'We're going to Lake Como – mind you, they say it's absolutely overrun with tourists now.' She picked a piece of lint from her dress.

'Don't wait a minute longer than you have to.' Olivia's face was grim. 'It's a wonder anyone in Harrogate has any teeth left. Old Dennis Adler has got a lot to answer for.'

Megan opened the door to the Vestry. The waiting-room seemed bigger and lighter than it did on the night of the launch party. Piano music played from speakers hidden in the walls, and the air was filled with a luxurious, musky scent. It was giving Megan spa vibes; she half expected to be handed a towelling robe and pointed towards the massage room.

'What can I get you to drink?' Cassandra Cleveland stood to greet her. 'Tea? Coffee? Prosecco?'

Prosecco? The most exciting thing Dennis Adler had ever offered had been a squirt of anti-bacterial hand gel. They were most definitely not in Kansas anymore, Toto. It was good to see Harrogate raising its game, Megan thought.

'Prosecco would be lovely,' she said. Granted, it was ten-thirty in the morning, but Megan was paying an arm and a leg for this check-up and she was bloody well going to get her money's worth. At the aesthetics clinic she went to in Leeds, her exorbitant Botox bill was softened by a gift bag containing truffles and luxury product samples.

'Of course.' Cassandra smiled, but there was no warmth in it. The woman wore heavy foundation (a shade too dark for her fair skin, in Megan's opinion) and it was creasing beneath her eyes. Megan had noticed the subtle up-and-down Cassandra had given her when she entered the waiting-room, and she wondered if her oversized white shirt had passed muster. Cassandra seemed like the jealous type – Megan had met enough of them to tell – so maybe Dr Cleveland was a bit of a player.

Megan sipped her prosecco and gingerly tongued each of her teeth in turn. Her last check-up with Dr Adler had been more than two years ago, but she didn't have any pain so hopefully she wouldn't need any work. Lake Como was less than a fortnight away and she couldn't turn up at the Grand Hotel Tremezzo looking like a chipmunk. An image of Olivia's swollen face flashed into Megan's head, and she shuddered.

'Dr Cleveland will see you now,' Cassandra said. Megan stood. It seemed a little odd to walk into the dental room carrying prosecco, so she knocked back the remainder in a single gulp and left the glass on the coffee table.

'Megan!' Dr Cleveland greeted her as though she were an old friend. 'So lovely to see you.' He patted the cream leather recliner. 'Up you pop.'

As Megan scrambled into position (was there any dignified way to get into a dentist's chair?) she noticed Cassandra pulling on a disposable apron and a pair of blue gloves. You'd have thought with the prices the Vestry charged they could have afforded a dedicated dental nurse, but perhaps the husband-and-wife double act was the 'personal touch' that was afforded such prominence in their glossy brochure.

'Open wide . . .' Dr Cleveland moved a probe rapidly around Megan's mouth. 'Do you floss?'

'Ngh-huh.' Why did dentists always ask you questions when you couldn't answer them? Megan gazed up at the ceiling, which was painted a deep navy and dotted with tiny lights like constellations. The leather recliner was extremely comfortable, and if it hadn't been for Dr Cleveland's fingers in her mouth, it would have been quite relaxing.

'Eight partially erupted, seven, six, five, four, three, two, one. Do you have a holiday booked this year?'

'Ngh-huh.' Megan tried to nod.

'Anywhere nice? One, two, three, four, five, six, seven, eight. Cassandra and I just had two weeks in Barbados – have you been?' Dr Cleveland scratched at Megan's gums, calling out numbers to Cassandra. 'Two . . . one . . . three . . .'

When he finished, he scooted his chair close to Megan's side. One hand rested on the arm of the recliner, and the other . . . the other brushed her leg.

Megan blinked. Had that really just happened?

'Do you want the good news or the bad news?' Dr Cleveland said.

Megan glanced at Cassandra but the woman's face was impassive. Surely Dr Cleveland wouldn't be inappropriate with a patient when his wife was in the room? And it had only been the lightest of touches; it could easily have been accidental . . .

'Um, both, I guess,' Megan said.

'The bad news is that you have some dental decay in three of your molars. The good news is that Cassandra can book you in to get it fixed.' Dr Cleveland's brow furrowed. 'Were you by any chance with Dr Adler before?'

'Yes.'

He sighed. 'I never like to speak badly of a fellow professional, but . . .' He left the accusation hanging.

Cassandra took Megan back to reception, where she opened the leather-bound book and offered Megan a choice of dates. 'You opted for our bronze treatment plan,' she said. 'Based on your dental assessment, I'd recommend we upgrade you to gold.' She flipped open a leaflet and tapped a glossy nail against an exorbitant monthly sum.

'I don't think I want to—'

'This will cover you against any further work Dr Cleveland identifies a need for.'

Megan thought about what else Dr Adler might have over-looked, and, deciding it was better to be safe than sorry, handed over her debit card.

The following Wednesday, brunch at The Ivy was the last thing on Alexis's mind. She had summoned the girls to her house, ignoring the grumbling responses on their WhatsApp group from Megan (*I'm literally dying for eggs Benedict, Lex!*) and Brianna (*Watch them give us a crap table next time . . .*)

Only Olivia showed any concern. *Didn't you go to the dentist yesterday?*, she messaged. *Is everything OK?*

Alexis didn't answer. They'd see for themselves soon enough.

The women arrived together, sweeping onto Alexis's drive in Olivia's Volvo XC90, and ringing the bell as Alexis stood in the hall, steeling herself to open the door.

'I hope she's OK.' Olivia's worried voice drifted through the glass. 'She flatly refused to meet anywhere else.'

'Did she tell you why?' Brianna said.

'Only that she'd been to the dentist and couldn't leave the house.'

'Seems a bit extreme,' Megan said.

Alexis opened the door and gave them a weak smile. Brianna's eyes widened, but she didn't say anything. Alexis knew she looked a state. She'd been crying all night and her eyes were puffy and red-rimmed. Silently, she led them into the kitchen, which was dominated by a vast quartz-topped island.

'Does it hurt?' Olivia hung her bag on the back of a chair. 'My teeth feel OK now, so hopefully—'

Alexis opened her mouth, pulling her lips back from the gums. Fresh tears streamed down her cheeks.

The others recoiled. Brianna screamed.

'Jesus Christ.' Megan covered her mouth with her hand.

Alexis's teeth had been filed into stumpy pegs, the gums around them red and swollen.

Olivia rushed to Alexis, pulling her into a tight embrace. '*Why?*' she said.

'Bone disease.' Alexis's voice was muffled by Olivia's linen dress. She pulled away. 'I need crowns on the lot. This is the preparation phase.' A whistle followed each letter s, and she started crying again.

'It's a fucking horror show, that's what it is,' Brianna said. 'Let me guess: something else Dr Adler failed to spot?'

Alexis nodded. 'The signs would have been there for years, apparently.'

'This is outrageous,' Olivia said. 'There must be something we can do.'

'He's retired.' Megan shrugged. 'It's not like he can be struck off.'

'We should make him pay.' Brianna looked at the others. 'This is costing us thousands. If he won't pay, we'll sue.' She whipped out a notebook from her bag. 'Who else do you know who used to go to Dr Adler? We'll round up all his ex-patients – we can't be the only ones he's fucked over – and we'll take him to court for medical negligence. Agreed?'

Alexis nodded. 'Agreed.'

'I'm in,' Megan said. 'Does anyone know where he lives?'

'He moved away,' Olivia said. 'I'll speak to the journalist who did his retirement interview in the *Advertiser*. She might know where he's living now.'

'I don't know if I want to go for my check-up tomorrow.' Brianna chewed at the inside of her bottom lip. 'What if Dr Cleveland says I need all my teeth filed down? I don't want to look like a monster.' She gave Alexis an apologetic glance. 'No offence.'

Olivia put an arm around Alexis. 'What's done is done,' she said briskly. 'Get fixed whatever needs fixing, then . . .' Her expression darkened. 'Then we'll deal with Dennis Adler.'

Sweat trickled down Brianna's back and her peppermint tea sat untouched on the glass coffee table in the waiting room at the Vestry. Maybe she could go abroad to find a dentist?

'Is the tea OK?' Cassandra looked up from her computer screen. Despite the warm weather, she was wearing a high-necked sweater under her white tunic.

'It's lovely, thank you.'

'Let me know if I can get you anything else.' Cassandra adjusted a gold watch on her wrist.

'Lovely watch,' Brianna said. 'Is it Cartier?'

'Yes.' Cassandra stretched out her arm to admire it. 'Anthony bought it for me yesterday.'

'How lovely.' Lots of people went to Turkey to have their teeth done, didn't they? Brianna took out her phone and opened Google.

'He's always giving me presents,' Cassandra said. 'Performance bonuses, he calls them.' She laughed, but it sounded forced, and Brianna looked up. For a woman regularly showered with luxury jewellery, Cassandra didn't look very happy about it.

A sharp buzzing sound interrupted Brianna's thoughts.

Cassandra jumped. 'He's ready for you,' she said.

'Actually . . .' Brianna didn't know what it was about the Vestry, but it was giving her the jitters. 'I think I've double-booked myself.' She waved her phone, as though she'd been checking her calendar, instead of Googling *Turkey teeth*. There had to be a dentist somewhere; Brianna didn't care if she had to fly halfway around the world. Dr Cleveland – and his spoilt unhappy wife – gave her bad vibes.

'We have to charge the full amount if you cancel within twenty-four hours of the appointment.' Cassandra gave what Brianna supposed was an apologetic smile. The woman looked dead behind the eyes, Brianna thought, and it crossed her might that Cassandra might be Valiumed to the hilt rather than unhappy. Or maybe she was simply a grade-A bitch. Some women, of course, were all three.

'OK,' Brianna said. 'That's fine.' Thank God she could afford it.

'And we're obliged to leave a review, of course.'

'A review? About me?'

'To let other dentists know you cancelled at short notice,' Cassandra said. 'It's part of the dentists' charter.'

'The dentists' charter? I've never heard anything so ridiculous.'

'Nowadays, dentists can afford to be selective about the patients they take on.' Cassandra twisted a loose ringlet around her index finger. 'Under three stars? Massive red flag.'

What was the world coming to? Brianna had recently been reprimanded by Airbnb after failing to strip the beds before checking out (an unfair demand, in Brianna's opinion; it was hardly a holiday if you still had to do chores), and Alexis now found it impossible to book a table at Grantley Hall since that time she argued over a corked wine. It was getting to the point where one didn't dare complain about anything.

But there were always other restaurants, other booking sites. There weren't always other dentists; at least, not ones with open appointment diaries. Brianna thought of the man in the *Harrogate Advertiser* who had pulled out his own teeth. She didn't know whether dentists blacklisted patients, but she didn't want to find out the hard way. 'Fine.' She took a deep breath. 'I'm ready.'

Dr Cleveland flashed his perfect smile as he helped Brianna into the leather reclining chair and turned on the bright light. Above it, the ceiling twinkled with stars, but Brianna noticed that several of the bulbs had already gone, and, in the corner, damp had bubbled the surface of the navy paint.

'Well, you don't need a filling.' Dr Cleveland's face was so close to hers, she could feel his breath moistening her cheeks.

'At's rate,' she said.

Dr Cleveland frowned and withdrew his fingers from her mouth.

Brianna swallowed. 'That's great,' she clarified.

He shook his head. 'It's beyond that. It's a shame it wasn't filled when the decay first took hold; it would have been a tiny filling. Unfortunately, we're going to have to take it out.'

Thank God it was right at the back. No one would see. Brianna's jaw tightened. Bloody Dennis Adler. One tiny filling, that's all it would have been, and now she was going to have to check every selfie in case it showed a flash of gum.

'I can do it right now, unless you have somewhere you need to be?'

Brianna hesitated. The back of her neck was prickling, but if she left now, she'd only be delaying the inevitable . . . 'No. That's fine. Let's get it over and done with.'

'Cassandra, could you prepare the sedation please?'

'Sedation?' Brianna thought back to the last filling she'd had, which had only required local anaesthetic.

'Here at The Vestry, we like our patients to be completely relaxed. Just lie back for me.'

'I don't think I need—' Brianna felt something tighten around her wrist.

'Simple restraints,' Dr Cleveland explained.

'No, this is—'

'Sharp scratch.'

Brianna was finding it hard to breathe. Her pulse was racing, and she wanted to say she'd changed her mind, that she'd leave the tooth where it was, but now Cassandra was placing a strap around her forehead, too, and she was pinned to the chair, and she couldn't find the words, couldn't make her lips move or, or, or . . .

The lights on the ceiling faded to black.

The stars above her twinkled as Brianna stared at her reflection in the mirror. Her skin was flawless; her hair fell in shiny waves over her shoulders. Light blush gave her cheeks a shimmer, and a rich gloss made her lips full and sensual. Brianna began to smile, but as her mouth opened, her eyes filled with horror. Her gums were swollen and raw and robbed of teeth, and as she shook her head, blood spilt from the craters and ran down her throat, choking her.

'No, no, no!' Brianna screamed, her head thrashing wildly from side to side.

'Easy now.' Dr Cleveland was releasing the straps that had kept her still while he worked. 'Sedation can make some patients a little disorientated.'

'My teeth!' As her hands were released, Brianna snatched them to her mouth, feeling for her teeth.

They were still there.

Brianna's face was numb and her gums throbbed, but she still had teeth. She let out a harsh sob. 'I thought— I thought—'

'Cassandra.' Dr Cleveland called out, and, almost immediately, his wife came into the room. 'Brianna's feeling unwell. Could you get her something to drink?'

'Right away.' There was an expression on Cassandra's face that Brianna couldn't read.

Dr Cleveland pressed a button and Brianna's chair moved slowly upright. Cassandra fetched a glass of iced water and then gently pressed a hot washcloth against Brianna's face.

'Oh, that's good.' Brianna was feeling calmer, although her terrifying nightmare was still lingering at the edges of her mind. It had seemed so real; she kept needing to check that her teeth were still there. Well, minus one . . . Brianna's tongue found the empty space where her molar had been removed. She remembered what she'd agreed with the girls.

'May I see my tooth please?'

'Of course.' Dr Cleveland picked up a small jar from the side. Brianna's tooth rattled against the plastic as he handed it to her. 'You're very susceptible to sedation – it was quite a struggle to rouse you. I tried to be as gentle as I could.'

There it was again: that odd expression on Cassandra's face. Was it jealousy? Megan had mentioned seeing some-thing similar.

'May I keep this?' Brianna held up the tooth. It would form part of the evidence she and the other women were compiling against Dr Adler: proof of all the rotten teeth he'd been too incompetent or lazy to treat.

'Keep it?' Dr Cleveland laughed. 'Whatever for?'

'I want to have it made into a necklace. It's very on-trend right now.' Brianna repeated the story she'd been given by Olivia, who could put a PR spin on just about anything.

'I've not come across that,' Dr Cleveland said, and there was a hint of suspicion in his expression. Brianna wished she'd thought of some other excuse – she couldn't think of anything less on-trend than tooth jewellery – but she was committed now.

'Lots of celebrities are doing it,' Cassandra said, as she washed her hands.

Dr Cleveland turned to look at her. 'Is that so?'

'I'm sure I read about a pair of earrings Gwyneth Paltrow had made from her son's baby teeth.' There was a faint flush on Cassandra's cheeks. Had Olivia invented something that was an actual trend? Personally, Brianna couldn't think of anything worse than wearing her teeth anywhere other than in her mouth but if it was good enough for Gwyneth Paltrow, it was a good enough excuse for Brianna.

'Well then . . .' Dr Cleveland held up his hands in mock defeat. 'It's all yours, Brianna.'

By the time Brianna got home, the anaesthetic had worn off and her gum was throbbing. The sedation had left her with a dull headache and a dry mouth, and she downed another glass of water. She felt sweaty from the nightmare and somehow grubby, even though she had showered that morning and all she'd done was drive to The Vestry and back. She turned on the shower and began peeling off her clothes, looking forward to stepping into the steamy cubicle.

Brianna stopped. Something wasn't right. She'd thrown her trousers and shirt in the laundry basket and was standing in her bra and pants. She stared down at the front of her underwear, then turned and looked over her shoulder, craning her neck to see her rear view in the mirror.

No, no, no . . .

Brianna swallowed hard. She turned back to the mirror, to her stricken face, not wanting to think about what this meant but unable to ignore it. Brianna had dressed herself properly that morning. She knew this not only because she was a grown woman who knew how to dress herself, but also because this particular pair of knickers had a ribbon at the front which tended to catch on the zip of her trousers as she got dressed, and it had done exactly that this morning.

Then how, Brianna thought, could the ribbon now be at the back?

Olivia's journalist contact had tracked down Dr Adler's new address. The retired dentist had moved to Scarborough and, three days later, Brianna was ringing the doorbell of a neat bungalow near the seafront. The others had offered to come with her, but Brianna wanted to go alone. She was experiencing a desire for justice she hadn't been aware of since leaving law school, and it felt good.

When Dr Adler opened the door, Brianna wasted no time in explaining her concerns about Dr Cleveland's ethics. She left out the bit about her pants, not yet ready to confront it herself, let alone share it with others.

'You'd better come in,' he said.

Five minutes later, they were sitting at the kitchen table and Dr Adler was peering through an eye glass at her extracted tooth. On the other side of the room, his wife was making coffee.

Dr Adler looked up. 'This is a perfectly healthy tooth.'

All over Harrogate, people were gossiping about Dr Adler's shoddy work. For years, they were saying, Dennis Adler had failed to spot decaying teeth and rotting gums, leaving poor Dr Cleveland to pick up the pieces. Except there was nothing poor about Dr Cleveland, was there? Not with the prices he was charging; prices no one could refuse because demand for dentistry far outstripped supply. It was a seller's market, and Dr Cleveland was taking full advantage – in more ways than one.

'Are you sure?' Brianna said. 'I don't mean to be rude, but—'

'But I'm an old man and why should you believe me over a Harley Street dentist?'

Brianna flushed. 'It's just that Dr Cleveland told me three more of my teeth need attention, and my friends have all had to have extensive work—'

'Listen.' Dr Adler held up a hand. 'A friend of mine runs the post-grad dentistry course at Leeds University. If you've got time to drop in on your way back to Harrogate, I'll give him a call and let him know you're after a second opinion.'

She exhaled. 'Thank you.'

'Brianna, is there something else worrying you about Dr Cleveland?' Dr Adler's wife turned as she spoke. Her eyes were shrewd.

'I— No. Well, maybe.' Brianna looked down at her hands.

'I told you there was something not right about that man.' Mrs Adler was talking to her husband now.

He smiled indulgently. 'You and your intuition.'

'I didn't know you'd met him,' Brianna said.

'We were back in Harrogate for lunch with some friends,' Mrs Adler said. 'They told us the mews was being renovated and we couldn't resist wandering across to have a look. Anthony Cleveland was there with his wife, talking to the builders, so we introduced ourselves.'

'I offered to tell him about some of the patients; pass on what I'd learnt about the politics of the town,' Dr Adler said. 'But he didn't seem at all interested. Said he'd "work it all out in time". He was quite rude, actually.'

'Remember how he snapped at his wife?' Mrs Adler shook her head. 'Like she was some kind of servant. It troubled me – I wanted to take her with us.'

Dr Adler was writing something on a piece of paper. 'This is the website for the General Dental Council hearings. It'll tell you if Dr Cleveland has ever been investigated or suspended.' He handed it to her. 'And in the meantime, don't let him anywhere near your mouth.'

'There's nothing wrong with my teeth.' Brianna looked at her friends. 'Not with the one Dr Cleveland took out; not with the ones I've got left. No gum disease, no cavities. And the chances are there was nothing wrong with any of yours, either.' It was horrific news to deliver, but Brianna couldn't help but feel exhilarated. In front of her, secured with a length of pink legal tape pinched from her husband's study, was a bundle of evidence against Anthony Cleveland. Brianna was done with being a corporate wife. She was a qualified lawyer and when this was all over, she was going back to work.

Olivia gasped. 'But I had twelve fillings!' If you didn't know Olivia, you might not notice anything was wrong, but Brianna knew the extensive dentistry had taken its toll on her friend. Her face was still swollen, and her habitually concerned expression had become pinched and anxious.

Alexis touched a hand to her mouth. Her new crowns had been fitted, but she still whistled when she talked, and the dark circles beneath her eyes told Brianna she wasn't sleeping well.

'He made me upgrade to a Gold package because my teeth were so bad,' Megan said, outraged. 'We had to cancel Lake Como.'

'That's not all.' Brianna took a deep breath and, before she could change her mind, she told them about finding her underwear on back to front.

There was a long silence.

'Mine . . . were twisted.' Olivia's voice was barely audible. 'I didn't think anything of it, just assumed I'd put them on that way, but now . . .'

'He touched my leg.' Megan looked at the others. 'I thought it was an accident, but . . .'

As the women took in the full ramifications of these revela-tions, they stared at each other in abject dismay. Olivia reached across the table and took first Brianna's hand, then Megan's, squeezing it tight. Opposite her, Alexis did the same, until the women were linked, their fingers interlaced and their knuckles white with silent support.

'We can't let him get away with this,' Olivia said.

'We're not going to.' Brianna broke the chain in order to open her laptop. 'I looked Dr Cleveland up on the General Dental Council register. He's not listed.'

'He's not even a dentist?' Alexis let out a wail.

'Oh, he was . . . But he wasn't called Dr Cleveland then.' Brianna turned the screen to face the others, and they saw a photograph of a much younger Anthony Cleveland above the caption 'Dr Anthony Rathbone'. 'Dr *Rathbone*,' Brianna explained, 'was struck off ten years ago following an investiga-tion into malpractice and a number of allegations from female patients in relation to his behaviour.' She tapped the keyboard and the screen changed to a photograph of 'Cassandra Cleveland, dental technician'. 'Three years ago, Anthony Rathbone married Cassandra and took her name.' She looked up at the group. 'He's been practising under a false identity ever since.'

'The man belongs in jail,' Olivia said. 'We have to go to the police.'

'He was arrested once before,' Brianna said. 'I found a tiny mention in a local paper. It seems he was released without charge. Not enough evidence.'

'The same thing will happen again, won't it?' Megan turned to the others despairingly.

'Men like him always get away with it,' Alexis said bitterly. 'A rap on the knuckles – if that – and he'll be free to move on and do the same thing somewhere else.'

'I've been thinking about that.' Brianna closed the laptop. 'There's only one way to guarantee he gets the punishment he deserves.' She looked at the others. 'And that's to administer it ourselves.'

Olivia stood at the beautiful reception desk and smiled at Cassandra. 'I'm here for my follow-up appointment.' Her heart was pounding so hard, it seemed impossible Cassandra wouldn't notice, but the dentist's wife simply nodded. She had a pink chiffon scarf tied around her neck today; the ends tucked into her crisp white tunic.

'Of course, take a seat and I'll let Dr Cleveland know you're here.'

'He doesn't drive a blue Porsche, does he?' Olivia settled herself on one of the velvet sofas, trying to appear relaxed. This was the riskiest part; the part where they had to get Anthony Cleveland exactly where they wanted him.

'Yes, why?'

'Does he leave it in the underground car park?'

'Yes.'

'Oh dear . . .' Olivia sighed. 'I saw some kids messing about with one as I arrived. I hope it's not the same—'

'He loves that car.' The pen fell from Cassandra's hand and onto the desk, where it rolled to the edge and dropped onto the plush carpet. Cassandra took no notice. 'They mustn't damage it . . .' She pushed back her chair with enough force to leave it rocking. 'Will you excuse me? I should— I have to—'

Cassandra was now a far cry from the calm, self-contained woman Olivia had seen on every other occasion. Was it the Porsche that Cassandra was worried about, or her husband's reaction? Brianna had relayed Mrs Adler's concerns over Cassandra, following the way Dr Cleveland had spoken to her; perhaps her fears had been justified.

Cassandra was halfway across the room now, and as she flung open the door and raced down the stairs, Olivia breathed a sigh of relief. Phase one was complete.

'Olivia!'

She jumped. Dr Cleveland stood in the doorway of the treatment room. He wore blue scrubs, the sleeves pushed up to reveal strong, tanned arms. Olivia tried to control her breathing. Could he see how terrified she was?

'I wasn't expecting to see you so soon after your last appointment.'

Olivia gathered her things and followed him into the surgery. She glanced over her shoulder as Dr Cleveland closed the door. No sign of Cassandra yet. Olivia hoped the kids she'd befriended downstairs would keep the receptionist out of the way for long enough. It had cost Olivia twenty quid and all of her persuasive skills.

'Are you experiencing pain?' Dr Cleveland said.

'Not at all.' Unless you counted the pain in her chest, Olivia thought, as her heart threatened to pound its way right through her ribcage.

'Then . . .' He looked confused.

It was now or never. Olivia felt nauseous, but Cassandra could be back any second and a plan was a plan . . . she dropped her chin and looked up at Dr Cleveland through heavily mascaraed lashes. 'I wanted to see you, actually.' Her voice was low and husky.

There was a long pause. Maybe he wouldn't fall for it, maybe they'd got all this wrong and Dr Cleveland was a faithful husband who would never—

'How very flattering.' A slow smile spread across the dentist's face. Bastard, Olivia thought. Olivia had drawn the short straw for phase two of their plan, none of the women wanting even to pretend to find such a vile man attractive.

'You fancied him,' Alexis had reminded Brianna. 'You said you'd let him fill—'

'Don't.' Brianna screwed her eyes shut. 'God, I feel sick at the thought. Anyway, you're the most attractive out of the four of us. You should do it – he won't be able to resist you.'

'Objection!' Megan had looked outraged.

'This isn't a courtroom drama, Megan,' Brianna said.

'Why is Alexis more attractive than me?' Megan demanded.

'It's not a competition.' Olivia had tried to keep the peace, but Megan was now rattling off her attributes.

'I'm slimmer, for one thing – no offence, Alexis—'

'Actually, quite a lot taken.' Alexis stood up. 'Fuck this, I'm not staying here to be insulted by a woman who can barely raise her eyebrows she's had so much Botox.'

'You bitch!' Megan jumped to her feet too. She turned on Brianna. 'This is all your fault – you started this.'

'I did not!' Brianna pushed back her chair.

'Enough!' The ear-splitting shout from the usually gentle Olivia had stopped them all in their tracks. Olivia put her hands on her hips. 'Sit, down,' she said. 'All of you.'

'But—' Alexis started, but Olivia glared at her.

'Now.' Olivia waited until all three women sank meekly into their seats. 'You're all behaving like toddlers. We have a job to do, and we won't get it done unless we work together. I'll seduce Dr Cleveland myself, all right?'

'You?' There'd been a twitch at the corners of Megan's mouth that Olivia hadn't appreciated.

'Yes, me.' Olivia had drawn herself tall. 'Is that a problem?'

'No, of course not.' Brianna hesitated. 'But . . . let's make a few tweaks, shall we?'

Consequently, Oliva was now not wearing one of her favourite comfy linen sack dresses, but had squeezed into a

185

low-cut stretchy number from Brianna's extensive wardrobe. Megan had teased her silver bob into loose waves, while Alexis created a smoky eye that even Olivia had to admit looked sensational. It seemed almost a shame to waste it on Dr Cleveland.

'I can't stop thinking about you,' she said now, fluttering the false eyelashes Alexis had carefully applied. Dr Cleveland glanced towards the door. 'Don't worry,' Olivia said. 'Cassandra's not there. She said she had some errands to run.'

'How convenient for us.' Dr Cleveland took a step towards Olivia.

She lifted a hand and put it flat on his chest, hoping it would stop him leaning forward to kiss her. The thought brought bile to the back of her throat. 'Perhaps,' she said, as seductively as she could manage, 'you could examine me a little more thoroughly this time?'

Dr Cleveland put his hands on Olivia's upper arms and stroked them both, all the way down to her hands. His thumbs brushed her breasts as they passed, and she shivered in fear. He smiled. 'You like that, huh?'

Olivia thought she might vomit. Gently but firmly, she pushed her hand against his chest, moving him backwards. Dr Cleveland raised an eyebrow but allowed himself to be manoeuvred into the reclining chair.

'We'll have to be quick,' he murmured.

Olivia dipped her head, her hair falling across his face. 'Oh, I'll be quick,' she said, and she slipped the restraint over his left wrist.

His eyes widened. 'What are you—' Dr Cleveland raised his other hand, but Olivia was ready for him. She raised her knee sharply up into his groin, and as he cried out in pain, she tightened the second restraint, pulling it with all the force she could muster until it locked into place.

Behind her, the door flew open, and Olivia snapped her head back, terrified that Cassandra would be standing there, that all this would be in vain. She breathed a sigh of relief when Megan, Brianna and Alexis burst in.

'You did it!' Brianna joined her by the chair. 'I've got to be honest, I didn't think you had it in you.' Olivia, who hadn't been sure she'd had it in her either, beamed.

'What the fuck are you doing?' Dr Cleveland shouted.

'Hold his head still for me,' Olivia said. 'I can't get the strap around it.'

'Get off me!'

'Should we sedate him?' Megan said. 'He's very loud.'

'You fucking bitches!'

'No.' Alexis picked up the drill. 'I want him to feel every single tooth.' She pressed a button and the room filled with a high-pitched whine.

'You can't do this.'

'Just watch us.' Megan selected a vicious-looking hook from the gleaming trolley next to the chair, then picked up a stainless-steel mouth opener. She tried to prise open the dentist's lips, but they were clamped shut. 'I can't get it in.'

'Leave it to me.' Olivia reached for Dr Cleveland's groin, took a handful, and squeezed hard. He screamed, his mouth opening long enough for Megan to slip in the opener. The four women grinned at each other.

'What the hell are you doing?'

They turned. Cassandra was standing in the doorway, hands on her hips. She took in the scene and her jaw dropped.

'Megan, you were supposed to lock the door!' Alexis said.

'I thought Brianna was doing it!'

'Get off him right now.' Cassandra took a step forward but Olivia met her halfway, their faces just centimetres apart.

'Your husband is getting a taste of his own medicine,' she said. 'This is for all the women he's assaulted, all the money the two of you have conned out of desperate patients.'

'You won't get away with this,' Cassandra said, but there was no conviction in her voice, and Olivia saw her eyes dart towards her husband, strapped into the chair.

'Yes, we will.' Olivia didn't move. 'Justice is finally being served.'

The two women stared at each other, then Cassandra turned. She reached into a cupboard and Olivia wondered if there was a panic button, if it would be a matter of minutes before the police descended. She braced herself for the sound of an alarm.

But then Cassandra turned back and there was a beat as all four women stared at her.

Cassandra was holding the biggest pair of pliers the women had ever seen. 'We'll need these for the molars,' she said.

'Cassie, what the hell?' Dr Adler's words were barely audible around the metal clamp, but there was no mistaking his fury.

'Do you think I didn't know?' Cassandra advanced on her husband, spitting out the words. 'All those women you fucked? All the ones you touched up while they were out for the count?'

'You're going to regret this,' Dr Cleveland said. 'If you do this, I'll—'

'Hit me again?' Cassandra tested the pliers in the air, closing them with a snap that made the others wince. 'I don't think you're in a position to make threats, do you?' The pink scarf around her neck had slipped, and Olivia saw an angry purple bruise at the base of her throat. She wondered what other marks had been hidden beneath the woman's heavy make-up and long-sleeved clothes.

'Let's begin, ladies,' Brianna said. 'Would you like to do the honours, Alexis?'

'With pleasure.' Alexis leant over Dr Cleveland, the drill poised for action.

'Hang on,' Megan said. 'Why does she get all the fun?'

Just as Olivia was about to start diffusing another argument, Cassandra spoke.

'There are thirty-two teeth in an adult mouth,' she said, her eyes fixed on her husband who was desperately trying to free his head from the restraints. 'By my calculations, that's at least six each.'

Olivia was beginning to like Cassandra. She ushered everyone into a semi-circle around the dentist's chair, then nodded to Alexis. 'Let's give Dr Cleveland the smile he deserves.'

TAKING STOCK

Abir Mukherjee

It's a nice street. The residents will tell you it's the nicest in town, even if those on the far side, in the grand old houses near the park, do look down somewhat on the newer builds closer to the main road. Still, the street as a whole has what estate agents call *character,* a virtue which makes it *sought after.* So thinks the sharp suited, bleach-toothed young man who's just stepped out of number six, The Hollies. He likes this street. The most sought-after in Harrogate. Surrounded by the park, seven minutes' walk to the Waitrose and not much more to the M&S. The house will be an easy sell, he thinks as he walks back down the gravel driveway to his Vauxhall. He's already got some potential buyers in mind: a double income family with quadruple expense kids; a retired couple with more money than sense looking to downsize to a five bedroom. And the old lady looking to sell, poor dear. She looks a bit like his gran, but he's not going to let sentiment get in his way. Not when there's a bonus at stake. He's already set her expectations low: 'cost of living crisis, you see, Mrs Phillips; interest rates through the roof, Mrs Phillips; a buyer's market, Mrs Phillips.' It's madness, he's told her, but he'll do his best. Get her something *reasonable.* Oh yes, this'll be easy. He's seen the concern in her eyes. She'll take the first offer he brings her.

There'll be a nice fat commission for the firm, and a healthy boost for hitting his quarterly sales target; and if things keep going well, this time next year he could trade in the Astra for that BMW he's had his eye on. He beams an altogether too bright smile, bought and paid for at a clinic in Turkey. He's having a good recession.

And it *is* a nice street. Mrs Phillips, now sitting in her kitchen with a cup of tea in hand thinks so too, and she should know. She's lived here long enough. Fifty-two years next March. Of course, it was a different street entirely back then. The new builds didn't exist and none of the other houses had been converted into flats. Not that she minds the flats, unlike some of the other residents, even if their cars do tend to spill out from their driveways onto the street. She'll be sad to leave it. Fifty-two years is a long time in anyone's book. She expected to be carried out of here in a box, just like her poor husband, Andrew, but that's not going to happen. Not now. Not since that letter fell through her door a week last Thursday, the one from Esher & Williamson, financial advisers.

She didn't even know Andrew *had* financial advisers.

She checks her watch and switches on the small TV that sits on the counter. *Sculpture Vulture* is on BBC2. She's an avid fan but today thoughts of Andrew, and the situation he's left her in, crowd her mind.

Cryptocurrency. What even was that?

'*Bitcoin, Mum.*' That's what David had told her. '*It's based on blockchain technology and algorithms.*' And still she has no idea. All she knows is that Andrew, the man she was married to for fifty-two years, who hadn't owned a computer since 1997, who needed her help even to send an email, had, apparently, invested their life savings in something that didn't really exist and which was traded by a company based in a tax haven.

Whatever possessed you, you silly old fool?

Except she knows the answer to that. Andrew never could resist a get-rich-quick scheme. Ever since Mrs Thatcher sold off the Crown Jewels, Andrew had picked up a knack for chasing a fast buck. British Telecom, British Gas, British Airways, even the companies now pumping sewage into rivers and onto beaches. If it was going cheap, Andrew was always first in line for a piece. Even now she has a dozen accounts with half a dozen building societies, with approximately £10 in each of them, which Andrew opened back in the nineties on the off chance of a free £500 if they became a bank.

And now?

Now all that money, the proceeds of Andrew's carpet-bagging *and* her hard-earned savings, was all gone, courtesy of a young American man with curly hair, who, if she understood the news correctly, was hailed as a financial genius by the great and the good, but turned out to be a crook or maybe an idiot. Mrs Phillips doesn't much care which it is. Idiot or crook, the money's gone, Andrew has racked up debts and she will need to sell the house.

It has not been an easy decision. She's discussed it with David. She hasn't asked him for help of course – he has a family of his own now – and even though she and Andrew had, until last year, been paying the grandchildren's school fees, it is a matter of pride to her not to ask for her son's help. Still, she had hoped he might offer . . .

'Sell the house, Mum. It's too big for just you anyway.'

Sell the house. The one he was born in – well, not born in per se, but she knows what she means. Sell the house he grew up in. As though the memories mean nothing to him.

On screen, the tanned presenter in the bow-tie shows off a garish-looking piece. It is worth several million pounds, apparently. Several. Million. Pounds. For a trinket. And here she is, about to lose the most precious thing she has left.

She has no option. She will sell the house and pay off Andrew's debts and then she will move into a retirement home. The alternative, moving in with David and Celia and their kids, is a non-starter. It would be lovely to spend more time with her grandchildren, but Celia would never be happy with her mother-in-law under the same roof and frankly, Ruth can't blame her.

She doesn't think much of the young man who has just left her house. Brown shoes. With a suit. In her day only spivs wore brown shoes with a suit. And that knot on his tie – the size of the Isle of Wight – like one of those footballers on the television. How can one trust such a person? Still, such is the way of the world these days. She has long stopped trying to make sense of it. Live and let live, that's her motto, and to be fair it's given her more peace than religion has.

The man now striding up her driveway does not, it's fair to say, subscribe to that philosophy. He is large and corpulent and wears suede loafers. Mr Francis Anderson, Frank to his friends down the King's Head or the rugby club bar or the nineteenth hole at the golf course. Frank by name, frank by nature, that's Frank's credo: a proud, plain-speaking Yorkshireman, at least by his own admission if no one else's. It is an attitude he revels in, affording him as it does license to be rude, sexist and casually racist without ever forcing him to confront his reasons for doing so, which, if he stopped to think about it, he might find were rooted in the insecurities and inferiority complexes that stem from a deeply unhappy childhood. But Frank Anderson will never contemplate such things, which is probably for the best.

He lives two doors down from Mrs Phillips in a house he shares with his second wife, a baby son twenty years younger than his other children and a revolving selection of paintings and sculptures – the stock for the art gallery he owns and runs in town. And now he has a favour to ask. In previous years he might have asked Norman from next door, but Norman's dead now, God rest his soul; passed away during Covid, and Frank hasn't really got to know the new people who moved in three years ago. Mrs Phillips though, she's been here forever. Quiet type. Bit zealous when it comes to the recycling, but a good sort. Trustworthy, and that's what counts. He rings her doorbell and waits, inspecting his fingernails as the seconds tick by.

Mrs Phillips puts down her mug and pads through to the hall. There is a man at her door, clearly a large man judging by the fractured outline in the frosted glass panel of the door. She opens it and is surprised, and somewhat irritated, to see Frank Anderson standing there, though she hides it with a half-smile. She hasn't seen much of him, not since the divorce. Not since his ex-wife moved out.

'Hello, Frank.'

'Ruth,' says Frank, in what he hopes is an appropriately sombre tone with which to address a recently widowed woman. Must be over a month since her husband passed, possibly getting close to two, he thinks. How long, he wonders, is it appropriate to maintain the sombre tone? And suddenly he thinks, is it too early to ask a favour of a grieving widow? Still, he's here now.

'I wonder if I might . . .' and only then does he think maybe he should lead by checking how she is. 'How are you holding up?'

Ruth Phillips gives him a nod and responds in the way an English widow should.

'Oh, you know, through the worst of it.'

Frank responds with nods of his own. Sage ones. Nods that he hopes acknowledge her bravery and the damn tragedy of it all. Nods that punctuate a silence that is becoming slightly awkward and that prompts Mrs Phillips to say more.

'Would you like to come in?'

Frank shakes his head.

'No, no. I'm sure you're busy . . . well, if it's not too much trouble . . . I might . . . I just wanted to ask a favour, that's all.'

Ruth Phillips invites him into the hallway and closes the door behind him.

'I'll pop the kettle on.'

Frank does not particularly want a cup of tea, he'd rather just say his piece and get on with his day, but this is England and no conversation between neighbours of passing familiarity, who know each other well but not quite well enough, can take place without the social lubrication of a cuppa.

He follows her through the hall. It is maybe only the second time he's been in here. Twice in over ten years. He notices the decor – the wallpaper, the quartet of fading, framed prints of birds on the wall, the blue and white plates high up on the skirting rail. Old-fashioned. The kitchen too is old-fashioned. Farmhouse style, he thinks it's called, warmed by the massive lump of an Aga against the wall. Timeless, it is. Not like his own kitchen, which Suze has had ripped out and changed twice since she moved in and is currently antiseptic white, and where he's not allowed to sit on the matching leatherette breakfast stools in case he scuffs them.

Ruth Phillips opens one of the Aga's lids and places the kettle on the hot plate. The water is still warm from when she last boiled it so it shouldn't take long to re-heat. She fetches a mug from the cupboard and turns to him. She wonders why Frank is here, but she is not the sort to be vulgar enough to ask, and so she reaches for small talk. *What is his new wife's name, again?* Fortunately, she's good with names and it comes to her almost at once.

'And Susan? She's keeping well?'

'Aye,' he says. 'As well as can be expected. Got her hands full with the little one, but you know Susan, she's a tough one.'

Tougher than she used to be, that's for sure. The arrival of little Frank junior seems to have changed her. Changed something between them. She's got a lot less time for Frank senior these days. And a lot less patience. He doesn't remember it being this hard with the other kids. He doesn't remember Deirdre snapping at him the way Suze does, but that was a very long time ago and there's no point dwelling on it and anyway, isn't that why he's here? His big plan for a reset with Suze.

'Little Francis,' Ruth says. 'Is he sleeping through the night yet?'

She thinks back to when David was a baby; the battles she had getting him to sleep. Feeding him in the middle of the night, then getting up at six to make Andrew's breakfast.

'Not yet,' Frank says, his tone even more sombre than when he was passing on his condolences at the front door, possibly because the pain now is his own.

The kettle starts to scream and for a split second he imagines it's Frank junior. Ruth Phillips turns her back to him once more, lifting the kettle from the stove top and putting it out of its misery.

'Milk?' she asks.

'Aye. And two sugars.'

Suze doesn't like him having sugar in his tea, or real milk for that matter, so he doesn't have it at home now. It's probably for the best, health-wise, but here, away from Suze's glare, he feels safe enough to ask for it.

Ruth fetches the milk from the fridge and pours. Re-screwing the lid, she leaves the plastic bottle on the counter-top, reaches for the sugar bowl and extracts two cubes. She still buys cubes. She's not sure why, but her mother used to do it and maybe she feels that her mother, God rest her soul, would look down in disappointment from on high if she lets standards drop. She stirs the mug, takes it over to Frank and hands it to him.

An awkward silence descends as Ruth picks up her tea and Frank eyes his own, aware that it will be uncomfortably hot to drink. And so he decides to tell her why he is here. He explains to her, between small, scalding sips of sweet tea, about the romantic weekend in Las Palmas that he's booked for him and Suze. Little Frank junior will be packed off to Suze's mother in Wetherby. He keeps to himself his hopes that this two day getaway might rekindle the spark in his second marriage. To be honest, even if it doesn't, he'll be happy enough if it just leads to a decrease in her hostility towards him.

He explains to Mrs Phillips that he would like her to keep an eye on the house. 'Got a lot of artwork inside,' he tells her. 'Stock for the gallery. And there've been some shifty-lookin' blokes spotted in the street, recently. *Loitering.*' The word falls from his mouth with the weight of a death sentence.

'Loitering?' she says.

'Loitering,' he confirms.

He senses her concern and wonders if he has over-egged the malevolence of the loitering.

'Don't worry, though. Everything's alarmed and connected to the alarm company's control centre. They'll call the police. It's just, if I could leave a set of keys with you and if you could maybe keep an eye out, that'd be grand.'

Mrs Phillips acquiesces. After all, it's what neighbours do. It's what they've always done in this street. She wonders why he hasn't asked Mr or Mrs Shah, their mutual neighbours whose house sits between them. Such a lovely family. They insist their children call her Auntie Ruth.

'It's no problem at all,' she tells him and he beams her a smile.

'Oh that's wonderful. Ta very much,' he says and feels that he must now somehow reciprocate her kindness. 'And if you ever feel like changing your decor or what have you, a bit of new art for the walls, you just let me know. I'll find you something special; waive the commission.' He gestures at the walls, illustrating just how much he could do for her, and manages to knock over a vase on the sideboard. It falls floorward and for a moment, Ruth Phillips has her heart in her mouth. Frank flails at it in a desperate bid to avert catastrophe, but he's not as fit as he used to be and his fat fingers manage only to knock it against the wall with a sickening crack.

He picks up the thing and examines it. There's a crack in it, but maybe that was there before? Best not chance it, he thinks.

'An' I'll get you a new one of them too.'

He leaves the keys and a note of the alarm code alongside the half-drunk tea and heads back to the front door. Ruth Phillips is a step behind, a gentle smile affixed to her face that, when he turns to her, reminds Frank of the Virgin Mary. *Our Lady of Harrogate*, he thinks as he says his goodbyes. *May she watch over my house and all that resideth therein.* He smiles at the witticism as he walks back down the street. It's very clever, even if he does say so himself. And then he sees Suze glaring at him through the bay window of his own house and the smile evaporates from his lips.

We need not worry much about the next thirty-odd hours. They pass unremarkably enough. Frank surprises Suze with the tickets to Las Palmas, and though her initial reaction is akin to having been stung by a wasp, to her credit, she calms down most quickly once he's shown her pics of the five-star hotel and she's called her mother to confirm that what Frank has told her about childcare for the baby is indeed true. A few hours later they are on their way to Manchester Airport via Wetherby, but not before an altercation over what to pack – hand luggage only, because those are the terms of the tickets Frank's bought, *and surely that's enough for two days; and can't she just be grateful for once?* It comes as a surprise, even to Frank, that this is the hill he has chosen to die on, but every man has his limits and his is paying an additional £79.99 to take a suitcase on board. The flight itself feels to him like the last plane out of Saigon or Kabul, filled as it is with screaming infants and well-oiled hen dos. Suze does not complain, indeed she might not even have noticed the mêlée, sedated as she is by almost half a dozen G&Ts.

The evening at the hotel in Las Palmas is short if not particularly sweet. The room is full board and while the wine is copious and the food plentiful, the former leaves Suze nursing a headache and the latter drives Frank to the bathroom. It's not all bad, though. For the first time in as long as he can remember, the two of them will get to sleep past 5 a.m., and when they do wake they will smile at each other.

Mrs Phillips too has an early night. She has received the contract from the estate agents and pored over its clauses, not because she is going to change anything or even spot anything amiss, but out of a vague notion that reading the small print is the right thing to do. She spends the afternoon tidying the house, preparing it for the many, many viewings which the young man with the unnaturally white teeth has already called to tell her he's lining up. He is more than excited to start showing people her house and will start bringing them round just as soon as she's signed the paperwork. She is upstairs by 9 p.m., wrapped up under the duvet with her hot-water bottle and a Richard Osman, in a bed that now, in the absence of Andrew, feels too big by half.

The next day, too, passes without event. Frank takes Suze shopping in the boutiques of Las Palmas and it almost feels like three years ago, when the world was a bed of roses and the only thorn in his mattress was his ex-wife.

Mrs Phillips visits Bettys Café Tea Room with a friend, as she has done regularly for the last fifteen years, whenever either of them has needed a shoulder to cry on or an ear to gossip into. Deirdre often comes armed with a rucksack-full of stories of old school acquaintances, spreading salacious details as thick as she does the jam on their scones, but today is one of those days when Ruth has the more interesting news: of Deirdre's ex-husband and the holiday he has planned to Las Palmas. She wonders whether to broach the subject at all, but she cannot keep such a thing from her friend. She mentions the fact in neutral tones and Deirdre nods, curious despite her better judgement. Before Ruth knows it, she and Deirdre are gossiping, dissecting Frank's relationship with that strumpet, Suze.

'He'll regret it, mark my words,' Deirdre says, and Ruth wonders if he already is.

They talk and talk, about Frank and how he's treated Deirdre. About the injustice of it all.

Let's skip forward, then, to the events that matter, the ones that occur the next day, or more specifically that next night. Big Frank Anderson is feeling good. His stomach has settled and Suze, God bless her, is feeling amorous, a combination of sunshine, red wine and several boutique purchases having rekindled in her feelings of, well, let's just say *warmth*, towards her husband. Frank swallows a blue tablet and for one awkward moment wonders if it's past its sell-by date. But no, even as he brushes his teeth he can feel the first stirrings . . . *down there*.

Moments later, he is back in the bedroom, dimming the lights, putting Chris de Burgh on the Bluetooth speaker and opening a bottle of room-service champagne, the price of which still irks him but it's probably worth it. And then he is on the bed, whispering sweet nothings in Suze's ear, when suddenly the strains of 'The Lady in Red' are guillotined and his phone starts ringing.

Frank ignores the interruption, continues about his business in the hope that it'll stop, and it does, eventually, only for Chris to sing a few more bars before it starts ringing again. Frank is now torn between his phone and his wife, and he is grateful when she breaks the impasse.

'Just answer it,' she says, in a tone that suggests he has mere seconds to deal with the caller otherwise that blue pill will have been for nothing.

He reaches for the phone. A number he doesn't recognise. 'Hello?'

'*Mr Anderson?*' An English voice on the other end. 'I'm calling from Shield Security . . .'

A minute later, all thoughts of romance now a memory, Frank is calling Ruth Phillips. It's late. He hopes the old woman is still awake, and as it rings he regrets not asking what's-his-name, Mr Shah next door, to watch the place instead.

Ruth Phillips answers on the fifth ring.

'Frank? Yes, I can hear the alarm going off. I'm putting on my coat. I'll pop round there now.'

For a moment Frank worries. If his place *is* being burgled, then is it safe for an old woman to go round? Maybe she should wait for the police? But then, there's his art to think of. Yes, it's insured, but still. This isn't going to be good for his premiums. And anyway, whoever's robbing him, the buggers will probably have scarpered as soon as the alarms went off. The old dear'll be all right.

'Just be careful, Mrs Phillips,' he says, impressed by the sincerity in his own voice. 'The security company people and the police should be there soon.' He hopes his statement is true, but the security people are coming from Wakefield and the police, well, do they even respond to burglaries these days?

She promises to call him as soon as she's managed to have a look around and he hangs up and turns to Suze. Her eyes are closed now, the wine having worked its soporific spell on her. Chris de Burgh is singing another song now, about another woman, not in red this time, but in black and out for revenge. He gets back on the bed and tries caressing Suze's face but she just turns over on her side and lets out a snore. He worries about the effects of his blue pill, and not just about the waste of money, but he'll have to live with it. He's in no mood for romance now.

Ruth Phillips wraps herself in a big coat and pulls the front door closed behind her. The ringing is louder in the street. It's been twenty minutes since the alarm went off and lights are already on in the windows of other houses.

Talking of lights, there's one flashing on the alarm box high up on the wall of Frank Anderson's house. Ruth takes her time. Armed as she is with Andrew's old five-iron, it's still best to be careful. She walks around the property, finds a smashed window at the rear but no sign of life. Whoever has done this has probably been and gone . . . or they may still be inside. After several minutes, she decides that the risk of attack by burglars is less troublesome to her than the damn ringing of the alarm. She takes Frank's key, unlocks the front door, switches on the hall light and methodically enters the code he's given her into the alarm box under the stairs.

A strange silence descends. She feels electric tension in the air and waits a moment, listening out for any hint of movement, but there is nothing. She does not feel scared, which is surprising, but then she has always been a woman of resilience. Now she matter-of-factly walks through the house, taking stock. The walls are covered in paintings. They're different from the ones at her place. These are modern and frankly rather ghastly. There is one of Queen Elizabeth II with bright pink lipstick smeared all over her mouth. How that constitutes art, Mrs Phillips is not at all sure. And maybe the burglars agree with her, for they haven't stolen it.

The living room too is decorated in a style she would struggle to call homely. It is hard and angular and the only softness is provided by a thin, zebra print rug on the wooden floor. So different, she thinks, from the days when Deirdre lived here. The room is pristine, the TV still on the wall, the artwork, such as it is, remains unmolested. Nothing has been taken, at least not in here.

It is only when she opens the door to a room at the back of the house that she notices. This, it is clear, is Frank Anderson's office. There is an elegant desk. Large, wooden and old-fashioned, with sets of drawers on either side and topped with green leather. The rest of the room though . . . well, it's a bit of a mess. Upended racks spill canvases and rolled-up prints across the floor. Frames have been smashed and paintings removed. It's hard to say what's missing, but she imagines whoever has done this knew what they were looking for. Then again, maybe they didn't. For something catches Mrs Phillips' eye. A row of sculptures on a sideboard against the far wall, one of which she now recognises. A Rodin bronze of two lovers entwined. It is called *Eternal Springtime* and is worth the better part of a million pounds, at least according to that lovely man with the bow-tie who presents *Sculpture Vulture* on the BBC.

She spends a few minutes tidying up, then stops, realising that her fingerprints are now all over a crime scene. Oh, she is a silly old woman. She heads back to the sitting room as her phone rings. She has, she realises, forgotten to phone Frank back. He is obviously worried. She answers and tells him what she has found.

Frank is pacing the balcony of his hotel room now, quietly of course, in his socks, so as not to wake Suze, but he's angry. This is not how he anticipated things would go tonight. A sleeping wife and a robbery at his house. Something in Frank seems to snap. Maybe it's the sea air in his lungs or the out-of-date Viagra coursing through his system, but he suddenly sees things clearly. That old Mrs Phillips has reassured him that only stock from his office has been taken and that the rest of the house is fine. Sounds like an inside job to him. But if so, who? The staff at the gallery? They've all been there for decades. Suppliers? But they wouldn't know he was going on holiday. The only others were Suze and her mum. He shakes his head. That's madness. He needs to stop being such a paranoid bugger. But the thought lingers. Festers.

He's lost a lot of stock and he's going to have to rebuild. That's going to take time and effort. Fine, he'll throw himself into it when he gets back tomorrow. As for him and Suze, well, he'll worry about that too when he gets home, but already he's considering his options. Even if she isn't involved in this, does he really want to spend the rest of his life with her? She's become a cold fish, and he doesn't like fish. He likes sugar. He consoles himself that he's always used good lawyers and that the prenup is watertight. If he were to, you know, start proceedings, he's confident Suze will get her hands on precious little of his wealth. Even less than Deirdre did. *Thank God for prenups*, he thinks to himself. *Belt 'n' braces, Frank. Belt 'n' braces.*

Mrs Phillips is back in her kitchen, watching the sun rise through the window, a mug of tea in her hand. The people from the security company were very nice to her. Even the policemen were understanding as she explained about the tidying up.

'*Not to worry,*' they told her. '*A professional job,*' they said. '*There wouldn't have been fingerprints to find. Probably won't be DNA evidence either.*'

Mrs Phillips reaches for her phone and calls her old friend, Deirdre, in Leeds. She tells her what has happened. Tells her everything. Deirdre says she will be round shortly, just as they had agreed the day before. She will take it from here. Mrs Phillips hangs up, takes a sip of tea and makes a mental note to call the estate agents at 9 a.m. sharp to tell that young fellow with the brown shoes and the white teeth that she's changed her mind. The house is no longer for sale. She takes a long look at the sculpture on the table in front of her, then looks out at the rising sun once again. It is October but to her it feels like springtime. *Eternal Springtime.*

MURDER AT THE TURKISH BATHS

Ruth Ware

The beautiful Victorian Turkish Baths of Harrogate have been one of the jewels of the city since they first opened in 1897. This story is set in the 1920s, when the baths were already a fixture of the town's social scene, and shortly after the opening of the brand new Bettys Tea Room, soon to be a Harrogate institution in its own right. Close to a hundred years later, the baths are still operating, their glorious interior virtually unchanged from Nell's day, so if you fancy stepping back in time, you can experience Nell's world by booking yourself in.

You expect to see a fair amount of odd things when you're a ladies' bath house attendant. In the eight years I've worked at the Harrogate Turkish Baths, I've found ladies playing leap-frog in the changing area and crying in the steam-room. I've found them doing other things in the steam-room too, but my auntie brought me up nicer than to talk about that. I've found a diamond ring in the caldarium and a sapphire one in the plunge pool – that was a story and a half. Once I found a fat rascal in the pocket of one of the robes – I have to admit, when I put my hand in and it came out sticky, I was expecting worse.

What you don't expect to find is a dead body. And what you really don't expect is for the body to be that of a man. Not on a ladies' day. We're very strict about that – and good luck trying to sneak past Mrs Patchett in the ticket booth. She's got eyes like a hawk.

So my first thought, when I saw the poor gentleman, was how on earth did he get in?

'Excuse me, sir!' I said, trying not to let my voice sound flustered. 'Excuse me, but you can't be in here!'

He didn't say anything. Which wasn't surprising, as I later found out, though of course at the time I didn't know that. They'd just put fresh water on the brazier and with the steam gushing from the vents, it was hard to see much, but peering through the mist I could just make out his shape – and I thought that maybe his eyes were closed.

'Excuse me!' I said louder, thinking he might be asleep. 'Sir, I have to ask you to leave! This is a ladies' day.'

He didn't move. Just sat there, slumped, on his red towel. And so, seeing there was no choice but to wake him up myself, I walked into the billowing clouds, crossed the tiled floor, and shook him by the shoulder.

Well *then*, of course, I realised. Not from the temperature of the body – the steam-room is hot enough that he felt warm to the touch. But from the fact that he keeled over sideways like a felled tree and lay there in a pool of his own blood. That was a bit of a giveaway. Oh and it turned out the towel wasn't red – it was white, like all the other towels. The red was . . . well, you can probably guess.

I didn't scream. I'm not the hysterical type. Auntie Vi always says that, she says 'Thank goodness you're not the hysterical type, Nell.' But I did let out a little yelp. Then I took a couple of deep breaths and realised that I'd better go and inform someone sharpish.

Outside the steam-room I closed the door and walked as quickly as I could to Mrs Patchett's ticket booth. I didn't run – there's very strict rules about that. When I got to Mrs Patchett's window, I said, 'Mrs Patchett, please could I have a word?'

Mrs Patchett looked up from her ledger and she didn't look best pleased at being interrupted in the middle of trying to make yesterday's takings balance.

'It'll have to wait, Nell. I'm two shillings out.'

'I'm afraid it can't, Mrs Patchett,' I said. I knew I sounded a little self-important, but really, it was important, wasn't it?

Mrs Patchett put down her pen and glared at me over her pince-nez.

'Nell Holliday, I hope for your sake someone's dead or dying.'

'Dead, actually,' I said. And then her pince-nez fell off.

Well, after that, things moved very quickly. The police came and they took the poor gentleman away. His name, it turned out, was Sir Clive Clithering – and when I heard the name, I realised I knew him. Well, I don't mean *knew* him, I don't run in those kinds of circles. But he owned a big tea-packing factory just outside Harrogate, and I'd seen him in the papers a fair bit.

What none of us could understand was how he'd ended up in the steam-room on a ladies' day. But Jeannie Wainwright – she's one of my best friends at the baths, and her brother Bob is an attendant on the men's days – said she thought it was all too likely.

'Well, yesterday was a Wednesday,' she said, as if that explained everything. Us attendants had been banished to the Winter Gardens tearoom, to keep out of the way while the police went about their business, and Mrs Patchett had told us not to gossip, but of course none of us intended to take the least notice of that. I frowned.

'What's that got to do with anything?'

'Wednesday night is when the boys have football practice. And the Baths team is playing Taylors this Saturday. Bob was full of fire and brimstone about how they were going to get their own back for the defeat last month.'

Of course. That made sense. The Turkish Baths football team is made up of most of the younger male attendants – with Bob as their star striker. They would have been shutting up as fast as they could after closing, so as not to be late for practice. It wouldn't be a surprise if something had been missed, and the idea was a kind of comfort in a way – I can't say I liked the idea of the poor gentleman sitting there overnight in a pool of his own blood, but at least us girls hadn't let a murderer into the baths. Or worse, a man.

After the police had taken their photographs and measurements, and gone on their way, Mrs Patchett came to find us and ask for volunteers for the clean-up. A good number of the girls shrieked and said the thought gave them the vapours and just the idea of being in a room where a man was killed was enough to make them feel quite faint.

In the end, the only hands that went up were me, Jeannie Wainwright and Betsy Binns, and Mrs Patchett picked all three of us. I didn't mind. In fact, I was quite curious to get back in the steam-room and see if things were as I'd remembered them.

When I opened the door for the second time that day, the steam-room looked different. Someone had shut off the brazier so the temperature in the room wasn't much above the rest of the baths, and the steam had gone entirely. It just looked like what it was – a tiled, rather chilly room, lined with benches.

Sir Clive had been sitting in the right-hand corner, and you could see where the blood had puddled and soaked into the bench before trickling down into the drain. The police had taken the towel – evidence, I suppose – and I'm sure I was glad, for there would have been no getting the bloodstains out of the nasty thing, as I knew all too well.

Betsy began sluicing cold water into the drain in the centre of the floor to try to wash out the clotted blood pooling there, but I was looking for something else – something I'd only half noticed when I'd come in the first time.

Because there on the tiled wall, were letters. A trailing C, an A and then something else that could have been a P, or could have been an R with its tail broken short. They'd been written in what looked like blood. And the sight of them made me feel . . . well, I don't know exactly. But like things didn't quite add up. In fact, the whole business was beginning to get murkier than the plunge pool on a Sunday night.

The next day, we were told that the baths were closed for the rest of the week, and we girls would be put on full pay, which I called handsome, though my Auntie Vi said management was only doing what was right. It's not like *we'd* murdered the poor man.

'You mark my words,' she said darkly as she pinned on her hat, on the way out of the door to her job as a typist at the *Harrogate Advertiser.* 'They'll find some way to put it back on the working man. It's always the likes of us who suffer at the end of the day.'

Auntie Vi is a member of the local communist party and says things like that. Though not when she's at work.

I didn't really believe her of course. But when I met Jeannie and Betsy for tea at Bettys later that afternoon and found Jeannie already in tears before the tea had even cooled, it seemed as if Auntie Vi had been right.

'What's happened?' I looked from Jeannie to Betsy, but Jeannie was sobbing too hard to speak, tears dropping into her clotted cream. Betsy shook her head.

'They've arrested Bob.'

'What? Bob *Wainwright*?' I didn't mean to sound so incredulous – but really it was hard to imagine Jeannie's older brother hurting a fly. I'd known him since I was eight. He'd been eleven, the tallest boy in his class, and Jeannie used to make him lift us up on his shoulders to scrump the best apples in Mrs Baxter's orchard. Mrs Baxter saw him running away and complained to his parents, and he'd got in awful hot water, but he'd never told on us. Just took the spanking and kept mum. Now he was twenty-six and just as sweet as those apples. I wondered sometimes if he remembered that afternoon. Somehow I doubted it. He had bigger fish to fry these days. I was just his little sister's friend.

'I don't believe it,' I said, sitting down at the table and pulling off my gloves. 'Bob? That's absurd. What's their evidence?'

'He was the one who shut up the steam-room, apparently,' Betsy said grimly. 'Among other things.'

I didn't have to ask how she knew all this. Betsy's sweetheart, Dick Bates, was a constable in the Yorkshire Police.

'When did they arrest him?' I asked. At the words *arrest him*, Jeannie gave a great despairing wail.

'This morning. There, there, Jeannie, do keep it down a bit. You'll get us thrown out and I haven't finished my Swiss roll. And you haven't touched your scone.'

'I don't *care*,' Jeannie said tragically. 'What does it matter about a scone? They're going to hang my brother.'

'They won't hang him,' I said firmly. I poured myself a generous measure of Earl Grey and put some jam on Jeannie's scone. If she wasn't going to eat it, there was no point in letting it go to waste – that wouldn't help Bob, would it? I took a big bite and said, through the crumbs, 'Tell me everything.'

Everything turned out to be an understatement, and when Jeannie and Betsy had finished, the case against poor Bob seemed a lot more damning than I'd originally expected.

It wasn't just the fact that he'd been the person in charge of shutting up the steam-room. It wasn't even the fact that he was the last member of staff on the premises, because Mr Simmons (the male Mrs Patchett) had left early to go to the football.

No, the real smoking gun was the fact that he seemed, unbelievably, to have been having an affair with Lady Caroline Clithering.

As I said to Auntie Vi that evening over tea, you could have knocked me down with a feather. We were having cold ham with piccalilli and boiled potatoes. Not my favourite but probably better than what poor Bob was having down at the gaol.

It wasn't that Bob wasn't good-looking, he was actually quite handsome – tall and blond, and always with a string of girls after him. But he didn't seem the type for an affair. And her a Lady at that!

It was Auntie Vi who filled me in on the details. It seems there's some point to working in a newsroom – you hear all the news that's *not* fit to print.

Because it turned out that Lady Caroline Clithering hadn't always been a Lady – she'd started out as plain old Carrie Jenkins, but had soon traded that in for the stage name of Caro Castanetti when she left school and began dancing professionally. From the Winter Gardens in Blackpool to the Liverpool Olympia, right down to the ballroom at the Harrogate Hydropathic, Caro Castanetti had rhumbaed and flamencoed and cha-chaed her way across the North West and finally into the arms of Sir Clive Clithering, newly widowed and out for a good time.

That was five years ago, and since then, all had not been well. Because what Sir Clive had wanted – a pretty, grateful, empty-headed little girl, ready to play mother to his orphaned daughter and gaze with admiration on the man who had plucked her from the gutter – was not what Lady Caroline had turned out to be. She was clever, sharp, and very easily bored – and neither she nor Sir Clive's teenage daughter Ruby wanted to play happy families. She put up a good pretence for a while – she was in show business after all – but within a year of marriage she was back drinking at the Hydro and dancing with any handsome young man who happened to be within arm's reach. And one night, that happened to include Bob.

'So the police are saying that Bob stabbed Sir Clive in the neck with a fountain pen,' I said, as I forked another potato into my mouth. Auntie Vi made a face, but it was more for form's sake than anything else. She's not squeamish, my aunt.

'What for, though?' she asked, a little sceptically. 'A crime of passion? They surely don't think that Bob expected to waltz off into the sunset with Lady Caroline! She knows which side her bread's buttered, that one, and it's not Bob's.'

I shook my head.

'No. And that takes us back to the letters on the wall. *C . . . A . . . R*. Because the obvious idea is that Sir Clive scrawled them with his last ounce of strength – trying to spell out *Caroline*. But according to Betsy's Dick, that's not the case. The police doctor says that Sir Clive would have died near enough straight away. He certainly wouldn't have been fiddling about scribbling letters on the wall – and why would Bob have let him, if he had? It's not like he'd be standing over a dying man, watching him doodle out accusations against the woman he loved.'

'I see,' Auntie Vi said, nodding. As usual she was one step ahead of my reasoning. 'So the police case is that Bob scrawled the letters after Sir Clive's death, to implicate Lady Caroline – but why?'

I shrugged.

'Maybe she was leaving him? Dick didn't say.'

'Hmm . . .' Auntie Vi rested her chin on her hand, and her expression was thoughtful. 'And there's no other clues?'

I shook my head.

'No. Well, there were two oddities that Betsy mentioned. The pen Sir Clive was killed with, it wasn't Bob's or his. It had the initials JH engraved on it. There's a Joe Howells who works at the baths but he wasn't on that day, he'd come down with a stomach flu.'

'And the other oddity?'

'The police found a streak of gum or resin on the luggage hatch of Sir Clive's car. Some kind of spirit glue, Betsy said.'

'That could have been there ages,' my aunt said a little dubiously.

'The chauffeur swears he'd had the car cleaned that very morning and would have spotted it – and neither he nor Sir Clive took any luggage to the baths.'

My aunt shook her head pessimistically.

'Well, that doesn't sound like much of a defence for poor Bob. It strikes me that he had means and he had opportunity. Which means that motive is the weak spot in the police case. I hope his lawyer realises that. Who is his lawyer, by the way?'

I opened my mouth – and then shut it again, realising that not only did I not know the name of Bob's lawyer, I didn't even know if he had one. Jeannie's family wasn't well off, not since her dad broke his leg at the quarry when she was nine. Bob earned a good wage at the baths, more than us girls, but between what he gave to his mother and what he spent on the weekends, I didn't think he'd have saved much. Maybe there was no lawyer. Maybe Bob had no one looking out for him at all. It was a sobering thought.

The next day the Turkish Baths were still closed so I did something a little foolish. I found myself standing outside Harrogate Police Station, wearing my best hat, and feeling more than a bit nervous.

Inside, I walked up to the desk, looked Dick Bates right in the eye and said, 'Hello Constable Bates, I've come to see Bob.'

We'd been at school together, me and Dick, and of course I knew him from courting Betsy, but I thought it better to act professional.

Dick shook his head.

'Sorry, Nell. No can do.'

I don't know if it was his tone or what, but something about the way he said it nettled me, and I felt my anger rise, pushing aside my nervousness.

'Tell me this, then,' I said, putting both hands on the counter. 'What crime has Bob Wainwright committed?'

Dick folded his hands and put on what I thought of as his *official* voice, a stilted drone that didn't sound like his normal tone at all and always made me want to burst out laughing.

'Said prisoner, Robert Stanley Wainwright, has been arrested on suspicion of—'

'That's right. *Suspicion*,' I snapped, interrupting him. 'Because he's not been convicted yet – and in English law, unless I'm very much mistaken, a man is innocent until he's found guilty. And Bob's not been found guilty of anything, as you well know.'

'Nevertheless—' Dick began austerely, but I'd had enough.

'Listen to me, Dick Bates. If you don't let me see Bob right now, I'll be telling Betsy about this. And you do *not* want to be getting the sharp end of her tongue. Bob's innocent until proven otherwise – and an innocent man has a right to visitors. *If* he wants to see me.'

It was a big if. And, truth be told, it was the part I was most nervous about. But when Dick Bates came back, truculent and irritated, from speaking with his boss, it turned out that Bob did want to see me. Or at least, was prepared to. Which came to the same thing.

As Dick led me through a maze of corridors and locked doors, I found myself wondering what I was going to say – why I was even here. All I knew was that I didn't believe that Bob Wainwright, Jeannie's Bob, the boy who had taken the rap for my scrumping all those years ago and never said a word – I didn't believe he was guilty of anything. And I wanted him to know it.

Eventually I was taken into a small interview room and sat down, and then a few minutes later I heard the clanking of irons and Bob Wainwright shuffled into the room in cuffs and leg irons. As he tried to lower himself onto the wooden stool opposite, I had to take a couple of good deep breaths and remind myself that I hadn't been brought up to get weepy about that sort of thing. Then the prison guard retreated to stand beside the door and I opened my mouth to speak – but Bob got in first.

'Nell, I'm so glad you came. Is Jeannie here too?'

I shook my head.

'Just me, I'm sorry, Bob.'

'You have to believe me, I didn't do it!'

'I know,' I said firmly. 'That's why I'm here. But why on earth do the police think you did?'

'You know about . . .' Bob swallowed. He looked ashamed of himself, as well he might. 'About Caro?'

'About you and Lady Caroline?' I knew my tone was tart, but I couldn't keep the disapproval out of my voice. 'Yes, I know. Oh, Bob, what were you thinking? A married woman.'

'I know.' Bob sounded wretched. 'I'm not proud of myself – but it was just a bit of fun at first. She said her husband didn't mind – that he didn't like dancing and didn't mind her amusing herself. Only then it turned from dancing to . . . well, other things. And now—' He stopped. His big hands were twisted on the table. I shook my head.

'You don't have to go into all that. But I still don't understand, why would they think you'd kill Sir Clive and try to frame Lady Caroline? What good would that do? Was she leaving you?'

Bob nodded, and his face was grey and weary.

'My solicitor said not to talk about it, but the police have got it all out of Caroline, so what's the point?'

'Not to talk about what?'

'She's pregnant. Caroline. She said it was his, but . . . well. The timing . . .' He stopped. His face was a picture of misery.

'Oh Lord.' I knew I shouldn't take God's name in vain. Auntie Vi would have scolded me, and quite right too, but the moment seemed to need it. 'Oh Bob, so they think she was going back to him, to have his baby, and you killed him in a fit of fury and tried to pin the blame on her, as an act of revenge?'

Bob nodded.

'I didn't do it though, Nell. I swear it. How could I mind her going back to him? She was a sweet lass, but she was his wife and I knew what we were doing was wrong. The baby only proved that – and maybe it was his, or maybe it was

217

mine, but it didn't really matter at the end of the day. The poor little scrap would have had a better life as lord of the manor at Clithering Hall than I ever could have given it. Do you believe me?'

I shut my eyes. What a mess. What a stupid mess. Then I opened them, and clenched my fists in my lap.

'Yes, I believe you. And before I'm done, so will the police.'

'Time's up,' said the officer from the door, his voice bored. I wondered if he'd been listening in.

Bob stood up, and the officer started unshackling his ankles so he could walk back to his cell.

'Thank you for coming, Nell. It means a lot.'

'It'll be all right, Bob,' I said, as he was led away down the corridor, looking forlornly over his shoulder. But I wasn't sure if I believed it.

The walk to Clithering Hall was a long one and I was out of breath by the time I got to the top of the hill, pushed open the big wrought-iron gates, and made my way up the drive.

I climbed the stone steps, put my finger to the bell-push, and took a deep breath.

Then I rang.

Deep inside the house I heard a low clanging, but it was with surprising speed that the polished door swung open, as if the footman had been waiting for me. When he saw me standing there, in my Sunday-best coat and hat, his lip curled, just a little.

'The servants' entrance is around the side, miss.'

'I'm not a servant,' I snapped back. 'And I'm here to see Lady Caroline.'

'Lady Caroline is not at home to visitors,' the footman said, austerely, and the big door began to close. I suppressed the urge to poke him with my umbrella and instead put a foot inside the door.

'Please tell her ladyship that Jeannie Wainwright is here to see her. About Bob.'

Well. It was a lie, but a white one. I was Jeannie's best friend after all, and I was here to talk about Bob.

The footman raised one eyebrow. Then he swung the door open again and gestured to a chair in the cavernous entrance hall.

'Please wait here, Miss. I will go and enquire. Do you have a card I might present to her ladyship?'

Of course I didn't. As he well knew. Engraved calling cards were for society ladies like Lady Caroline, not the likes of me. The urge to poke him in his buttoned waistcoat was gone, replaced with a strong desire to snap that he wasn't any better than me just because his employer had given him a pair of shiny shoes to wear with his uniform, and nor for that matter was Lady Caroline. But I only smiled sweetly and said, 'I seem to have come out without one today. Just tell her, Jeannie Wainwright. Bob's sister.'

'Very good, Miss,' he said. And disappeared.

Well. The next few minutes were nerve-wracking, I don't mind telling you. Worse than turning up at the police station uninvited. I had no business at all demanding to see Lady Caroline – and there was every likelihood she'd send me packing.

Instead, though, the footman came back with a sour expression on his face that told me, even before he spoke, that I'd won.

'Please come this way. Her ladyship will see you in the blue drawing room.'

*

Lady Caroline was waiting in the blue drawing room when the footman showed me in, and I don't mind admitting that my hands, inside my best kid gloves, were sweating something horrid. But I reminded myself that the woman sitting in front of me, dressed in silks and with a languid expression on her face, had been born Carrie Jenkins, and probably into a home a lot like mine.

'Your Ladyship,' I said, wondering whether I was supposed to curtsey. The footman had withdrawn and shut the door behind him.

'Jeannie?' Lady Caroline said faintly. 'Jeannie Wainwright, you said?'

The curtains in the room were half drawn and she had to peer through the dim light to look at my face. I felt myself blush.

'Well, Your Ladyship, I have to confess, my name's actually Nell. Nell Holliday. Jeannie's my best friend – but I thought you'd be more likely to see me if I gave her name.'

'But—'

'I *am* here about Bob,' I said, cutting in before she could decide I was an imposter and ring the bell to get me ejected. 'Did you know he's been arrested for the murder of Sir Clive?'

'Oh, poor Bob,' Lady Caroline said. 'So I heard. I can't think why he'd do such a thing, I'm sure. It's utterly inexplicable.' She was lying on the sofa with a handkerchief over her brow, but she shot me a very sharp look from under its folds. It was clear she knew exactly what the case was against Bob, and was sizing me up to see if I knew it too.

'Lady Caroline, listen to me,' I said, urgently. 'I don't believe that Bob did this, and I don't think you believe it either. And I know you don't owe Bob anything,' I raised my voice as she started to protest, saying something about barely knowing the poor man. 'But if his case goes to court, your reputation will be ruined as much as his. The police case against him is all about you – and you must know that. Now tell me, is it true about the baby?'

'Oh!' Lady Caroline had sat up at my first words, but now she fell back against the cushions, her eyelids fluttering. 'Oh, it's true that I'm expecting poor darling Clive's child. But I can't see what that has to do with anything.' Another sharp look from under the handkerchief, and then her eyes closed. 'And I never even got the chance to tell him, that's what makes it all the more heartbreaking! At least I will have his baby to remember him by.'

And his money, I thought. But I didn't say that.

'Look,' I said at last. 'You can stick to your story that you don't know Bob from Adam—' She opened her mouth to say something, but I barrelled on, determined to finish. 'But we both know that's not true, or you wouldn't have let me in. So I'll tell you a thing that *is* true. They're going to hang him. Do you understand that? They're going to hang him by the neck for something you and I both know he didn't do. Whatever went on between the two of you, I don't think you want that on your conscience. So if you know anything about what really did happen to your husband, for God's sake, tell me.'

'I don't, I truly don't,' Lady Caroline said, and now she put the handkerchief aside and sat up, her hands clasped over her heart. It was hard to know if she was telling the truth . . . but if I'd had to put a tenner on it, I'd have said she was. 'I swear to you, Nell. I'd tell you if I did, but I've racked my brains and I can't think of anything. The only people to benefit from his death are myself, and his daughter by his first marriage, Ruby. But we were both here at the hall. I was listening to a concert on the wireless, and Ruby was practising lines for her play – she's an actress you know. Really very talented, though of course poor darling Clive didn't approve. He never did understand the lure of life behind the footlights. Of course *I* did, though I gave it all up for him.'

'Could I speak to her before I go?' I asked. It was pushing my luck, but as Auntie Vi often said, shy bairns get nowt, and to my surprise, Lady Caroline nodded languidly.

'You can certainly try, but I can't guarantee she'll talk to you. She's in the garden room. Ask Rogers to show you the way.' She pressed a little button by her side, then lay back on the couch and resettled the handkerchief over her brow. 'Now if you'll excuse me, I really do have the most terrible headache.'

The interview was plainly over, so I showed myself out to where Rogers the footman was standing in the hallway. He escorted me to the garden room, which turned out to be a pleasant sunny room with big glass windows. The door was ajar, and inside I could see a tall red-headed girl in a black dress, declaiming in a loud voice.

'I am the son of a butler and a lady's maid, the combination of all— no, wait. Bother.' She stopped, and then picked up the book lying in front of her. 'Drat. Why can't I get that line? The happiest of all combinations. The *happiest*.' She coughed, put down the book, and then spoke again. 'My lady, I am the son of a butler and a lady's maid, the happiest of all combinations.'

'Very good,' I said from the doorway. '*The Admirable Crichton*, yes? I saw it at the Royal Hall two years ago.'

The girl swung round angrily.

'Who the devil are you, and what are you doing spying on me?'

'My name is Nell Holliday. And I'm not spying. I was visiting your mother.'

'My *step*mother,' Ruby said. 'Goodness me, I'd have thought anyone who could add two and two would be able to see she didn't give birth to me. What do you want? Can't you see I'm busy?'

Something told me that I wasn't going to get the chance to interrogate Ruby the way I had Caroline. She didn't look like the type to answer direct questions.

'I just wanted to say you're very good,' I said instead. Another one of Auntie Vi's sayings – you catch more flies with honey than with vinegar. 'I've never known a lady to do amateur dramatics before.'

Unfortunately it was the wrong thing to say, and Ruby Clithering's face twisted in a scowl.

'Amateur? I'm going to be a professional actress. Or rather I *was*. Now poor darling daddy's gone . . . I don't know what I'll do.'

She sat down on the chair and put her face in her hands.

'The death duties are going to be awful. I expect the house will have to be sold. My childhood home, gone. And poor daddy, my biggest supporter – killed by that awful man.'

Biggest supporter? It was a far cry from how Lady Caroline had described Sir Clive's views on his daughter's chosen career. The question was, which of them was lying?

'You think he did it then?' I asked. I tried to keep my voice casual. Ruby looked up, her face shocked.

'Of course he did! What other explanation is there? They were having an affair, you know. Him and Caroline. Daddy turned a blind eye to the rumours, but I heard the servants gossiping. And then she left, and poor daddy suffered the consequences. And now – now I have no one. No one at all.'

She burst into tears. I muttered something about being terribly sorry for her loss and edged out of the room down the corridor to show myself out.

*

Rogers the footman was standing in the hallway looking bored when I entered, but he straightened up and opened the front door for me rather smartly.

I had my foot on the step when something occurred to me, and I turned.

'Is it true what they're saying, that the house is going to be sold?'

For a minute, his face struggled between the professional mask of decorum, and his real feelings – and then the feelings won out, and his lip twisted.

'I should say so. Going from what we've pieced together in the servants' hall, Sir Clive left his fortune split between his daughter and his missus – and with that and the death duties, there's going to be precious little left at the end of the day. Neither of them can afford to buy out the other, so they'll have to sell the house and split the proceeds. I dare say her ladyship and Miss Clithering will be all right, but good luck for us poor sods. Out on our ears.'

'That's bad luck,' I said sympathetically. 'They're always looking for attendants down at the baths. And it's good pay.'

The footman gave a laugh. He looked a lot more human now he'd softened up a bit.

'No thanks. If I'm chucked out of here, I'm off to London. I've got a mate down there earning sixty quid a year.'

'Well, good luck,' I said. And then, thinking I might as well push my luck, I added, 'Listen, tell me if this is impertinent, but did anyone else leave the house that day? Apart from Lord Clithering, I mean?'

The footman shook his head.

'I'm afraid not. Just Sir Clive – and Jack Hobbes, the chauffeur of course. And the usual deliveries – milk and fish, and the boy with the evening papers. But all the servants live in, and none of the family left apart from his lordship. And there's no way in or out of the hall apart from the main gate.'

I nodded, and then took my leave to traipse down the hill to Harrogate. As I looked back, thinking of all the working men and women in that big house who'd be out of a job now Sir Clive was gone, Auntie Vi's words came back to me: *They'll find some way to put it back on the working man. It's always the likes of us who suffer at the end of the day.*

It looked like she was right.

That night at tea, I couldn't eat my cheese and onion pie, though it's normally my favourite. Auntie Vi watched me pushing the pieces around my plate and sighed.

'Spoilt your appetite, Nell?'

'Actually, no,' I said. 'More . . . just a lot on my mind.'

I'd been thinking all day about my conversations with Bob, Caroline and Ruby, trying to make the pieces fit together. I had the feeling that I was missing something . . . a piece which would make sense of the whole mess.

'I just . . . I don't believe Bob did this. But I can't see who else would have a motive,' I said. Auntie Vi put down her knife and fork and looked at me seriously.

'Now, Nell, I can tell you're all in a tangle. Talk me through it, and maybe together we can straighten it out.'

I sighed.

'Well, to begin with, the murderer must be someone who hates Lady Caroline. That CAR, that can only mean one thing?'

Auntie Vi nodded.

'Yes, an attempt to throw suspicion on Lady Caroline.'

'Right. Which rules out Lady Caroline herself. Then there's Sir Clive's daughter, Ruby. There didn't seem to be any love lost between her and her stepmother, but both Lady Caroline and the footman say none of the family left the house that day.'

'Besides, doesn't the killer have to be a man?' Auntie Vi said. 'I mean, how would a woman get entry to the baths on a men's day?'

I considered the question.

'I suppose it must be. From what Bob says, Mr Simmons was on duty until he locked up at five o'clock, and left. Anyone coming in before that would have had to pass Mr Simmons.'

'One of the servants up at the hall?' Auntie Vi asked. I sighed.

'I don't know. There's the chauffeur, Jack Hobbes – we know he was there because he accompanied Sir Clive to the baths. But like the rest of the staff, he stands to lose a lot by Sir Clive's death – if the hall gets sold they'll all be out on their ear. But I suppose one of them might hold a grudge. Oh, Auntie.' I put my head in my hands. For the first time, I was starting to wonder if I had this all wrong. 'It feels like nobody did this.'

The next day, the baths reopened and I worked a full day, thinking about everything Auntie Vi had said. On my way home, I passed the Women's Institute Hall and there outside was a big poster. 'Opening night! The Harrogate Women's Institute presents: *The Admirable Crichton*. A play by J.M. Barrie.'

Underneath was the all-female cast list – and at the top was Ruby Clithering.

On a whim, I entered the hall, paid my sixpence and sat and waited for the play to begin. As soon as the curtain came up I knew one thing: Ruby Clithering was no amateur. She was very, very good. By the time the play finished, I knew another: who had killed Sir Clive. I just wasn't sure why. And as Auntie Vi had pointed out, a case without a motive was no case at all.

*

Twenty minutes later I was knocking at the door of Ruby's dressing room, out of breath, and praying that she would still be there.

'Who is it?' The voice that came from within was totally different from the deep plummy tones of the character she'd played on stage – it was Ruby's sharp, upper-class accent and no mistake.

'It's me, Miss Clithering. Nell,' I said. 'I've got you some flowers.' And blooming hard they'd been to come by, at almost ten o'clock at night. In fact, I'd pinched them from in front of the town hall – something I wasn't proud of, but a man's life was at stake.

'Come in,' Ruby said, and I opened the door and closed it behind myself. Ruby was sitting in front of the mirror, taking off her make up.

'Congratulations, Miss Clithering,' I said, holding the flowers out. 'You were very good. I quite believed you were born to service.'

'Thanks,' Ruby said. She flung the flowers carelessly on the divan, then turned back to the mirror. She had pulled off the moustache and wig she'd worn for Crichton, and was dabbing at the spirit glue with a rag soaked in surgical alcohol. 'Ugh, this stuff is terrible for my skin.'

'You were particularly convincing . . .' I took a deep breath. 'As a man.'

There was a long silence. Then Ruby looked at me in her mirror and her expression was hard.

'Thank you, but if you'll excuse me, I'm very tired. And Hobbes, the chauffeur, is waiting for me outside.'

'Of course,' I said. My heart was beating in my chest. I prayed I could pull this off. 'Just one question – will you be travelling inside the car, or in the luggage compartment?'

'In the luggage compartment?' Ruby gave a short sarcastic laugh. 'Why on earth would I want to do that?'

'I don't know,' I said. 'But you did the other day, didn't you? When you smuggled yourself down to the Turkish Baths while your father sat in the back seat quite oblivious. The glue on your moustache was wet and it transferred onto the car. And then you entered the baths disguised as a man, wearing your Bill Crichton costume and wig, borrowed Joe Howells' uniform from the staff room and waited until the place was almost closed before you stabbed your father. Why did you do it, Ruby? Was it because your stepmother was pregnant and you stood to lose everything if the baby was a boy?'

There was a long, long silence.

Then Ruby laughed. It was a low, horrible laugh that made my blood run cold.

'You don't know anything. As if I cared about money. The only thing I ever cared about was acting – and I'd been trying to persuade my father for years to let me have acting lessons, but he just kept saying I was a hack, an amateur who'd never make it on the professional stage. He even had the nerve to say the Women's Institute only let me in their amateur dramatics society because of who *he* was. Everything revolved around him and his damn money. Money! Who cares about money? Art, that's the only thing that matters.'

'So – why then? If not for the money, why?'

'You were right about the first part, for what it's worth,' Ruby said bitterly. 'I did stow away in the luggage compartment. I did dress up as a man and gain entry to the baths. I borrowed an attendant's coat and followed father around the baths and I thought, this is it. I've fooled everyone, even him. He'll have to finally admit that I'm a better actress than he ever thought possible. At the end of the afternoon, I found him in the steam-room. I went up to him, pulled off my wig and I said, *'Now do you see, father? How's this for acting?'* And do you know what he did?' Her face twisted. 'He began to laugh. He laughed. He laughed at *me*. He said, *'Any fool can dress up as a servant, it just shows you're common as they come.'* And suddenly, I couldn't bear it any more. There was a pen in the pocket of the coat, I don't know whom it belonged to, but my hand closed over it like it was meant to be – and I stabbed him in the neck. It was a fountain pen with a sharp metal nib and it went in like . . . well. Easier than I would ever have thought possible. I stood there, watching as he bled out all over the floor. I couldn't quite believe what I'd done. And then I heard footsteps in the hallway outside – and I panicked. My first thought was to throw suspicion on someone, anyone. Caroline seemed like the obvious choice – she had a bloody good motive after all. So I started to write *CAROLINE* on the wall of the steam-room in my father's blood. Only then I realised the footsteps were coming closer – I almost didn't have time to duck down into the steam. But whoever it was didn't come in, they just opened the door and called out, *'Closing time! All out please.'* As soon as they'd gone, I ran. I didn't know about Caroline and the attendant of course.' Her face twisted again. 'Poor bastard – but it can't be helped.'

There was a long silence, and then Ruby seemed to shake herself out of introspection. She picked up her bag and shrugged into her overcoat.

'Now, if you'll excuse me, the chauffeur is waiting for me. I need to go.'

I shook my head. When I spoke, I hoped I sounded braver than I felt.

'I'm sorry, Ruby. You're not going anywhere. You're coming down to the station and you're repeating everything you told me to the detective inspector.'

'What?' Her face was incredulous. 'You must be insane. Why would I do that?'

'Because if you don't, Bob Wainwright will hang.'

Ruby shook her head impatiently.

'Well I'm sorry about that, but as I say, it can't be helped. And frankly, serves him right for cuckolding my father.'

'Then I'll have no choice but to tell everyone what you told me.'

'And if you do,' Ruby spoke sweetly, 'it will be my word against yours. And I'm a Lady, and you're nothing but a bath attendant.'

I kept my temper. After years working at the baths, that's something I'm very good at. And besides, like Auntie Vi always says, there's nothing to be gained by lashing out.

'What would I have to gain by lying?'

'What would you gain?' Ruby's voice was mocking. 'It's obvious you're in love with that Wainwright fellow. You practically make goo-goo eyes every time you talk about him. Why would anyone believe the word of a moonstruck girl, trying to save her sweetheart?'

As she said the words, I felt something flash through me. It was a realisation that she was right. I did love Bob. Perhaps I always had, ever since he'd lifted me on his shoulders to reach the sweetest apples and then taken the beating that was mine and Jeannie's. Bob was a good man, a sweet man. And I loved him, even if he'd never love me back.

'Maybe you're right,' I said quietly. 'Maybe no one would believe the word of a moonstruck girl. But they'd believe the word of her best friend. *And* of Police Constable Bates.'

And then I pulled the door wide and let her see who was standing outside: Betsy and Dick Bates.

'Ruby Clithering,' Dick began. He had put on his best official voice, and although it was pompous and droning and all the other things that had irritated the life out of me in the police station, now the sound of it made me want to cheer.

'Ruby Clithering, I am arresting you on suspicion of the murder of Sir Clive Clithering . . .'

'So,' my aunt said thoughtfully. It was Sunday, and we were doing our usual walk along the Stray. 'All's well that ends well?'

'I suppose so,' I said. I felt lighter than I had in days. 'They found Ruby's fingerprints on the fountain pen, so there was no doubt really, not even when she retracted her confession.'

'And Bob's been released?'

I nodded. I hadn't seen him yet, but that didn't matter.

'What do you think will happen about the baby?' Auntie Vi asked, and I shrugged.

'Lady Caroline seemed pretty set on saying it was her husband's – and who knows, maybe it was. I don't think Bob minds.'

'You don't think the baby has a right?' Auntie Vi asked quiz-zically. 'To know the truth about his or her father?' And she shot me a look that was . . . well, I'd struggle to put a word to it. A little bit curious, a little bit worried, a little bit shy maybe. As though there was something she couldn't quite find the words to say. But I thought I knew what that something was, and I stopped and took my aunt's hands in mine.

'I don't think it matters who the father is, Auntie Vi. All that matters is that it has a ma who loves it. There's worse things in life than being a bastard.'

'You knew, then?' Auntie Vi said. There was a catch in her voice, and I nodded.

'I did. I think I've always known. But it doesn't matter. I've had all I ever needed, Auntie Vi, and that's you.'

Auntie Vi smiled, but there were tears in her eyes.

'I wish I could have said. There were so many times I wanted to call out, *that's my girl!* Your first nativity play. Your school leaving certificate. I'm so proud of you, Nell. But times were different then – it was another century. An unmarried girl . . . it just wouldn't have done. You'd have carried that all your life.'

'I know,' I said. I squeezed her hands. 'But I've nothing to be ashamed of, and nor have you.'

Auntie Vi wiped her eyes, and then she looked up, over my shoulder, and I saw her face change. There was a lightness in her expression, and when I turned around, I felt my own heart skip a beat.

For coming up the Stray, his hands filled with apples, was Bob Wainwright.

Acknowledgements

An anthology is always better than the sum of its moving parts – and there were a lot of moving parts here, from the initial impetus from Simon Theakston, chairman of the Theakston Brewery, Managing Director Richard Bradbury and Sharon Canavar, CEO of Harrogate International Festivals, to the team at Orion – led by Publisher Sam Eades, to the authors who gave so willingly of their time and talent.

A huge thank you to all.

For me, as editor, it has been a long and exhilarating journey. This collection represents a high-water mark for crime anthologies – rarely has such a roll-call of prominent crime and thriller writers come together in one edition. With this much experience on hand, editing the collection was simply a matter of firing the starter pistol and watching the bodies pile up. The end result not only looks fabulous, but within these glossy covers is a truly wonderful selection of short stories. We hope you've enjoyed reading them.

A thank you to others involved in the process: Dan Herron in contracts at Orion; Rachael Lancaster for the terrific cover design; and my agent Euan Thorneycroft at AM Heath.

Finally, thank you to the many readers, critics, reviewers, bloggers, book-groupers, podcasters, booksellers, bookshops and word-of-mouth enthusiasts who have consistently supported the Theakston Old Peculier Crime Writing Festival over the past two decades. Your help has made this the world's most fabulous annual gathering of crime and thriller nerds. Long may it continue!

Harrogate International Festivals is an arts charity. Charity no. 244861.